Donna Leon

The Golden Egg

Grove Press
New York

First published in Great Britain in 2013 by William Heinemann

Printed in the United States of America
Published simultaneously in Canada

ISBN: 978-0-8021-2242-1
EISBN: 978-0-8021-9359-9

Atlantic Monthly Press
an imprint of Grove Atlantic
154 West 14th Street
New York, NY 10011

Distributed by Publishers Group West

groveatlantic.com

19 20   10 9 8 7 6 5 4

Praise for *The Golden Egg*

"[Readers] will savor the pleasures of dialogue as elliptical in its way as Henry James and a retrospective shock when they finally appreciate the import of the tale's unobtrusive opening scene and its sly title
—Kirkus Reviews

"It is with a smile that we receive, open, and read the latest in Donna Leon's wonderful mystery series featuring Commissario Guido Brunetti. These character-driven novels, which transcend the mystery genre, are travelogues of Brunetti's Venice and character studies of the human condition that go beyond nationality and station."
—Bookreporter

"Rating: A."
—Deadly Pleasures

Praise for Donna Leon

"[Leon] has never become perfunctory, never failed to give us vivid portraits of people and of Venice, never lost her fine, disillusioned indignation."
—New York Times Book Review

"Few detective writers create so vivid, inclusive, and convincing a narrative as Donna Leon, the expatriate American with the Venetian heart. . . . One of the most exquisite and subtle detective series ever."
—Washington Post

"Hers is an unusually potent cocktail of atmosphere and event."
—New Yorker

"No one knows the labyrinthine world of Venice or the way favoritism and corruption shape Italian life like Leon's Brunetti."
—Time

"For those who know Venice, or want to, Brunetti is a well-versed escort to the nooks, crannies, moods and idiosyncrasies of what residents call *La Serenissima*, the Serene One. . . . Richly atmospheric, [Leon] introduces you to the Venice insiders know."
—USA TODAY

"Donna Leon is the undisputed crime fiction queen."
—Baltimore Sun

Also by Donna Leon

For Frances Fyfield

lasciate,
che al mio core, al mio bene
io porga almen gil ultimi baci. Ahi, pene!

leave me,
to give my beloved, my son,
one last kiss. Ah, what suffering!

Giulio Cesare
Handel

1

It was a peaceful night at the Brunetti home, and dinner progressed in harmony. Brunetti sat at his usual place, his son Raffi beside him; opposite Brunetti sat his wife, Paola, and beside her their daughter, Chiara. A plate of *fritto misto* to which vegetables, particularly Chiara's current favourite, carrots, had been added with a liberal hand had initiated the peaceful mood; the conversation had maintained it. School, work, a neighbour's new puppy, the first Labradoodle to be seen in Venice: the topics flowed into and from one another, and then on to yet others, all of them tied in some way to the city in which they lived.

Though they were Venetian, the conversation took place in Italian rather than in Veneziano, Brunetti and Paola having decided that the children would learn the dialect anyway from their friends and on the street. This had indeed happened, and so the children spoke Veneziano as easily as did their father, who had been raised speaking it. Paola had picked it up – and it was perhaps to her credit that it embarrassed her to confess this – from the servants who had filled her family's *palazzo* when she was growing up, rather than from her parents, and so she spoke it less fluently than the others. She felt no embarrassment – quite the contrary – in having achieved almost native fluency in English from her childhood nanny and was pleased that she had managed to pass the language on to both her children, though the transmission had been aided by classes with a private tutor and summer study in England.

Families, much in the manner of churches, have rituals and rules which puzzle non-members. They also place high value on things which members of other groups do not prize to the same degree. If the Brunettis had a religion, aside from a formal adherence to some of the outward, decorative manifestations of Christianity, it was language. Puns and jokes, crossword puzzles and teasers were to them what communion and confirmation were to Catholics. Bad grammar was a venial sin; deliberate corruption of meaning was mortal. The children had taken pride in reaching the stages of awareness where they, too, could partake in the progressively more serious sacraments; raised in this faith, they did not think to question its values.

Later, when the plates from which they had eaten the finocchio and orange salad were removed from the table, Chiara set her water glass down with a thump and said, 'They all lived happily ever after.'

'Clorinda's eyes met Giuseppe's, and together they gazed happily down at the baby,' Paola said immediately in a voice she pumped full of emotion.

Raffi looked across at his sister and mother, tilted his chin and studied a painting on the other side of the room, and then said, 'And so it was: the radical procedure left even the doctors who performed it astonished: indeed, for the first time in history, a baby had successfully been delivered from a man's body.'

It took Brunetti but a moment to say, 'As he was wheeled into the delivery room, Giuseppe had time to say, "She is nothing to me, my love. You are the only mother of my child."'

Chiara, who had listened to the contributions of the others with growing interest, added, 'Only the strongest of marriages could survive such an event, but Clorinda and Giuseppe knew a love that passed all understanding and leaped over every obstacle. Yet for a moment, Clorinda wavered. '"But with Kimberly? The friend of my heart?"'

Back to Paola, who said in the cool voice of the narrator, 'In order to preserve the rock of honesty upon which their marriage was founded, it was necessary for Giuseppe to confess the lengths to which his desire for a child had driven him. "It was meaningless, my love. I did it for us."'

'"You brute," Clorinda sobbed, "you betray me like this. What of my love? What of my honour?"' This was Raffi's second contribution, to which he added, '"And with my best friend."'

Leaping at the opening this created, Chiara broke in out of turn and said, 'He lowered his head in shame and said, "Alas, it is Kimberly's child."'

Paola banged her hand on the table to get their attention and demanded, '"But that's impossible. The doctors told us we would never have children."'

Incensed at having had his turn stolen – and by his wife – Brunetti broke in to say, doing his best to sound like a pregnant man, '"I am with child, Clorinda."'

For a moment, no one spoke as they all ran their way backwards through the dialogue and accompanying narrative to see if they fulfilled the family requirement for a story filled with cheap melodrama, cliché and outrageous characterization. When it was clear that no one had anything to add to the beginning of the story, Paola got to her feet, saying, 'There's ricotta-lemon cake for dessert.'

Later, as they sat in the living room, having coffee, Paola asked Brunetti, 'Do you remember the first time Raffi brought Sara here, and she thought we were all mad?'

'Clever girl,' Brunetti said. 'Good judge of people.'

'Oh, come on, Guido; you know she was shocked.'

'She's had years to get used to us,' Brunetti said.

'Yes, she has,' Paola said, leaning back in the sofa.

Brunetti took her empty cup and set it on the table in front of them. 'Is this grandmotherhood calling?' he inquired.

Without thinking, she reached aside and poked him in the arm. 'Don't even joke about it.'

'You don't want to be a grandmother?' he asked with feigned innocence.

'I want to be the grandmother of a baby whose parents have university degrees and jobs,' she answered, suddenly serious.

'Are those so important?' he asked, just as serious as she.

'We both have them, don't we?' she asked by way of answer.

'It is the usual custom to answer questions with answers, not with more questions,' he observed, then got up and went into the kitchen, remembering to take the two cups with him.

He came back a few minutes later, carrying two glasses and a bottle of Calvados. He sat beside her, and poured them each a glass. He handed her one and took a sip of his own.

'If they have degrees and jobs, it means they'll be older when they have children. Perhaps wiser,' Paola said.

4

'Were we?' Brunetti asked.

Ignoring his question, she went on. 'And, if they get a decent education, they'll know more, and that might help.'

'And the jobs?'

'They're not so important, I think. Raffi's bright, so he shouldn't have trouble finding one.'

'Bright and well-connected,' Brunetti clarified, not thinking it polite to refer directly to the wealth and power of Paola's family.

'Of course,' she said, able to admit to these things with him. 'But bright's more important.'

Brunetti, who agreed, confined himself to a nod and another sip of the Calvados. 'The last thing he told me was that he wanted to study microbiology.'

Paola considered this, then said, 'I don't even know what it is they do.' She turned to him and smiled. 'Do you ever think about that, Guido, about all those disciplines we name every day: microbiology, physics, astrophysics, mechanical engineering. We mention them, we even know people who work at them, but I wouldn't be able to tell you what it is they actually do. Would you?'

He shook his head. 'It's so different from the old ones – literature, philosophy, history, astronomy, mathematics – where it's clear what they do or at least what the material is they're working in. Historians try to figure out what happened in the past, and then they try to figure out why it happened.' He put his glass between his palms and rubbed it like a lazy Indian making fire. 'All I can figure out about microbiology is that they look at little growing things. Cells.'

'And after that?'

'God knows,' Brunetti said.

'What would you study if you had it to do all over? Law again?'

'For fun or to get a job?' he asked.

'Did you study law because you wanted to get a job?'

This time, Brunetti ignored the fact that she had answered a question with a question and said, 'No. I studied it because it interested me, and then I realized I wanted to be a policeman.'

'And if you could study just for fun?'

'Classics,' he answered without a moment's hesitation.

'And if Raffi chose that?' she asked.

Brunetti reflected on this for some time. 'I'd be happy if that's what he wanted to study. Most of our friends' kids are unemployed, no matter what degrees they have, so he might as well do it for love as for any job it might get him.'

'Where would he study?' she asked, more a mother's concern than a father's.

'Not here.'

'Here Venice or here Italy?'

'Here Italy,' he said, not liking to have to say it, just as she didn't like to hear it.

They turned and looked at one another, forced to confront this inevitability: kids grow up and kids leave home. If the phone rang after midnight, it would no longer be possible to take it down the hall and look into their rooms to have that immediate, corporeal assurance that they were there. Asleep, awake, reading under the covers with a flashlight; unconscious, sulking, happy or angry: none of this mattered in the face of the certainty that they were safe, at home, there.

What babies parents are. All it took was that ringing sound in the night to freeze their hearts, turn their knees to jelly. It didn't matter if it turned out to be a drunken friend complaining about his wife or the Questura asking

6

Brunetti to come in because a crime had been committed in the city and he was the man in charge. Even a call that ended with a sincere apology for having dialled a wrong number at that hour had the same battering effect on these hostages to fortune.

What the cost, then, of having one of their children in a foreign city in a foreign country? They were brave people, Guido Brunetti and Paola Falier, and they had often made fun of the streak of melodrama that ran through the centre of the Italian character, yet here they were, both of them, just one step short of pouring ashes on their heads at the thought that their son had begun his university career and might someday go off to some other city to study.

Paola suddenly leaned sideways against the arm of her husband. She placed her hand on his thigh. 'We'll never stop worrying about them, will we?' she asked.

'It wouldn't be natural if we did,' Brunetti said, smiling.

'Is that meant to comfort me?'

'Probably not,' Brunetti admitted. Time passed and then he added, 'It's the best thing about us, the worrying.'

'Us two or us humans?'

'Us humans,' Brunetti said. 'Us two, as well.' Then, because solemnity was not a dress either of them could wear for long, he added, 'If he decided to become a plumber, he could study here and continue to live at home, you know.'

She leaned forward and picked up the bottle. 'I think I'll seek solace here,' she said, pouring herself another glass.

2

As Brunetti walked to the Questura, he gave no thought to last night's language game and remained impervious to the crisp autumn day; his mind was taken up with less diverting matters. An email had reached him just as he was leaving his office the previous evening, telling him that his immediate superior, Vice-Questore Giuseppe Patta, wanted to speak to him the following morning. In typical fashion, Patta had given no information about the topic of their meeting: Patta always liked to have the advantage of surprise, and he believed that not to reveal what he wanted to discuss would assure that. In this he failed to take into account the sense of fair play that lay deep in the heart of his secretary, Signorina Elettra Zorzi, who invariably gave a few minutes' warning to the person she conducted to her superior's office.

Brunetti had once commented on this to her, and she had replied that it was no more than telling the Christians in the Colosseo which door the lions were hiding behind.

This morning, it seemed, they were hiding behind the door to the offices of the Vigili Urbani, those unarmed officers whose job it was to see that city ordinances were obeyed. 'It's about the pavement in front of that mask shop in Campo San Barnaba,' she said after she and Brunetti had exchanged polite greetings. 'There's been a complaint from one of the other shopkeepers in the *campo.* They're paying taxes to put their tables outside and use the space as *un plateatico,* but the people in the mask shop aren't, and they insist that there's only one way that could happen.'

Brunetti often walked through the *campo* and knew the shop, and as he cast his memory back over the years he realized that, yes, the pavement in front had, as time passed, been increasingly covered by the amoeba-like extension of the tables on which the Made in China masks were displayed. Because this was a matter that did not concern the police, but only the vigili, Brunetti had ignored it. If paying for the vigili's blindness was cheaper than paying the tax, what merchant would not opt for it?

'But why is he concerned about something like that?' Brunetti asked, indicating Patta's door with a quick turn of his head.

'He had a phone call late yesterday afternoon; a few minutes after, he came out and asked me to send you an email.'

'Who called?'

'The mayor.'

'Aha,' Brunetti said softly.

'Aha, indeed,' she echoed.

'About the shop?' he asked.

'I'm working on . . .' she began and then effortlessly transferred to a much cooler voice to finish the sentence, 'in his office and waiting for you, Commissario.'

With Patta, Brunetti knew, there existed no lily that was not in need of gilding, and so he said, voice rich with passionate – however false – intensity, 'I saw his mail a moment ago, so I came down immediately.'

Whereupon the door to Patta's office was pushed fully open from the inside, and the Vice-Questore appeared. Brunetti often reflected that, in an opera, some sort of trumpet voluntary would sound at the appearance of this man. So handsome, so noble of bearing, so impeccably well dressed: one had no choice but to admire him, much as one would admire a well-wrought urn. Today, in acknowledgement of the approach of cooler weather, Patta wore a grey cashmere suit of such exquisite cut that, had they but known the final destination of their wool, scores of rare and endangered Kashmir goats would have fought to be the first to be shorn. The cotton of his shirt was blindingly white and served to reflect light up towards his still-tanned face.

As sometimes happened to him, Brunetti had to fight down the urge to tell Patta how beautiful he was. Conscious of how fraught his dealings with his superior already were and how prone Patta was to misinterpret what was said to him, Brunetti confined his enthusiasm to a smile and a pleasant 'Good morning, Vice-Questore.'

With every show of utter uninterest in their conversation, Signorina Elettra returned to her computer, her bearing making it evident that she found it more absorbing. She seemed to disappear, as if she actually occupied less space in the room, a tactic which Brunetti both admired and envied.

Patta turned and went back into his office, saying over his shoulder, 'Come in here.'

Brunetti's sensibilities had grown a hard callus over the years, and he was now virtually invulnerable to Patta's manner. Casual disregard, the absence of respect for anyone he considered an inferior: these things no longer caused Brunetti concern. Violence or its threat might have offended or angered him, but so long as Patta chose passive, rather than active, disrespect, Brunetti remained untroubled.

'Sit,' Patta said as he walked around his desk. As Brunetti watched, the Vice-Questore crossed his legs and then, as if remembering the crease in his trousers, immediately uncrossed them. He met his subordinate's neutral glance. 'Do you know why I want to talk to you?'

'No, sir,' Brunetti said with every evidence of ignorance.

'It's about something important,' Patta said, glancing aside after he spoke. 'The mayor's son.'

Brunetti refrained from asking how the mayor's son, whom Brunetti knew to be an untalented lawyer, could be important. Instead, he tried to look eager for the Vice-Questore's revelations. He nodded with calculated neutrality.

Again, Patta crossed his legs. 'Actually, it's a favour for his son's fiancée. The girl – young woman – owns a shop. Well, half owns a shop. She has a partner. And the partner has been doing something that might not be entirely legal.' Patta stopped, either to draw breath or to search for a way to explain to Brunetti how something not 'entirely legal' might refer to the bribery of a public official. Clam-like, Brunetti sat in his safe place and waited to see what route Patta would choose.

The straight and narrow, as it turned out, at least in the fashion that term was understood by the Vice-Questore. 'For some time, the partner has been persuading the vigili to ignore the tables outside the shop.' Patta stopped, his use of the word, 'persuading' proof that he had exhausted his store of frankness.

'Where is this shop, Dottore?' Brunetti asked.

'In Campo San Barnaba. It sells masks.'

Brunetti closed his eyes and gave every appearance of searching through his memory. 'Next to the shop with the expensive cheese?'

Patta raised his head quickly and stared at Brunetti, as though he'd caught him trying to steal his wallet. 'How do you know that?' he demanded.

Calmly, calmly, with an easy smile, Brunetti said, 'I live near there, sir, so I pass through the *campo* often.' When Patta said no more, Brunetti prodded, 'I'm not sure I understand your involvement in this, Dottore.'

Patta cleared his throat and said, 'As I mentioned, it's her partner who's been dealing with the vigili, and only now has this young woman realized that he might have been inducing them to ignore the space they use in front of the shop.'

In response to an intentionally dull look from Brunetti, Patta added, 'It's possible they don't have all the permits to use that space.'

Hearing 'inducing' and 'it's possible', Brunetti wondered what he would have to do to make Patta use the word 'bribe'. Hold his hand over a flame? Threaten to rip off one of his ears? And had Patta any intention of revealing the identity of the partner?

'You have friends who work there, don't you?' Patta asked.

'Where, sir?' Brunetti asked, unsure whether Patta meant the office that granted the permits and, if so, why the mayor couldn't just walk down the hall in the Commune and do his son's dirty work for him.

'The vigili, of course,' Patta said with a certain lack of patience. 'They're all Venetian, so you must know them.' Though he had been working in Venice for more than a decade, Patta still thought of himself as a Sicilian, an opinion in which he was joined by everyone else at the Questura.

'I do know some of them, Dottore,' Brunetti said and then, suddenly tired of the conversation, asked, 'What would you like me to do?'

Patta leaned forward and answered in a softer voice. 'Speak to them.'

Brunetti nodded, hoping that his silence would be answered with further information.

Patta, perhaps realizing a certain lack of precision in his instructions said, 'I'd like you to find out if the vigili involved are trustworthy.'

'Ah,' Brunetti allowed himself to say, making no sign of the wild hilarity evoked in him by Patta's choice of word. Trustworthy? Not to reveal that they had been accepting bribes from the business partner of the mayor's future daughter-in-law? Trustworthy? Not to reveal that a request for information had come from a commissario of police? Trustworthy? Brunetti found it interesting that it seemed never to have occurred to Patta to wonder if the same thing could be said of the mayor, or his son, or his son's fiancée.

A long silence settled on the room. A minute passed, quite a long time when two men are seated facing one another. A sudden obstinacy overcame Brunetti: if Patta wanted something from him, then he would have to ask him for it directly.

Some of this must have conveyed itself to Patta, for he finally said, 'I want to know if there's any danger this might become public, if this girl is going to cause him trouble.' He shifted in his seat and added, 'These are difficult times.'

So there it was: the girl might cause the mayor – who

was to run for re-election the following year – trouble. This was not about law: it was about reputation and probably about re-election. In a land where no one was without sin, everyone feared the first hand that reached for a rock, especially if the hand emerged from the cuff of a uniform. Once that started, there was no knowing when the next hand reaching for a rock might emerge from the pale grey uniform sleeve of the Guardia di Finanza.

'But how can I find out?' Brunetti inquired politely, as if he were not already busy making a list of the various ways he could.

'You're Venetian, for God's sake. You can talk to these people: they trust you.' Then, aside, to some invisible Recorder of Injustices, Patta said, 'It's a secret club you have, you Venetians. You do things among yourselves, in your own way.'

This, Brunetti forbore to say, from a Sicilian.

'I'll see what I can find out,' was all he said. He got to his feet and left the office.

When Brunetti stepped out of Patta's office, Signorina Elettra glanced in his direction and raised one eyebrow. Brunetti doubled the gesture and made a circling gesture with one hand to tell her to come up to his office when she could. Face still bland, she turned back to the screen of her computer, and Brunetti left the room.

He stopped in the officers' squad room and asked Pucetti to come upstairs with him. Inside, when the young officer was seated, Brunetti said, 'You have much to do with the vigili?'

He watched Pucetti try to figure out the reason for the question and liked him for that. 'My cousin Sandro is one, sir. So was his father until he retired.'

'You close to them?' Brunetti asked.

'They're family, sir,' Pucetti said.

'Close enough to ask them about bribes?'

Pucetti weighed this up before he answered. 'Sandro, yes; my uncle, no.'

Curious, Brunetti asked, 'Because you couldn't ask him or because he wouldn't tell you?'

'A little bit of both, I think, sir. But mostly because he wouldn't tell me.'

'How long did he work for them?'

'Forty years, sir. Until he retired.'

'So you're a police family?' Brunetti asked with a smile.

'I suppose you could say that, Dottore. Sandro's brother Luca is in the Guardia Costiera.'

'Anyone else?'

'No, sir.' Then, with a smile, Pucetti added, 'My mother has a German Shepherd. Does that count?'

'I'm afraid not, Pucetti. Not unless it's been trained to smell bombs or drugs.'

Pucetti's smile broadened. 'I'm afraid all he can smell is food, Dottore.' Then he asked, 'What do you want to know about the vigili, sir?'

'It's about that mask shop in Campo San Barnaba. I've been told the vigili have been ignoring the *plateatico* they use.'

Pucetti glanced away, no doubt hunting for the shop in his route-walking memory. He looked back at Brunetti and said, 'I'll ask Sandro, sir.'

Brunetti thanked him and sent him back to the squad room. Glancing at his watch, he saw that it was well past the hour to go down to the bar at the bridge for a coffee. Signorina Elettra would come up in good time, he was certain.

3

In order to distract himself from continuing to think about Patta's request, Brunetti went downstairs and asked Vianello if he'd like to come for a coffee. The Inspector closed the file he was reading and got to his feet. They walked along the *riva* side by side, occasionally moving out of the way of the people walking towards them. Vianello talked about his vacation, which he had delayed until November and was now trying to organize.

Inside the bar, they exchanged pleasantries with Sergio, the owner, who now worked only a few days a week. They ordered two coffees; while they waited, Vianello pulled a pamphlet from his pocket and placed it on the counter in front of Brunetti. He saw a long expanse of white sand, the usual palm trees bending down towards it, and in the far distance the beaches, equally white, of small islands.

'Where's this?' Brunetti asked, tapping a finger on one of the trees.

'The Seychelles,' Vianello answered just as Sergio brought them their coffees. Vianello ripped open a packet of sugar and poured it into his cup, then added, 'Nadia wants to go there.'

'You sound as if you don't want to,' Brunetti said as he stirred sugar into his own coffee.

'I don't,' Vianello answered.

'But you've got this,' Brunetti said, licking his spoon clean and using it to tap the brochure.

'Nadia got it,' Vianello clarified.

'And you're carrying it around.'

Vianello took a sip of coffee, swirled the cup twice, and finished it. He set it on the saucer and said, 'I'm carrying it around, but I'm also carrying around the receipt for the hotel in Umbria we've reserved for the first two weeks in November.'

'Can you cancel the reservation?' Brunetti asked.

Vianello shrugged. 'I suppose I can. Nadia went to school with the owner, and he knows how crazy my schedule can be. But I wanted the kids to see it.'

'Any particular reason?' Brunetti asked.

'Because it's a working farm. Not one of those places where they keep a donkey in a field and sell you apples to give to it,' Vianello said with contempt. 'They've got cows and sheep and chickens, all those animals my kids think live inside the television.'

'Come on, Lorenzo,' Brunetti said with a smile, 'they're a little too old for that.'

Vianello smiled, 'I know. But the animals might as well be on TV. How are city kids supposed to know what an animal is and what it does or what it's like to work the land?'

'You think that's important?' Brunetti asked.

'Of course it's important,' Vianello said, perhaps too

fiercely. 'You know it is. Everyone's always telling us we should respect nature, but if kids never see it, how are they going to respect it? All they get are some crazy ideas that television gives them.'

'That's television's job, I think,' Brunetti observed.

'What is?'

'Giving people crazy ideas,' he said, then asked, 'What are you going to do?' He knew Vianello's wife and was surprised that she'd had an idea like this. 'Are you sure Nadia really wants to go to the Seychelles?'

Vianello asked Sergio for a glass of tap water and did not speak until the barman set it in front of him, when he said, 'She got the brochure and said that it would be wonderful to get away from the cold.' He drank the water, set the glass back down. 'Doesn't that sound like she wants to go?' He did not look at Brunetti as he asked this.

'Are you going to tell me the real reason?' Brunetti surprised Vianello, and perhaps himself, by asking. 'Why you don't want to go?' Before Vianello could protest, Brunetti said, 'I know, I know, the kids need to be exposed to nature.'

Vianello picked up his glass and was surprised to find it empty. He put two Euros on the counter and turned towards the door.

Outside, they fell into step and started back to the Questura. Brunetti, content to have asked his question, waited for his friend to speak. A boat puttered past them, a mottled brown dog standing at the front, barking with the joy of the boat's forward motion.

'We shouldn't do things like that,' Vianello finally said.

'Like what?'

'Travel those distances,' Vianello said. 'Just to go and lie in the sand and look at the sea, I mean.' The barking diminished, and Vianello went on. 'If you're a neurosurgeon and you have to go somewhere to save a life, then get on a plane and fly. But not to lie on the beach. It's not right.' Then, happy to think of further justification, Vianello added, 'Besides, the sun's bad for you.'

They walked a few more steps. 'Right in an ecological sense?' asked Brunetti, unable to resist the impulse to take a poke at Vianello's growing enthusiasm.

Eventually Vianello said, 'Yes.'

Brunetti slowed down and then stopped. He rested his forearms on the metal railing beside the canal and turned back towards the leaning tower of the Greek church. Another boat entered the canal from the right, passed them, then the Questura, and went on its way.

Brunetti stood there, watching the boat approach the far turn and thinking about Vianello's use of the word 'right'. It was a smallish boat, and there was no appearance of cargo in it, so the man might well be going down to Castello to meet his friends for a drink and a game of cards. Like all motors, however small, this one would leave a slick of oil on the water, adding to the pollution and thus to the eventual death of the *laguna*. So, under Vianello's system of judgement, would the man's trip be condemned as not 'right', or was there a factor of quantity to be considered? Or, as Vianello had stated, necessity? How much could we do before it became wrong?

The priests, he remembered, had taught him and his friends that gluttony was one of the cardinal sins, but Brunetti had never known what gluttony was. More accurately, though he had grasped that it meant eating too much, he had never understood where 'too much' began. How could wanting a second helping of his mother's *sarde in saor* be wrong? Which sardine would push him over the edge from pleasure to sin? It was this perplexity that had led the young Brunetti to the realization of how strongly the priests associated pleasure with sin, and that had put an end to that.

'Well?' Vianello asked when the boat had disappeared and Brunetti had still not spoken.

'I think you should go to Umbria.'

'And my reason for wanting to go there?' Vianello asked.

'It's a perfectly legitimate one,' Brunetti answered and, pushing himself back from the railing, headed towards the Questura.

Vianello hung back; not hearing his footsteps, Brunetti stopped, turned to him and raised his chin interrogatively. 'You think it's legitimate or you agree with me?' Vianello asked.

'I think it's legitimate and I agree with you,' Brunetti said, walked back to Vianello, and clapped him on the shoulder. 'I don't know what good it's going to do for the planet or for the universe . . .' he said and his voice trailed away.

'But?' Vianello asked.

'But if you don't go, then you avoid doing something that's harmful, and that's a good thing.'

Vianello smiled and said, 'I didn't think of it that way. All I knew was that it wasn't right.' After a moment, he added, 'Besides, I've always wanted to learn how to milk a cow.'

That stopped Brunetti in his tracks. He took a close look at Vianello to see if he was joking. Finally he said, 'You're serious, aren't you?'

'Of course,' Vianello answered.

Turning back towards the Questura, Brunetti said over his shoulder, 'You paid for the coffee, so I won't tell Signorina Elettra you said that.'

4

Since he would be passing her office, Brunetti decided to save Signorina Elettra the trip to his; besides, he was curious to learn whatever she might know about the reasons behind Patta's request. Good as his word, he decided to say nothing to her about Vianello's bucolic desires. The relaxed smile she gave him as he went in told Brunetti that the Vice-Questore had gone off on crusade against wrongdoing in some other location.

'What have you managed to find about the mayor's son?' Brunetti asked, having no doubt that she had been in pursuit of that information.

She pushed back a vagrant curl and turned her screen towards him. 'As you can see,' she said, pointing to the printed form he saw there, 'it took him eight years to finish university and another three before he passed the state exams.'

'And now?' Brunetti asked.

'He works in the law office of a friend of his father's.'

She scrolled down to another document and pointed to the screen. 'He also has a job as a regional counsellor.'

'Doing what?' Brunetti asked, then, remembering that he was talking about a political position, changed it to, 'Meant to be doing what?'

'He has been appointed to serve as liaison between students and the regional department of sport.' Her delivery was as neutral as Médecins sans Frontières.

'What does that mean?' Brunetti asked with curiosity he did not have to feign.

She typed in a few words and hit the ENTER key: a new document appeared on the screen. The young man's name was at the top and, below it, a row of figures. 'And this is?' Brunetti asked.

'It's the payment that was made to his bank account by the regional treasury last month,' she said. She turned the screen further in Brunetti's direction.

The young man's base salary was four thousand four hundred Euros a month; added to this was a fixed sum of nine hundred Euros for office expenses and one thousand nine hundred for a secretary.

'Dare I ask the name of his secretary?' Brunetti asked.

'Lucia Ravagni,' Signorina Elettra answered.

'Is she by any chance the part owner of a shop in Campo San Barnaba?' he asked, almost as if a voice had whispered the necessary question into his ear.

'Yes.'

'If he's a lawyer and she's running a shop, when is it that they find time to work as a regional counsellor and a secretary? And where?' Brunetti asked.

'There's an office assigned to them in the Uffici Regionali.'

'"Assigned?"'

'A friend of mine who works in one of the offices on

the second floor – their offices are on the first – says they are seldom in evidence.'

'No doubt keeping a careful eye on sporting events,' Brunetti suggested.

'Or students,' she added in the bright tone she used in response to life's many absurdities. But then Signorina Elettra's voice grew serious and she asked, 'Why do we tolerate this? Why do we let them appoint their friends and their wives and their children and not go after them with clubs?'

Brunetti, as he did with increasing frequency, chose to treat her outburst seriously. 'I think it's because we're a tolerant people and understand human weakness. And because, for most of us, the only people we trust fully are members of our families, so we understand when other people do, as well.'

'Do you trust yours?' she asked in an uncharacteristic display of curiosity.

'Yes.'

'Everyone in it?'

'More than I would the state, or most of its representatives, yes,' Brunetti said and then, to extricate himself – perhaps both of them – from the unwonted intimacy of the conversation, said, 'I'd like you to find out anything else you can about them.'

'I've asked some people,' was her answer.

Very conscious of the fact that, as a civilian employee, Signorina Elettra had no official role in the work of the police and had taken no oath to the state, and thus should in no way be made privy to the investigations of the police, Brunetti said, 'The mayor wants Patta to be sure that nothing is made public about the bribes her partner has been paying the vigili.'

She hit a key, and the screen grew dark. Idly, she turned

it towards her but kept her eyes on Brunetti. 'I wonder what's going on.'

'Indeed,' Brunetti said.

As if surprised by her own realization, she said, 'There's something of the purity of a syllogism in my eagerness to work on this.'

'Meaning?'

'I want bad things to happen to politicians. The mayor is a politician. Therefore, I want bad things to happen to the mayor.'

Her smile positively glowed. 'It leaves me little choice, does it?' she asked.

'As a syllogism, there is no flaw in it,' Brunetti said, logic having been one of his heart's delights at university. Then, soberly, 'But it deals with emotions, not really with facts, doesn't it, so I'm not sure that it is within the mandate of the syllogism. At least as a means of proof.'

Her look was sober when she said, 'There is no error of fact, Dottore: not in the first premise, and not in the second, and certainly not in the conclusion.' Then, lightly, 'I'll let you know whatever I find.'

It made no sense. It made no sense. It made no sense. Brunetti repeated this to himself as he climbed the steps to his office. Then, for the last flight: no sense, no sense, no sense. What did the mayor have in mind when he asked Patta to see if things could be kept quiet? The more people who were told to keep something quiet, the greater the certainty that it would become public information. Or was the mayor, like so many of his colleagues, convinced that he was somehow above the normal rules that governed human behaviour? Why else would politicians continue to speak so openly of their crimes and misdemeanours on *telefonini* that even they must know were open to the ears of many of the forces of order? Why continue to discuss bribes with the men who paid them? Why give thousands of Euros to prostitutes and, when caught, claim it was a payment made to keep them from falling into prostitution? How stupid they must believe us to be; what contemptible sheep we are to them.

Surely, not all politicians could be like this. Were this the case, Brunetti realized, the only options open to a decent person would be emigration, or suicide.

His phone was ringing when he entered his office. Believing it might be Patta, suddenly returned to the Questura, he answered with his name.

'You know the boy who doesn't talk?' Paola asked. 'At the dry cleaner's?'

His mind still on politicians and Patta, Brunetti could think of nothing more than, 'What?'

'The boy who worked in the dry cleaner's. The deaf one.' He could tell from her voice that Paola was troubled, but it took him a moment to recall the boy, who sometimes used to be seen in the back room of the shop, folding things or standing idly, head moving back and forth as his eyes followed the motions of the iron that imposed order on shirts and dresses. Brunetti's memory of him was hazy, save for the folding and for the odd, arrhythmic way the boy moved.

'Yes,' he finally said. 'Why?'

'He's dead,' Paola said, sounding saddened by the news. But then she said, 'At least that's the rumour in the neighbourhood.'

'What happened?' Brunetti asked, wondering what sort of accident could have befallen him and how his deafness might have contributed to it. Many of the delivery men who pushed their wheeled metal carts around the city cried ahead to warn people to get out of the way: because he could not hear, the boy might have been run over, crushed, anything. Or knocked down the steps of a bridge or into the water.

'A man at the bar where I was having coffee said he saw an ambulance in front of a house this morning, and when they came out they were carrying one of those plastic boxes. He knew that's where he lived – the deaf boy – so he asked the men if that's who it was. All they told him was that it was someone from the first floor, a man.' She paused, then asked, 'They carry dead people in those, don't they?'

Brunetti, who had seen too many of them, confirmed this.

There was a long silence, and then Paola said, 'I don't know what to do.'

Her remark confused Brunetti. If he was dead, there was nothing she, or anyone, could do. 'I don't understand.'

'His family. Do something for them.'

'Do you even know who his family is?'

'It's the people at the dry cleaner's, isn't it?'

Brunetti felt a flash of irritation that his time was being taken up with this, and that was followed by a flash of shame. Was he meant to reprimand his wife for an excess of compassion? 'I don't know. I've never paid attention.'

'It must be,' Paola said. 'He was pretty useless as a worker. I always figured he was the son of the woman who runs the place or maybe of the one who irons. No one else would have hired him.' After a moment, she added, 'Though I haven't seen him there for a long time. I wonder what happened?'

'I've no idea,' Brunetti said. 'You can't very well ask, can you?'

'No. No.'

26

'Maybe the newsagent?'

'You know I can't ask him,' Paola said.

Four years ago, Paola and the newsagent had got into a heated discussion when she asked him why he sold a certain newspaper and the man replied that it was because people wanted it. That had led Paola, a woman not known for moderation in argument, to ask if he'd use the same justification if he sold drugs, before putting down the money for her newspapers and walking away.

It had been Brunetti, after she recounted the incident at dinner, who had told her that the man's son had died some years before of an overdose, information that had reduced Paola to tears of shame. She had gone back the next day and tried to apologize, but the man had turned his back on her and returned to untying a parcel of magazines. Since then, it had fallen to Brunetti to buy the newspapers.

'Would you ask him? Or someone else in the neighbourhood?' she asked.

Before he agreed, Brunetti wanted to know: 'Is this curiosity or concern?'

'Concern,' she answered immediately. 'He was such a miserable creature. I don't even know how long I saw him there. Or on the street. Or standing there in the back room, folding clothes or watching them work. And always looking so terribly sad.'

Brunetti remembered the boy's awkward gestures, the odd jerking of his head that suggested other problems more serious than the deafness that had cut him off from the world.

'Was there anything else wrong with him?' he broke in to ask.

'What do you mean? Isn't being a deaf mute enough?'

'Was he mute, too?'

27

'Did you ever hear him speak?'

'No,' Brunetti answered, unsure whether this meant he had to be dumb, as well as deaf. 'I told you; I hardly noticed him.'

Paola sighed, 'I'm afraid that's what most people will say. How awful, eh?'

'Yes. It is.'

'Oh my God,' Paola said. 'I don't even know his name if I want to ask about him. He's just the boy who doesn't talk. Didn't talk.'

'I think people will know who you mean.'

'That's not what I'm talking about, Guido,' she said, words that would usually be spoken angrily but now radiated only sadness. 'That's what's so awful. Think about how old he must have been. Thirty-five? Forty? More? And we all referred to him as a boy.' Then, after another pause, 'The boy who doesn't talk.'

'I'll see if they know anything downstairs,' Brunetti volunteered. 'And at the hospital.'

'Thanks, Guido,' she said. 'I know it sounds as if I'm being a baby over this, but it's terrible – to have a life like that, and then die, and people don't even know your name.'

'I'll see what I can find out,' Brunetti said and replaced the phone.

He picked it up immediately and dialled the number of the morgue. Identifying himself to Rizzardi's assistant, he asked if they had had a man brought in from San Polo that morning.

'He's with him now,' the man explained, quite as though Rizzardi were a normal doctor and were in the examining room having a look to see what the problem was.

'I'm in my office. Would you ask him to call me when he's finished?'

'Of course, Dottore.'

Paola was right, he realized. To have lived a life, even a life cut short in the middle, and not to have a name to be called by, to live among people who did not know your name – Brunetti had no word to describe it. If the man – he would call him a man now, not a boy – had been mute as well as deaf, how had he communicated with the world around him? How had he expressed even the most simple desire, save by pointing at the thing he wanted? But what if he were cold or hot or wanted something to eat: was he reduced to a life of pantomime? Had someone taught him to read? To write? To sign? And if not, then how did he establish contact with the world?

It daunted Brunetti, the pathos of it.

The phone rang, and when he answered he heard Rizzardi's voice. 'Ciao, Guido. Franco said you called about the man from San Polo.'

'Yes. My wife called me and told me he was dead. We knew him. Sort of.'

Rizzardi did not ask for clarification, leading Brunetti to wonder whether all any of us ever do is sort of know people. He continued, 'So I called to ask you to tell me what you can about him.'

'His name is,' Rizzardi began, said, 'Wait a minute,' and set the phone down. He was back in a few seconds and said, 'Davide Cavanella, or at least that's the name written on the papers that came with him. Someone at the address must have given it to them.'

'What caused his death?'

'It could be suicide,' the pathologist said.

'Suicide?' repeated an astonished Brunetti. 'But he was a deaf mute. And he may have been retarded.' He had no idea why those two things should exclude the possibility of suicide, but they did.

'I'm not sure I see the connection,' Rizzardi answered mildly. 'If anything, I'd think those poor devils would be more likely to kill themselves than the rest of us. At least we have the comfort of complaining about our lives and having people listen to us.'

'Are you joking, Ettore?' Brunetti asked.

After a brief pause, Rizzardi said, 'I might have been, when I said it, but I think it's true. I don't know about you, but it helps me to be able to complain or to be angry and have people tell me I'm right to think the way I do.'

'Me, too,' Brunetti agreed. Then he asked, 'How'd he die?'

'It started out the most peaceful way, and then it got ugly,' the pathologist said.

'What does that mean?'

'He took sleeping pills, quite a lot of them, with what I think was hot chocolate and something sweet: biscuits or cake. And a lot of these pills are brightly coloured.'

'Excuse me?'

'You said he might have been retarded,' the pathologist explained. 'The pills might have looked like sweets to him.'

Brunetti considered this possibility and then asked, 'And then?'

'He fell asleep on his back, and then he started to vomit,' Rizzardi began, paused and then asked, 'You know what happens, don't you?'

'Yes.'

It was some time before Rizzardi spoke again. 'It must be awful. You think you're going to go to sleep peacefully, and then you end up choking to death. Poor devil. Terrible. Terrible.'

It had happened to Brunetti only once, choking, when he was a young man and a piece of bread got caught in his throat. Luckily, he'd been eating in a trattoria, and even more luckily, the waiter serving the next table had dropped the plates he was carrying and grabbed Brunetti from behind, yanking him to his feet and enclosing him in an iron grip. A terrified Brunetti had coughed up the piece of bread, followed quickly by everything he had eaten that day. Draped across the table, his sleeve in a plate of pasta, Brunetti had slowly gasped himself back to life and, returned to it, had been astonished to find himself in an almost empty room.

Decades later, he could still remember the terror that had gripped him and the certainty that he was going to die. One thing that had astonished him at the time was his perception that everything was happening with courtly slowness. His hands had moved at a snail's pace to grasp his own throat; the plates the waiter let fall when he started towards Brunetti had floated to the floor as slowly as snowflakes. And the sharp jolt of pressure to his chest that had saved his life had taken for ever to come.

He still remembered that strange prolongation of time, and the sense, when he looked up from the table, breathing almost normally, that time had slipped back to its normal pace.

' . . . no sign of organic damage,' he heard Rizzardi say.

'What?' Brunetti asked.

'I didn't find any sign of organic damage.'

'But he died,' said a confused Brunetti, trying to recall what little he knew of physiology. 'Choking would stop the oxygen, wouldn't it?' Beyond that, he had no idea what the actual cause of death would be. Lack of oxygen to the brain? Or to the lungs and then to the brain? But what did that *do*?

'Oh, there was that,' Rizzardi said. 'I was talking about his ears. I didn't see any sign of injury or scarring from

illness that would have caused the deafness.' The pathologist continued, reflectively, 'But if it was genetic, then
there'd be nothing to see, anyway. There was no sign of
damage to his vocal cords, either.'

Brunetti, still puzzled as to what the actual physical
cause of death might have been, didn't react to this and
only asked, 'Would the pills have killed him, anyway?
Even without the choking?'

'I think so.'

'Only think?'

With a voice into which he put an almost parental calm,
Rizzardi said, 'I'm waiting for the results of the lab tests.'

'Let me know when you get them, will you?' Brunetti
asked.

'I'll send the report to you,' Rizzardi said, then added,
as if he had the power to read Brunetti's mind, 'The
choking cuts off oxygen to the brain, and that shuts down
the whole system. It can happen in a few minutes. That's
enough.' That said, the pathologist put down the phone.

The very words, 'a few minutes', renewed Brunetti's
memory of and terror at his own experience. What would
it be like to choke for minutes? And had this poor dead
man experienced the bizarre elasticization of time?

5

Brunetti had time to tell Paola only the bare facts of the man's death before the kids arrived for lunch, which put an end to the subject. Over a salad of carpaccio of red beet, ruccola and parmigiano, Chiara asked permission to go on a school trip to Padova that coming Saturday, and over involtini of chicken breast, which she ignored and replaced with cheese, her parents gave their permission for her to go. As soon as everyone was finished, Chiara went to her room to study, and Raffi went off to play soccer with friends on what the family agreed was probably going to be one of the few remaining mild afternoons of the autumn. Brunetti returned to the Questura.

Signorina Elettra had left before lunch, having selected herself as the person to attend an afternoon presentation by the Guardia di Finanza on the newest techniques for detecting and combating identity theft and computer hacking. When Brunetti had learned of this, he had expected protest from those police officers who might more rightfully have been chosen to attend. Not a whimper.

Had it been any other employee, Brunetti realized, he would have looked askance at her self-selection, but the ways of Signorina Elettra, though they were not beyond reproach, were assuredly beyond question: like his sense of time when he had choked on the piece of bread, her prerogatives had expanded.

Dutifully, Brunetti spent the afternoon going through the files that had accumulated on his desk during the last weeks, reading through them methodically, or at least allowing his eyes to pass methodically over the words. Because he had lived for more than two decades with a woman who responded to infelicities of language with the ardour of a shark greeted by a bleeding wound, Brunetti's interest was kept alive, if not by the subject matter of the documents, then by the language in which these subjects were presented. A man who had beaten his wife senseless, causing her to lose the sight of one eye, spoke during his questioning of his 'difficulty in sustaining a life-affirming relationship'; the wife of a prominent lawyer, caught at the doors of the Armani shop wearing a short leather jacket with the price tags carefully sliced from it, maintained that she had 'serious problems in recognizing the arbitrary distinctions in ownership between shop and client', and maintained that she was, anyway, merely stepping into the *calle* to see how the colour looked in the light of day. The fact that the bag she wore across her shoulder held five T-shirts and two pairs of slacks did nothing to clarify her rhetoric, though it did clarify the situation. It had taken her husband less than two hours to arrive at the Questura with a certificate from a psychiatrist, attesting the woman's pre-existing 'difficulties in ownership assignment', and thus she had been released.

34

Brunetti suspected he should be troubled, or at least embarrassed, by the amusement these phrases provoked in him, especially in the first case, but he was not. Politicians made no discernible sense when they spoke, few doctors used the word 'cancer' with patients who had it, and the word 'immigrant' could no longer be prefaced by 'illegal'. Detach language from meaning, and the world was yours.

Shaking his head when he found himself entertaining thoughts like this, he got to his feet and walked over to the window. The cat condominium still stood in front of the church of San Lorenzo. At this distance, Brunetti could not see any of the residents in front of it, but the sight of the tiny structure cheered him, as it always did. Unruly creatures, cats, and profoundly, incorrigibly disobedient. Were Paola not allergic, they would have one, perhaps two. Out loud, he found himself saying, in English, as did she, '"For he is an instrument for the children to learn benevolence upon."' And so they are, Brunetti supposed.

He returned to his desk and to the reports, forcing himself, like a swimmer in icy water, to stick at it and move ahead, though his destination seemed to move farther off, the more he struggled to reach it. It was a call from Paola that hauled him to the shore.

'I called Donata Masi,' she said, naming a colleague from the university who lived in Campo dei Frari and thus, Brunetti realized, close to the dry cleaner's.

'What did she tell you?' he asked, knowing what the subject matter had to be.

'That he wasn't the son of either of the women there. She said she asked about him, years ago, and they told her they let him pretend to work there because they felt sorry for him.'

'Pretend how?' Brunetti asked.

'Oh, you know. Folding clothes up and sometimes taking parcels home for people. Ironing flat things.' He wanted to ask how this could have gone on for years, with never an official inspection of the place to see who was working there, but his wife was hardly the person to know, and so he let it pass.

'Anything else?' he asked.

'No,' Paola said, sounding disappointed. 'I asked her if she knew his family, but she clammed up and said she didn't want to get involved. So I changed the subject and asked her about a committee meeting we have tomorrow.'

Brunetti wasted no time by asking what it was Donata didn't want to get involved in. The possibility that officialdom in any of its manifestations might interest itself in a matter – any matter – was enough to cause a cordon sanitaire to form around the subject. People stopped talking, people knew nothing, people forgot. Let officialdom be represented in the form of the police, and forgetting quickly turned into total amnesia. The newspapers had recently been filled with accounts of women who had been raped by the Carabinieri who had arrested them or, in some cases, who had been raped by the officers to whom they had gone to report a crime. Trust the police?

'And so?' he asked.

'So I don't know what to do,' Paola admitted.

He allowed his sadness to seep into his voice and said, 'There's nothing you can do, Paola.'

It took her a moment to answer. 'The least I can do is let his family know he's remembered by some of us. Not just by the women in the dry cleaner's, but by some of us who saw him all these years.'

'And what will that do?' he asked. He knew he should not, but at times he lost all patience with her eternal desire to do the noble thing.

36

'It won't *do* anything, Guido,' she said fiercely. 'It's not supposed to *do* anything. He's dead, so there's nothing anyone can *do*. But at least there can be some acknowledgement that people knew him and that he wasn't just some poor dumb creature passing through life without anyone paying attention to him.'

The little Brunetti had observed of the dead man suggested that this last description was in fact closer to the truth, but he lacked the will to say it. He evaded confrontation by saying, 'I'll ask downstairs and call the ambulance service and see what information they have about his family. If he has any. His name was Davide Cavanella.' Before she could ask, he said, 'Rizzardi gave it to me.'

'Was he allowed to live alone?' she burst out.

'Paola,' Brunetti said with great steadiness, 'I'll make a few phone calls and see what I can find out about him. All right?' It wasn't a test of wills, not really, but it was a test of whether she could still be reeled back from the edge of the verbal excess she invariably regretted.

Her silence told Brunetti that she was as aware as he of how each of them was expecting the other to behave. 'All right,' she said at last. 'Call me . . .' she started to say, and then changed it to, 'No, tell me about it when you get home.'

He used an affectionate name and replaced the receiver.

He phoned downstairs first to find out if the call about the man's death had come to the Questura. Nothing of the kind, he was told. The Ospedale Civile gave a similar answer and referred him to the Carabinieri at Riva degli Schiavoni. After some time, they told him that they had received a call at 6.13 that morning and, informed that the person was dead, had sent the city hearse which was under the authority of the Ulss system, though it hadn't been sent from the hospital.

Brunetti took a few deep breaths to restore himself to the calm necessary to deal with bureaucracy and dialled the number the Carabinieri had given him. And it was from them that he finally learned the address of the dead man: San Polo 2364. As was often the case, the number meant nothing to Brunetti until he had looked in *Calli, Campielli e Canali*, where he saw that it was in one of the small *calli* beyond Campo San Stin.

He opened his bottom drawer and started to pull out the phone book, irritated with himself that he had not thought of this simple solution first. His hand stopped when he remembered that the man was deaf: perhaps it was no solution at all. But perhaps he lived with a family member: someone must be able to answer a phone. Brunetti looked at the far wall and summoned up the memory of the man: expressionless face, forever concentrated on something no one else could see, or hear; mouth always a bit open, perhaps to aid breathing; a restless lack of coordination that affected his walk and the way he repeatedly patted the cloth when he tried to fold the garments in the back room of the dry cleaner's.

He opened the book and looked through the Cs until he found Cavanella, Ana, at that address. Before even deciding to do it or knowing why he should want to, Brunetti dialled the number. It rang six times before a deep voice that was probably a woman's answered with '*Sì.*' There was no interrogation in the word, no curiosity.

'Signora Cavanella,' Brunetti began.

'*Sì,*' she repeated.

'This is Commissario Guido Brunetti. I'm calling to . . . .' Before he could finish the sentence, Brunetti was speaking to silence: the woman had replaced the phone.

He looked at his watch. It was just after five, so if he assigned himself the task of going to speak to her in person, he would be so close to home when he finished the interview that there would be no sense in his returning to the Questura.

He took the Number Two to San Tomà, walked past the Frari, down the bridge and along the canal towards Campo San Stin. He crossed it and turned right at the second *calle*. The name he wanted was on the third door on the left. He rang it and waited.

After what seemed a long time, he heard a shutter open above him. Brunetti stepped back and looked up. A woman with a cloud of too-red hair stood at the first floor window, looking down at him.

'Who are you?' she asked with no preliminaries and less grace.

'I'm Commissario Brunetti, Signora,' he answered politely, suddenly not at all sure just how it was he had ended up here, staring up at her uninviting expression. 'There are some questions we have to ask you,' he improvised. As he spoke, he studied her face – she was barely five metres from him – looking for signs of resemblance to a man he had to confess he barely remembered and, aside from his odd, robotic movements, probably would not have recognized.

'About what?' she asked. Brunetti wondered what she thought the police might have come to ask about, but then his mind caught up with the absolute lack of emotion in her question and it occurred to him that she might have been pushed – either by grief or the drugs used to combat it – into a place beyond all emotion or the ability to register it.

He backed into the *calle*, so that he could speak to her without having to look almost directly above himself.

'What do you want?' she asked.

'To speak to you, Signora,' he said, though he had still

39

given no conscious thought to what he wanted to say to her.

She considered his statement, said '*Va bene*', then closed the window and turned away.

Brunetti returned to the door and waited; and continued to wait. After a few minutes, the door was pulled open. The woman stepped forward and stood in the doorway, repeating, 'What do you want?' Her voice was neutral, devoid of interest. He could have been trying to sell her a set of cooking pots or to convert her to the love of Jesus.

'First, to express my condolences, Signora, and then to ask if there is any help you might need from any agency of the city.' Brunetti knew he had only the authority of humanity to offer the first and no authority whatsoever to offer the second. But he had told Paola he would try to help, and he would do that in whatever form he could.

She looked at him directly and Brunetti had the strange sensation that she was waiting for his words to be played back so that she could understand what they meant. In a situation such as this, Brunetti's first impulse was usually to speak again, but he remained silent, curious to see how long it would take her to answer him. A long time passed: she looked blankly at him, while Brunetti studied her.

She might have been in her fifties, but he wasn't sure at which end of them he found her. The red hair stopped two centimetres from her scalp and slipped into white for the rest of the way home. Her eyes were a clear blue, the skin around them virtually unlined. Her nose and well-defined cheekbones were further evidence that she might once have been a great beauty. And it was in the angled line of those bones that he caught a fleeting glimpse of the dead man.

She was taller than average, though the thickening around her waist suggested that she might once have been taller still. Her hands, he noticed, had inordinately short fingers and the shiny skin that comes to hands that have spent a lot of time in hot water.

Brunetti realized that she had no intention of speaking: he could stand there for the rest of the afternoon and still she would not say anything to him. 'Would you like to come to see Davide, Signora?' he finally asked.

At the mention of the name, she took a half-step backwards, as though trying to escape the name or the grief it brought her. She held up one of those thick, work-branded hands to ward off his words, stepped back into the house, and closed the door.

6

Though the woman's retreat meant Brunetti could go home early, his failure to get her to speak to him left him dissatisfied and, strangely enough, uncomfortable about going home when he should still be at work. He told himself not to behave like a schoolboy whose teacher might call and find him still at home when he was meant to be at school and, screwing up his courage, went to a bar in Campo San Polo and took a seat outside. He ordered a spritz, sure it would be the last of the season: a month from now, the thought of ice and chilled Aperol – chilled anything, for that matter – would set his teeth on edge. But the late afternoon sun was gentle on his face, and he was happy to sit in it and watch the world go by, busying itself with things he no longer had to concern himself with today.

He studied the *campo*, glad it was one of the big ones, where kids could play soccer or ride their bicycles, the second in violation of some city ordinance that no one liked or bothered to obey. His drink came, and he let it sit in front of him for a while so as better to savour the first taste of it. He fished up the slice of orange and bit into it, then followed with the first bitter-sweet-cold-bitter sip. Three swallows landed near his feet. He leaned across to the next table and took a potato crisp from the bowl left behind by the last clients, crumbled it between his fingers, and tossed the pieces to the busy birds, which fell upon them. He took another sip and studied the birds.

A shadow fell across his table and his drink. Looking up, he was momentarily blinded by the sun, but when his vision cleared he saw Lieutenant Scarpa, Vice-Questore Patta's assistant, standing above him. 'Good afternoon, Commissario,' the Lieutenant said. 'Busy with the birds?' The Lieutenant was in full uniform, with his dark woollen jacket, but seemed remarkably cool. As if suddenly recalling that he was speaking to a superior officer, he removed his hat and held it, elbow bent, stiffly at his side.

'Yes, Lieutenant,' Brunetti said with an easy smile, 'the owner says they've been stealing potato crisps from the bowls on the tables, so I came over to investigate the case.' He pointed to the bird on the far left and added, 'I suspect that one's the ringleader, so I'm going to stay here and finish my drink while I keep my eye on him, just to be sure.'

'I'll look forward to reading your report,' the Lieutenant said, gave a lazy salute, replaced his hat, and walked away, heading in the direction from which Brunetti had arrived.

Paola had picked up many English expressions from the nannies who had lived with her family while she was growing up, and one of them sprang to Brunetti's mind: 'A ghost walked over my grave.' Or was it a goose? And how was it that a speaking person could have a grave? Regardless of the sense of it or who did the stepping, it perfectly described the effect of Scarpa's presence. The fact that the Lieutenant was walking towards San Stin made Brunetti uncomfortable.

He finished his drink, paid the waiter, and walked home. Paola was in the kitchen, washing salad; she looked up in surprise when he walked in. He kissed the right side of her forehead and said, 'I found his address and went there, but the mother . . .' his voice trailed off for a moment. 'She refused to talk to me, closed the door in my face.'

Paola poured the water out of the bottom part of the spinner and, replacing the salad, began to spin it dry. 'What did she say?' She asked above the whirling noise.

'Nothing,' Brunetti answered. 'It was all very strange.'

'Why didn't she speak? If she came to the door, then she heard the bell, and that means she's not deaf.'

'No, no,' Brunetti answered. 'She can hear and she can speak. But all she did was ask me why I was there.'

'Did you tell her you were a policeman?'

'Yes. I told her on the phone, and again when I went there.'

'Then why wouldn't she talk to you?'

'Fear of the police, shock, grief, you name it,' he answered. 'You know people don't like to talk to us.'

'But she came to the door?' Paola asked, and when he seemed confused by the question, she added, 'Or else how could she have shut it in your face?'

'I told you: it was all very strange,' Brunetti repeated.

'How did he die?' she asked.

'He took sleeping pills,' Brunetti said, seeing no reason to tell her more.

The information stunned her. 'You mean he killed himself?'

Brunetti shrugged. 'He could have taken them accidentally. But they killed him.'

Paola said nothing for a very long time, then finally asked, 'Are you going to have to talk to her?'

'I just tried to, but she wouldn't speak to me.'

'No, I mean talk to her officially,' Paola clarified. 'As the police. Are you obliged to because he died like that?' He had seen no report from the men from the ambulance, which meant it was probably bogged down on someone's desk; he'd locate it in the morning.

'Yes. In a case like this, we'd usually want to exclude the possibility of suicide.' She gave him a strange look but said nothing. She took the leaves out of the spinner and put them in a large salad bowl. In an ordinary voice, she said, 'Would you get me a glass of wine?'

'White?'

She looked out the window before she answered, in the direction of the Dolomites, though they were hidden by the combination of pollution and fog that descended on the Veneto for a good portion of the year. 'No, I think it's time to start drinking red again,' she said, and bent to pull a frying pan out of the cabinet.

Brunetti did as he was told and chose a bottle of simple Cabernet. White might have been better as a follow-up to the spritz, but if Paola wanted red, then red it would be.

She put the frying pan on the stove, glanced at her watch, and took the glass he offered her. She sipped, nodded her thanks, and asked, 'You think there's time to watch the sun set?'

It had already happened when they got to the living room, so they contented themselves with sitting on the sofa and watching the light disappear in the west. Before Brunetti could do the husbandly thing and ask Paola how her day had been, she said, 'Her behaviour's strange, isn't it?'

Superstition stopped him from asking Paola how she

would behave if she were to lose her son; indeed, it banished the question even before it was fully formed in his mind. 'How's she supposed to behave?' Brunetti asked. 'I don't know if he's her only son, or only child.' He considered this, then said, 'Not that it matters, does it?'

Eyes still on the light that continued to diminish beyond the rooftops, she shook her head and sipped at her wine.

Brunetti began to wonder how much of their interest, now, was concern and how much was curiosity and why one was noble and the other base. Before he married and became a father, he was able to mouth platitudes about how horrible the death of a child must be for a parent, but now he could not say those things, nor could he allow himself to think of them. Like a medieval peasant, he refused to open his door to the carrier of plague.

The light grew dimmer still. Paola looked into her glass and said, 'I've been thinking about what you said. About suicide.' She took a very small sip. 'I wonder if it's possible that he got to the point where his life was so bad, he couldn't stand it any more?'

Brunetti thought about this and said, 'He'd have to know it was bad, wouldn't he?'

She turned her head to him sharply, mouth open. But before she could ask him what he meant, Brunetti saw her hear her own question and begin to consider it. Finally she said, 'Of course. If that's the only life he knew, then it was just that: life. Something worse would have to have happened, I suppose.'

They remained silent, each trying to imagine what could be worse than the life they had observed, until Paola said, 'Or maybe he simply found them and thought they were something else and ate them.'

'Rizzardi suggested that. It would depend on how much he understood.' Saying that, Brunetti realized that this was the unfathomable puzzle here: how enter into another's mind save by words?

'Only God knows that, I'm afraid,' Paola said. Then, 'But it might explain the mother's behaviour.'

'Guilt?'

Paola took another sip, shrugged, and finished the wine. 'I think I'll start cooking.'

'Good idea,' Brunetti said.

The meal was quiet: the children sensed the sobriety of their parents' mood and responded in kind. Chiara spoke of an argument she'd had. A friend had wanted Chiara to call and ask her parents if she could come to dinner at Chiara's house and stay on to study so that she could see her boyfriend; Chiara had refused, and now the girl wasn't speaking to her any more.

'Why'd you refuse?' Raffi asked, not surprised, just curious.

Chiara speared a shrimp from her risotto and studied it, as though asking it to supply her with the correct answer. 'Her parents have always been very nice to me. It didn't seem right to lie to them.'

Brunetti waited for Paola to put on her Socrates costume and ask Chiara what she would have done if her friend's parents had not been nice to her, but she remained silent, finishing her own risotto.

'Isn't there any mineral water?' Raffi asked.

'No, and there won't be any more,' Chiara answered, then added, 'This house is a mineral-water-free zone.'

'Declared so by you?' Raffi asked calmly. After all, he'd known her all her life, and little could surprise him from or about his sister.

'Yes.'

'Why?' Raffi asked.

'Because there's no guarantee of what's in it.'

'Water, presumably,' Raffi said with his mother's detached irony.

'Yes, water. Certainly,' Chiara said, striving for that same tone but falling short of it. 'And lots of other things, none of which we know about.'

'And this?' Raffi asked, holding up the pitcher he now realized must contain tap water. 'Aside from too much chlorine, that is?'

'That's tested, at least,' Chiara said. 'The water we were drinking last week, in case you bothered to read the label on the bottles,' she told him, 'is not.' Here began a dynamic Brunetti had been observing for years. Chiara was gearing herself up for an argument: it was audible in her tone. Raffi was getting ready to beat her argument aside by use of superior age and information.

Brunetti tuned back in. '. . . from Puglia, from a spring that is four kilometres from a chemical factory that was shut down by a court order three weeks ago.' Raffi tried to speak, but she rammed through whatever it was he started to say and kept going. 'Because they have been dumping chemicals into the earth for thirty years. Which means – though a lawyer would say it only suggests – that the chemicals are now in the groundwater and thus in the mineral water. And if you want to believe that the list of mineral quantities on the bottle labels even flirts with the truth, you are welcome to do so. I'll drink tap water.'

Brunetti realized that, had she been a true avatar of Paola, she would here have picked up the pitcher and filled her glass. But she was new to this and so she speared another shrimp and ate it, ignoring the dramatic possibilities offered by the pitcher. In a few years, Brunetti thought, she'd think of that and do it and, sooner or later, she'd be unbeatable.

Raffi, not to be daunted, asked, 'You sure it's not because you're tied of carrying the bottles up the steps?'

'I don't have anything to do with plastic bottles,' Chiara said loftily. Before Raffi could argue, Paola declared a truce by getting to her feet and asking him to help her carry the plates from the table.

The cake with fresh blackcurrants and whipped cream sealed the peace accord. Brunetti, a mere spectator to the discussion, said nothing of his delight that Chiara had put an end to his having to carry glass bottles of mineral water to the fourth floor, a realization that made all the sweeter his second piece of cake.

7

When he reached his office the next day, he found a note on his desk, asking him to call Dottor Rizzardi. After he and the pathologist had exchanged greetings, Rizzardi said, 'This Cavanella doesn't exist.'

'I beg your pardon,' Brunetti said. 'You did an autopsy on him yesterday.'

Rizzardi weighed that for sarcasm and apparently heard none. 'I'm sorry, Guido; I was probably speaking for effect. The secretary here called the Ufficio Anagrafe to report his death, but they have no record of him at that address.'

'Then he's resident somewhere else,' Brunetti said, almost embarrassed at having to state the obvious.

'Not in the city,' Rizzardi said tersely. 'The office checked when we asked: he's not now and has never been resident in Venice.'

'Then in the Veneto, I'd guess,' Brunetti said, thinking back to the very few words he had heard the mother say and recalling the telltale Veneto cadence.

'That's not our job, Guido,' Rizzardi said with unexpected force. 'We don't have to identify them, only find the cause of death.'

'I went to his home,' Brunetti explained, 'but his mother refused to talk to me.'

Rizzardi did not comment on that. He stated the rules: 'Until we have an identification, we have to keep him here.'

'I know,' Brunetti answered. Then, thinking of how the man might be identified, he asked, 'How old do you think he was?'

'I'd guess he was in his early forties,' Rizzardi said. Then, as an afterthought, letting the doctor in him speak, 'He was in excellent physical condition. His teeth showed signs of very little work. No sign of surgery, organs in perfect shape.'

'Are you sure about the age?' Brunetti asked, amazed that a face could so long have remained untouched by time and care, but he knew better than to question the pathologist's judgement.

'It's surprising, I know,' Rizzardi agreed. 'I've seen it before. The less contact people have with the world, the less they age.'

'He wasn't a hermit, Ettore,' Brunetti said, trying for lightness.

'All I know about him is what you told me, Guido: he was deaf and simple-minded,' Rizzardi said. 'I've seen cases of it before, and I'm trying to give you an explanation based on experience. With retarded people – or whatever we're supposed to call them now – and the blind, they don't seem to age the way the rest of us do, or at least their bodies don't show it the way ours do.' When Brunetti failed to comment, the pathologist clarified, 'From looking at his organs, and his teeth, that's my estimate.'

In some way Brunetti did not understand, Rizzardi's explanation made sense. Less contact with the world: less suffering. But less joy. 'Thanks, Ettore. It might help. I'll try to confirm at least his name. I'll call you when I do.'

'It's what was on the paper that came with him,' Rizzardi said. 'I don't know anything more than that.'

'I'll call.'

'Good,' Rizzardi said, and was gone.

Brunetti pulled the cover sheet of a report on an attempted escape from the local prison towards him. Because the escape had failed, he saw no reason to keep or pass on the report. He flipped it over, wrote Cavanella's name and address at the top, and began to make a list. He'd need to locate a birth certificate, or a baptismal certificate. There was the dead man's *carta d'identità*, which would most likely be in his house, and a card for the medical services he was sure to have been receiving. Brunetti doubted that Davide Cavanella would have a criminal record, but he could check that, as well. School records.

He sat and puzzled over the places where a person might be hidden. He had played the game as a boy, he and his friends lurking and disappearing in the *calli* and entrance ways of his neighbourhood and, as they grew older, farther and farther from home. The memory came to him now of how he had hidden, one spring day, beneath the canvas cover of a boat moored not far from his home and managed to fall asleep under it.

It was a desperate, high-pitched voice calling his name that woke him and catapulted him out from under the cloth. His mother stood on the Fondamenta della Tana, wearing her house slippers and her apron, her hair hanging partly loose on one side. At the sudden sight of her amidst his friends, Brunetti saw the grey in her hair for the first time and noticed how very poorly she was dressed, with a patched apron and a sweater darned at both elbows. For the first time in his life, seeing her there, in front of his friends, Brunetti felt ashamed of her, and then of himself for feeling this.

When she saw him, his mother came to the edge of the *riva* and reached down a hand to help him scramble back up. Her grip was firm, and he was surprised that she could so easily haul him up beside her.

He stood in front of her, head bowed, almost as tall as she, and muttered, 'I fell asleep, *Mamma*. I'm sorry.'

He had seen the looks on the faces of his friends. To be guests of her hospitality was one thing, but to see her out here, dressed for the kitchen and screaming her son's name . . . that was quite different. What would they think of him? And of her?

He saw her right hand move, and he stood rigid, fearing the blow he knew he deserved. Instead, she ruffled his hair and said, 'Then it's a good thing I came and found you, isn't it, *tesoro*, or else you might have been baked like a chicken in the oven down there and no one knowing what was happening to you.' She waited for him to respond, perhaps to laugh, but he was paralysed by love and unable to speak.

'And no one to baste you with olive oil, either,' she said with a laugh. Taking his hand in hers, she turned and led him back towards home, inviting all of his friends to come back with them and have a piece of the cake she had just pulled out of the oven.

Had Davide Cavanella's mother baked for him and his friends? Had she invited them back to the house in San Polo? Brunetti's train of thought stopped on the *riva* of his imagination and asked him why he thought Davide Cavanella had friends. Apparently speechless, how could he communicate enough to make a friend other than by using sign, had he known to use it?

Brunetti drew lines from the pieces of information he thought he needed and connected them to the people or places that might provide them. Applications for all of his documents would be – or should be, he reminded himself – kept at the Ufficio Anagrafe. Their own files would have records of any arrests, though Brunetti still found this difficult to believe. Signorina Elettra could certainly find any other indications left to bureaucracy by Cavanella's passing through this world.

But where could he find out if Davide had had any friends, and if his mother – if the woman who opened the door was his mother – had baked cakes for him or for him and his friends? He got to his feet and went downstairs to start Signorina Elettra in pursuit of the answers to the first questions.

Brunetti began by asking her if the presentation the previous day had been interesting.

Did she sniff? 'Amateurs,' she said, then looked up and asked, 'What is it, Commissario?'

When he had explained that Cavanella was not registered as resident in the city, though he had lived there for decades, he handed her the list of the information he wanted.

She studied it for long moments, then set it to the side of her computer, saying, 'You know you could do this officially.' He did not understand the reluctance he sensed in her. Usually a chance to make a visit – an unauthorized visit, it must be admitted – to the database of any city office was to invite Signorina Elettra to a few hours at the fairground. 'Or perhaps Pucetti, or even Vianello, could find all of this for you,' she said, moving the list slightly to the left.

'If you'd rather not,' Brunetti began, giving voice to the unthinkable.

She placed the very tip of one red-nailed finger at the centre of the list, smiled up at him, and said, 'All right, Commissario: I'll confess.'

He smiled his readiness.

'A friend,' she said, using the masculine form of the noun and thus rousing his interest, 'is arriving at the airport at two, and I thought I might go out to meet him.'

'Does he know where you work?' Brunetti surprised them both by asking.

She answered almost without thinking. 'Yes, I thought it best to tell him from the beginning.'

Interestinger and interestinger, Brunetti thought. The beginning of what? 'Then perhaps Foa could take you out on the launch.' Before she could question this, he explained, 'He can drop you off and wait for you both. I think it's good that we show the luggage handlers we're still interested in them.' The police had failed to stop the theft of property from suitcases for years now, and it was very unlikely that the sight of a police launch moored to the dock would have any effect on their continued depredations, but it was the best excuse he could come up with at such short notice.

'But they're over in the main terminal.'

'The word will pass to them, you can be sure.'

She smiled. 'I'd certainly hope so.'

'Have Foa take you home,' he added casually, perhaps too casually, for she looked at him and smiled.

'I'll have him take me to the Misericordia,' she began, paused to allow Brunetti to try to remember how close to it she lived, and then added, 'We can walk from there.'

Brunetti had long wondered what Signorina Elettra would think of his interest in her private life. It would be too much to say that her behaviour was at times provocative, just as it would be difficult to find a more suitable word to describe it. He had been too obvious in his offer of Foa's help, but there was no way now for him to retract the offer.

He picked up the paper. 'I'll ask Pucetti to do it through official channels.' Then, with a smile, he added, 'The practice will be good for him.'

'Probably slow him down,' she said and got to her feet.

She stopped at the door and said over her shoulder, 'It won't be necessary for Foa to take me, Commissario: I've got some things to do first, so I'm leaving now.' She did not explain what those things were, nor why she was leaving to do them four hours before she had to be at the airport. Brunetti raised a hand in acknowledgement and farewell, vowing to himself that he would tell no one what she had said.

He went to the officers' squad room and explained the anomaly of Cavanella's missing residence, then gave Pucetti the note of his name and address and the places where documents might be found. The young officer was puzzled to learn that Davide Cavanella was not registered as a resident of the city. 'If you've seen him here for years, Commissario, then he's got to be in the system somewhere,' the younger man said. 'If he was deaf, then he probably went to that school in Santa Croce. And there's got to be some association for people who use sign.' He added that to Brunetti's list, expanding the possibilities. 'If they live near San Stin, maybe the *parroco* knew them. And if he worked at this dry cleaning place, then they'd have records.' He added these to the list.

'I suspect they let him stay there out of charity,' Brunetti offered. He knew these women were his first good hope

56

of discovering anything about the dead man. He tried to remember when he had first seen Davide – no, call him by his surname, as though he were a real adult and not a person frozen in childhood – Cavanella there. Ten years ago? Longer than that?

He asked Pucetti for a phone book, which the young officer produced from a drawer in his desk. Only one dry cleaner's was listed in San Polo. Brunetti wrote the number in his notebook, reluctant to call them until he got back to his own office.

He handed the book to Pucetti, saying, 'All right, check the Anagrafe, or the school, and call the *parroco*.'

'How old was he?' Pucetti asked, sitting down in front of one of the three computers in the room.

'Rizzardi guessed him to be in his early forties.'

Pucetti raised his eyebrows. 'I thought he was much younger.'

'Why?'

'I don't know. I guess it was the way you talked about him.' Pucetti shook his head and typed in the address for the Comune di Venezia.

Quickly he found the site of the Ufficio Anagrafe, but there seemed to be no way to search for the name of a person. Pucetti switched to another page, typed in the name, 'Davide Cavanella', glanced at the paper Brunetti had given him and copied the man's address, but in the absence of a Codice Fiscale number the search could not progress.

Brunetti bent over the screen and asked Pucetti to scroll back to the opening page. When he saw the phone number, he picked up the phone and dialled it.

He gave his name and rank and said that he was calling to try to identify the dead man who had been found in San Polo the day before. He offered the woman he was speaking to the opportunity to call him back at the Questura, but she said that would not be necessary, and what was the man's name?

'Davide Cavanella, and he was probably in his early forties.'

'Then,' she said, 'he would have been born in the seventies.'

'Yes.'

'We're computerized back to the fifties,' she said, a note of pride audible in her voice. 'So if he was born here, we'll have him.'

Brunetti contented himself with making a polite noise while he left her to it. The sounds she made came through the phone, a combination of humming and clicks of displeasure or surprise. After a few minutes, she spoke to him in the voice of a person whose attention was somewhere else. 'I can't find him, Commissario. Are you sure of the spelling? Cavanella with a final A?'

'Yes.'

'Davide?' she asked.

'Yes.'

Again a hum-filled pause, some soft clicks in the background, and then she was back. 'I'm sorry, Commissario, but he wasn't born in Venice or Mestre; not between 1965 and 1975, he wasn't.'

'Can you check the entire province?' Brunetti asked.

This was the point when most bureaucrats tired of the novelty of answering questions for the police. Usually, they'd happily answer a few questions, do simple research if asked, but once things became complicated and time-consuming, they started naming supervisors and the need to get authorization or citing rules Brunetti always suspected they invented that instant.

'I'm not authorized to do that, Commissario,' she

answered in a different voice, the voice he knew so well. 'Not without an order from a magistrate.'

Brunetti thanked her and hung up.

Pucetti looked up, pulling his eyebrows together in interrogation.

'Nothing, neither here nor in Mestre, from 1965 to 1975,' Brunetti explained. Pucetti shrugged, as if this were the sort of answer bureaucracy always gave. 'Can you,' Brunetti began and then foundered on the appropriate verb. Get into? Access? Open? The real verb was 'break into,' but Brunetti was reluctant to use it, not wanting the corruption of subordinates added to his conscience. 'Get further information from the social services?'

'Of course, sir,' Pucetti said, and Brunetti didn't know if he was serving as an occasion of sin or as the person who lightened the weights carried by a racehorse. 'I can even do it with this thing,' he said, waving dismissive fingers over the keys and adding a noise that condemned the computer to ignominy. 'It's easy to find who's collecting pensions.' Then, in a voice from which all boasting was absent, Pucetti added, 'Once you know how to do it.' Brunetti nodded, his face impassive. 'I'll have a look around, sir,' Pucetti said and turned to the screen.

'Yes,' Brunetti answered and said he would be in his office.

Upstairs, he turned on his own computer and started a search through the phone books of the provinces of Friuli and Treviso, but there were no listings for anyone with the surname Cavanella.

He called down to the front desk and asked the man on duty there to connect him with the office that saw to the sending of the hearse.

This was quickly done, the roster was checked, and within minutes Brunetti found himself talking to the pilot.

'The call came from the Carabinieri a little before six, Commissario,' the pilot, Enrico Forti, told him. 'All they said was that a woman had called to say she had found her son dead in his bed and that we were to pick him up and take him to the hospital. That's the routine, sir.'

'And when you got there?'

'She was at the door. People always are: I guess they hear us coming. The motor, you know.'

'A woman with red hair?' Brunetti asked.

'Yes, sir.'

'How was she?' Brunetti asked.

After a moment, Forti said, 'I'm not sure I understand what you mean, sir.'

'How did she behave? Was she crying? Did she have trouble talking?'

The pilot was slow to answer Brunetti's questions. Finally he said, 'You have to understand, sir, that we answer all sorts of calls. Death hits people differently. You never know how it'll affect them.'

Brunetti waited.

'She was upset: you could see that. She said she had gone into his room and found him, and he was dead, and she called 118, and they told her we'd come.'

'And so?' Brunetti asked, trying to sound interested and not impatient.

'She was crying. She let us in and took us up to the apartment and back to his room. And he was in his bed, just like she said. It was pretty ugly: it always is when they die like that, sir. So we covered him and put him in the carrier, and we took him down to the boat and to the hospital. For Dottor Rizzardi.'

'Did she ask to go with you?' Brunetti asked.

'No, sir. She just stood there while we took him out, and then she closed the door before we took him to the boat.'

'Do you remember what the room looked like?' Brunetti asked.

Forti paused to remember and then said, 'It was awfully small, sir, and with only one tiny window, and the house opposite is very close, so there wasn't much light. Not that there would be, not that early.' He glanced at Brunetti, then added, 'It's in my report, sir.'

'Did the Carabinieri send a squad, do you know?'

'Probably not, sir. We called them and told them it looked like an accident, so I doubt they'd bother.'

On the tip of Brunetti's tongue was the temptation to remind Forti that doing one's job – and checking the scene of an unaccounted death was included in that – was not dependent on whether it was a bother or not, but instead he thanked him for his information and hung up.

He found the phone number of the dry cleaner's in his notebook and dialled; the phone was picked up on the fifth ring. '*Lavasecco*,' a woman's voice answered, not bothering with the name.

'*Buon dì, Signora*,' he said, 'This is Commissario Brunetti.'

Instead of greeting him, she said, 'Your wife's jacket and three pairs of your slacks are ready, Commissario. But your grey jacket has a stain on the right sleeve that didn't come out, so we're putting it through again.'

'Ah,' said a momentarily confused Brunetti. 'Thank you, Signora, but that's not what I wanted to ask you about.'

'Davide?'

'Yes. I saw him in your shop over the years, and I wanted to come by and talk to you about him, you and your colleague.'

'Renata doesn't come in until after lunch, Commissario, if you want to talk to us both. This is a slow period for us: everyone's got their winter things back already, and it's too soon for them to be wearing them again. All we get these days is linen. People mostly wash their summer things themselves. Must be the financial crisis.'

In recent months, criminals had taken to blaming their activities on the financial crisis. The Euro sank; salaries remained the same. What else could I do but rob the bank? Brunetti wondered what next would be blamed on the financial crisis. Bad taste?

'Of course, Signora. Thank you,' Brunetti said, checked his watch, spent an hour reading through some of the papers on his desk, and then went home for lunch.

8

Clouds gathered as they were having lunch, so before leaving to go to the dry cleaner's, Brunetti took a grey pullover from his drawer and slipped it on under his jacket. As he kissed Paola goodbye, she asked, 'Is this the first sign of winter?'

'A bit early for that, I'd say,' Brunetti answered. 'But I think it's the hardening up of autumn.'

'Nice phrase,' she said, stepping back from him and studying his face. 'Did you make it up?'

Puzzled, Brunetti had to think about that. 'I must have,' he said. 'I don't remember having heard anyone say it.'

'Not bad,' she commended him and moved towards her study.

As he opened the door to the *calle*, Brunetti felt that autumn had grown even harder while they were at lunch. He was glad of the sweater and wished he had thought to take a scarf, as well. He didn't have to think about how to get to the dry cleaner's but followed what he thought of as his own GPS – Guido's Personal System – and was there in ten minutes.

When he entered, he was enveloped in the familiar smell: slightly sharp, vaguely chemical, but so familiar as not to cause alarm. Two women clients stood in front of the counter, the owner behind it, making change from the cash register. A paper-wrapped parcel lay flat on the counter between them. Half visible behind the curtain that separated the back room stood the tall woman he had seen ironing there for years. Her short hair was as well coloured as it was cut, the same blonde it might once have been. Surely more than sixty, her body had remained thin and agile, perhaps due to the bending and lifting her job required of her.

'God knows what his mother's suffering,' he heard the woman who was paying say just as he walked in.

The woman to her left made a puffing noise, as if lifting a heavy weight, but said no more. The first woman turned towards her, and Brunetti watched her decide to say no more. She took her change, thanked the woman behind the counter, and picked up her parcel.

As she reached the door, the owner said, 'Next Tuesday, Signora.'

Her parcel rustled as she opened the door, and then she was gone.

When the door was closed, the second client said, 'God knows *if* the mother's suffering, I'd say.' She was full-bodied and round-faced, with plump red cheeks: in a fairy tale, she'd be the good grandmother.

As if she had not heard the remark, the owner said, 'It was a green silk suit, wasn't it? And your husband's brown jacket?'

The woman accepted the change of subject and asked, 'How do you do it, Signora? How do you remember everything? I brought them here in April.'

'I like the suit,' she answered. 'And your husband's had that jacket for a long time.' Before her client could interpret that as a criticism, she added, 'You never see quality like that any more: it'll last another ten years.' She went to take the clothing from the racks at the back of the shop.

The client smiled, placed a pink receipt on the counter, and opened her purse.

The owner came back, folded the suit and the jacket, wrapped them in light blue paper, and taped the parcel neatly closed. She took the money from the woman and after a polite exchange of goodbyes, the woman left.

Her comment remained in the space left by her departure. Before Brunetti could speak, the curtain was pulled fully open and Renata, whose name Brunetti had learned only some hours before, emerged.

She nodded to him but spoke to her colleague. 'I heard her. How could she say something like that? The poor boy isn't buried yet, and she's talking like that about his mother. She doesn't deserve that.'

'People have always talked about her like that,' her colleague answered with heavy resignation. 'But with her son dead, you'd think they could stop it.'

As though only mildly curious, Brunetti asked, 'Like what?'

The women exchanged a long look; in it Brunetti read the struggle between the desire to remain silent out of some sort of female solidarity and the urge to gossip.

Renata opted for gossip by leaning forward and grasping the edges of the narrow counter. Bracing her weight on stiff arms, she settled in for the long haul.

He saw the glance the owner gave her. Nothing at all was to be gained in getting involved in the affairs of other people. Authority existed only to cause trouble, to impale you on the thorns of bureaucracy, to make you lose time at work, and in the end to force you to hire a lawyer and spend years freeing yourself of the consequences of any revelation of information. The State was your Enemy.

As if unaware of all of this, Brunetti addressed the owner directly. 'Signora, at the moment all we know is that he died in his sleep. It looks as if it was an accidental death. I tried to speak to his mother, but she didn't – or perhaps she couldn't – answer me.' When it seemed they had no questions, he shook his head to suggest confusion, or resignation in the face of things we could not understand. 'I don't know how to say this,' he began, ignoring the look they exchanged and hoping to pull the conversation temporarily away from the mother, 'but it's always been our assumption – my wife's and mine, that is – that you let him stay here out of what I suppose I can only call the goodness of your hearts.' He smiled his approval of their action. 'I think that was very generous of you. No, it was more than that.'

'He was just a poor creature,' Renata said, then looked at her employer as if to ask belated permission for her comment. At the other woman's nod, she went on. 'It was Maria Pia's idea to let him help.' The other woman made a gesture, as if to dismiss the remark, but Renata went on. 'It wasn't easy,' she continued, then turned to Maria Pia and asked, 'Was it?'

'No, I suppose it wasn't. But he needed something to do.' She glanced quickly at Brunetti, at the other woman, then back at Brunetti. Keeping her eyes on his, she asked, 'It wasn't against the law, was it, letting him stay here?'

Believing there probably was a law that made it illegal to allow someone to pretend to work in your place of business, Brunetti said, 'Of course not, Signora.' He smiled at the absurdity of the idea, waved it away negligently. 'It was a kind thing for you to do.' To establish his position as a sympathetic supporter of her behaviour and to dispel any question of legal peril, he added, 'Any decent person would approve. Any decent person would have done the same thing.'

She smiled in evident relief: if a commissario of police said it was not illegal, then it could not be, could it?

'How did he . . .' Brunetti began, wondering how to phrase it. 'How did he begin here?'

Maria Pia smiled. 'He used to come in with his mother sometimes. And stand there and watch the things going around in the machines,' she said, pointing to the round glass window of the cleaning machine that had been in motion every time Brunetti came here.

'And then Pupo saw him,' Renata said. The women exchanged a smile that conveyed nothing but sadness.

'Pupo?' Brunetti inquired.

'The cat,' Maria Pia said. 'Didn't you ever see him here?'

Brunetti shook his head.

She pulled out a *telefonino* and switched it on, pressed buttons, summoning up memories and the images that captured them. Finding what she wanted, she came around the counter and stood beside him. 'Here,' she said, flicking photos across the screen as though she had done this all her life. He looked at the small rectangle and saw a photo of her holding an enormous cat in her arms, the largest cat he had ever seen. Its ears made it look like a lynx.

'What's that?'

'They're called Maine Coon Cats,' Maria Pia said, pronouncing the name in Italian, smoothing her hand across the surface of the phone and showing him more photos of the same enormous animal. He stood on the counter, slept on the ironing board, stood with his paws on either side of the window of the machine, intent on the spinning clothing. Then he appeared in the arms of Davide Cavanella.

'Pupo,' Brunetti said.

'Davide was the only person he really liked. Other than us,' she said.

'Not our husbands and not our children,' Renata added. 'Only Davide.'

'It was one of the reasons we let him stay here,' Maria Pia said, abandoning the pretence that he'd worked there.

'What happened?' Brunetti asked.

'Pupo was already ten when Davide came. Then last year he got sick with an ugly disease. Davide was his doctor: Pupo let him give him the shots.' Brunetti raised his eyebrows and Maria Pia went on: 'We showed him how to do it, and Pupo didn't seem to mind when he did it.'

'And then?'

'And then we had to take him to the vet and have him . . .' Unable to name the disease that killed Pupo, neither could she name what they had had to do.

Looking at the photo of the two of them together, Maria Pia finished the story. 'Davide never came back after that.' She switched off the phone and put it in her pocket.

'I think some of our clients didn't approve of his being here, anyway,' Renata said, shifting her weight from one foot to the other. Before her employer could speak, she went ahead: 'Like that Signora Callegaro. With her green suit and her husband's jacket he's too cheap to get cleaned more than once a year.' She pushed herself away from the counter, to stand up straight while making her denunciation. 'The stuff's been here all summer, and she comes in now. To sniff around.' And then, almost spitting, 'Spy.'

She turned to Brunetti. 'She complained about him once.' She stopped speaking, but a quick glance showed Brunetti that her employer's face was calm.

'About what, Signora?' he asked.

'She came in here, must have been two years ago, straight from the market, and she had two big bags with her. She came to pick up her cleaning, but when Maria Pia put it on the counter and started to wrap it, she said it was too much to carry and she'd come back for it.'

'What did you do?' Brunetti asked, addressing the question to the space between them so that either of them could answer him.

Maria Pia chose to interrupt here to explain what had happened. 'I know where she lives; over by Ponte dei Pugni, so I told her that Davide could carry the bags for her, and she could take the cleaning.'

'And she complained about that?' Brunetti asked.

'No, no,' Renata said and grabbed the story back. 'She said it would be all right, so Maria Pia went to the back and got Davide and told him to go with her, and they left.' Though curious about how she could have 'told' him anything, Brunetti said nothing.

'He came back, just the same as ever, so we forgot about it. Then, the next time she came in, she said he had frightened her.'

'How?' Brunetti asked.

As with any old couple, the story passed between them and now Maria Pia continued. 'She told me he carried the bags back to her house and up the stairs. They live on the fourth floor. She opened the door and pointed to the floor to tell him he could leave them there, but he pushed past her and found the kitchen and put them on the table. And then he took all of the things out of the bags and lined them up on the table. She came in and told him he could leave, that she'd do it herself, but she said he ignored her.' She looked at Maria Pia, as if to ask whether a deaf person could do anything other than that.

'When he was done, he folded the bags and put them on the counter, and when she tried to give him some money – this is what she told me, though I doubt she'd give anyone anything: it's no accident those two are married – he ignored her and left.'

When it seemed she had nothing more to add, Brunetti said, 'But what did she complain about?'

Renata made a huffing noise. 'She said she was frightened when he went into the house, that she didn't know what he'd do. I suppose she meant to her.' She rolled her eyes to suggest the lunacy of this possibility or the woman's fear.

Brunetti limited himself to shaking his head in sage acknowledgement of humanity's weaknesses. Turning to the proprietor, he said, making himself sound puzzled and not really curious, 'I'm not sure I understand, Signora. If he was deaf, how did you make him understand that he was supposed to carry the bags home for her?'

Maria Pia shrugged and answered, 'I picked up the bags and handed them to him, and then I pointed to the woman and made walking movements with my fingers.' She then did just that, walking her first two fingers halfway across the counter.

'I'd done it before. Or he'd done it with other clients, so he understood. He took the bags and went and stood by the door, the way he always did.'

'And then?' prodded Brunetti.

'He went out with her and came back, and I thought everything was all right. I should have known better. With her.' Another huffing noise from Renata.

'And what did you do, Signora?' Brunetti asked, wondering if Signora Callegaro's complaint had been enough to frighten her.

'What could I do? I apologized to her and said he was

70

perfectly harmless. She'd seen him here for years: she should have known that,' she said with mounting anger.

'Did you think about telling him not to work here any more?' Brunetti asked before he realized how habitual it was to use that word: 'tell'.

'No, of course not,' she said, the anger now veering in his direction. 'He'd been here a long time, and he was a good boy. He tried to help; he wanted to help.' Brunetti saw Renata nod in agreement. 'I couldn't just toss him away because someone didn't like the way he behaved. Let her take her husband's jacket somewhere else to have it cleaned.'

Brunetti smiled. 'Good for you, Signora,' he said without thinking.

They both smiled: Renata's nod of approval pleased him.

'Did she ever come in again when he was here?' he asked, again directing the question to both of them.

'Only once,' Maria Pia answered.

'What happened?'

Renata interrupted. 'I saw her come in: I can see a lot from back there,' she said, waving towards the curtain. 'So when she came in, I grabbed Davide's arm and told him to move back, out of sight.' She raised her hands, palms inward, and made brushing motions that would cause anyone to move back from her.

'Did he understand?'

'Of course,' she said, surprised. 'He understood a lot of things.'

About sleeping pills? Brunetti wondered.

He decided to risk a question about the mother. 'That woman, Signora Callegaro, said something about Davide's mother. It sounded like she knew her. And had a bad opinion of her.'

'She has a bad opinion of everyone,' Renata said angrily.

Brunetti turned towards Maria Pia. This was enough to encourage her to say, 'The mother, Ana, doesn't have a very good reputation.' Neither, it seemed, did Signora Callegaro, though Brunetti chose not to say this. His silence induced her to add, 'Most of us around here have known her a long time, and once you know a little about her . . . well, then you have some sympathy for her.'

'Why is that, Signora?' Brunetti asked, unable to disguise his real curiosity.

Maria Pia looked at her colleague, as if to ask her how it happened that she had already said this much.

The opening of the door distracted them all and turned their attention to the new arrival. It was a young girl, no more than thirteen, pink slip in hand. '*Ciao*, Graziella,' Maria Pia said, and turned to the long row of clothing. In a moment she was back with two silk dresses far too mature in style to be for the girl and a pair of black silk slacks equally unsuitable in size. The girl stood, looking around at the three adults, silent.

When the parcel was wrapped, she handed the pink slip and a fifty Euro note to Maria Pia, took the change, nodded her thanks, picked up the parcel, and left.

'What were you saying about the mother, Signora?' Brunetti asked.

The look Maria Pia gave him told Brunetti that time had run out, even before she said, 'It's just gossip, Commissario, and I don't think it's right to repeat it.' She turned to Renata and asked, 'Isn't that right?'

Renata looked at her employer, at Brunetti, and nodded. 'Yes. People are saying he choked on something: that's how he died. So she's had enough, I'd say.'

'Was he her only child?' Brunetti managed to inject sufficient pathos into the question for Maria Pia to answer, 'Yes.' But nothing more.

Brunetti accepted the futility of trying to learn anything else from the women: to continue to ask questions would only irritate them. 'Thank you for your help, Signore,' he said. Then, in a lighter tone, 'I'm not going home now. I'll ask my wife to send one of the kids over.'

'Good,' Renata said. 'It's always good to see them. Is your son still with that nice girl?'

'Sara?'

'Yes.'

'Years, it's been,' Renata said. 'Good family. Good girl.'

'I think so, too,' Brunetti said, thanked them both again, and left.

9

As he walked towards the vaporetto stop at San Tomà, Brunetti considered what the three women had said about Ana Cavanella: Signora Callegaro had cast doubt on her love for her son; Renata had defended her; and Maria Pia had said anyone familiar with her story would feel sympathy for her. But what was the story?

Maria Pia had also said that the people around there had known her for a long time. It should therefore be easy enough to find out about her: all he had to do was find someone who could begin to ask questions. But it had to be the right person, and they had to be the right questions. A woman, one who spoke Veneziano, not young and not flashy: a woman who looked and sounded like a lower middle-class housewife and mother, the sort of woman who would have stayed home to raise her children while her husband went out to work. Who more likely to feel sympathy with a woman who had lost her son? Who more likely to be honestly interested in the woman and her story?

He stopped at the squad room and found Vianello, asked him to come up to his office for a moment. Pucetti started to get to his feet when he saw his superior, but Brunetti held up a hand and patted the air a few times, signalling that he would talk to him later.

On the stairs, Brunetti asked, 'You read the report on the man they found in Santa Croce yesterday?'

'The suicide?' Vianello asked.

'He was a deaf mute,' Brunetti said. Vianello paused in mid-step, then his foot hit the stair at an odd angle and he shifted off balance for a second.

'You think it's strange, too?' Brunetti asked.

On the landing, Vianello stopped again. 'It's not that it's strange: it's just that I've never heard of a deaf person killing himself.' He gave this some thought, then added, 'Maybe that's because there are so few of them.'

They went into the office, and when they were seated, Brunetti asked, as if posing a theoretical question, 'Do you think Nadia would be willing to do a favour?'

Vianello smiled and said, 'You're an evasive devil, aren't you?' When Brunetti made an interrogative face, Vianello laughed and said, 'Aren't favours usually done *for* someone?'

Brunetti, found out, could do nothing but nod.

'Who's this one for?' Vianello inquired. 'Specifically?'

'Me,' Brunetti answered, then changed it to, 'All of us.'

'Justice in person, sort of?' Vianello asked.

'If you want to put it that way, yes.'

'What's the favour?'

'I spoke to the women at the dry cleaner's near my house. I've known them for years: it's where I used to see the man who died. They let him help them there.'

'And?' Vianello asked.

'His mother refused to talk to me. The women told me

75

she's lived in the neighbourhood a long time. And it seems she doesn't have the best reputation.'

'In a woman, that always means one thing,' Vianello observed.

'True enough,' Brunetti agreed, then went on. 'I must have pushed too hard with them because at a certain point they both stopped talking, and I knew I wouldn't be able to get anything more out of them.'

'Which means?' Vianello asked in the same level voice.

'That we need someone else to ask them questions, someone less threatening.'

'What makes you think they'd talk to Nadia?' Vianello asked, not bothering to ask for confirmation that this was the favour Brunetti wanted. 'She doesn't live near there.'

'I know. But she's Venetian: anyone who listens to her knows that.' Vianello looked doubtful, so Brunetti added, 'And she's *simpatica*. People trust her instinctively: I've seen it happen.' Before Vianello could object, Brunetti added, 'None of the female officers is old enough for people to trust them.'

Vianello gazed away. Brunetti watched the Inspector consider the idea and its implications. Though she would be, in a sense, working for his own employers, even Vianello was not free of the citizen's instinctive distrust of the state. Brunetti watched his friend as he contemplated the ways Nadia might be put in the public eye, how a record of what she heard and reported might somehow be used against her and, ultimately, against him.

Brunetti thought he saw the instant when Vianello's face registered the thought of Lieutenant Scarpa and the consequences of his learning of Nadia's involvement – unauthorized involvement – in a police investigation. Immediately after – there was not even the beating of a heart – Vianello said, 'I think I'd like to suggest an alternative candidate.'

Brunetti ran through the list again, this time even considering his colleague, Claudia Griffoni, only to exclude her at once because she was Sicilian. 'Who?' he finally asked.

'Just as you said, "*una donna simpatica e veneziana*".' With a smile, Vianello added, 'And this one lives in the neighbourhood.'

Baffled, Brunetti wondered if Vianello had some other branch of the service in mind. Was there a woman Carabiniere who could be enlisted to help them? He shook his head as a sign of his confusion and said, 'Tell me.'

'Paola,' Vianello said, and, as Brunetti's face made it evident he still did not understand, the Inspector added, 'Your wife.'

The word 'but' formed itself in Brunetti's mind. Luckily, he did not speak it, for he realized he would do so only in the sentence that insisted he could not ask *his* wife to do such a thing. Or would not. He looked away and then back at his friend. 'I see,' he said, admitting the truth.

Brunetti was silent, as if to allow a sound, or a smell, to dissipate, and then he said, 'There's no record of Davide Cavanella's birth.'

'If he's Venetian, that's hard to believe,' Vianello said.

'He could have been born anywhere,' Brunetti replied. 'His mother's from the neighbourhood and she speaks Veneziano, but that doesn't mean he had to be born here.'

'How long have you seen him around?' Vianello asked.

'Ten, fifteen years.'

Vianello glanced away, taking this in, then asked, 'Has she started looking in other places?' He didn't bother to name Signorina Elettra nor to suggest what the other places might be.

'Pucetti's working on it.' Before Vianello could express

77

his surprise, Brunetti explained: 'Baptism records, health card, school records, pension for him and for his mother, hospital records,' then added, 'Simple things,' thus acknowledging that he had left the extra-legal explorations to Signorina Elettra.

'There's no getting away from them, is there?' Vianello said in a voice slowed by deep reflection. Before Brunetti could ask, the Inspector continued, 'They can go into my bank account now and find out where I spend my money and what I spend it on. Or they can check my credit card and see what I've been buying.'

Brunetti opened his mouth to speak, but Vianello held up his hand to stop him. 'I know what you're going to say: that we get and use the same information.' He smiled at Brunetti, reached over to pat his arm, as if to persuade his friend that he was not about to begin raving.

'Think of the chip in our *telefonino*,' Vianello went on. 'It leaves a record of where we go. Well, where it goes.' Again, he held up his hand. 'I know. We use that information, too. But who leaves his *telefonino* behind? Even that fool who killed his wife kept it in his pocket when he dumped her in the woods,' he said, referring to a recent case they had solved in no time because of this very simple error on the part of the murderer.

'Then what are you talking about?' Brunetti asked.

'That the way we think about it has changed, and we don't question it. We've come to think it's normal that other people know what we're buying or reading or where we've been.' Vianello paused, giving Brunetti a chance to object.

He did not, so Vianello added, 'And the internet? Every time we look at something, we leave a permanent record behind: that we read it or glanced at it, or bought it or tried to buy it, or, for all I know, looked at the timetable for going there.'

Brunetti was unsettled by the feeling that he had looked at another person but seen what he saw in the mirror every morning, heard a voice speaking and recognized it as his own. To the best of his knowledge, he had never left traces behind when breaking a law. He had, however, grown increasingly nervous about the red, howling trail of law-breaking that Signorina Elettra might have left behind her. It wouldn't even have to be Lieutenant Scarpa who discovered it for her – and anyone connected with what she had done – to be ruined: a well-intentioned journalist could land them all in court, disgraced and unemployed, and without a future.

He pushed this thought away, as he had so many times over the years. 'This won't get us anywhere,' he said.

Like the other partner in an old marriage who by now knew all the patterns, Vianello pursed his lips and gave a half-tilt of his head. 'Let's call Pucetti, then, and see what he's found.'

As it turned out, the young officer had found nothing. Like Dottor Rizzardi, Pucetti had failed to find evidence of the passage through life of Davide Cavanella: he seemed, as far as officialdom was concerned, to have sprung into life only by leaving it. Before his name was written on the form that accompanied his body to the morgue at the Ospedale Civile, it had not been entered in any official register kept by the city of Venice. There was no birth certificate; the files of the Church had no registry of his baptism or first communion. He had not attended school in the city, neither the public grammar schools nor the special school in Santa Croce for deaf children. He had never been issued a *carta d'identità*; he had never been registered with the health service, nor had he ever been in hospital. He had never applied for a driver's licence, passport, gun permit, or hunting licence.

Knowing little about the dead man, Pucetti had also searched for evidence of his marriage or the birth of his children, and in those offices had found the same void.

When Pucetti, sitting beside Vianello in front of Brunetti's desk, had finished his list of non-information, the three men sat in silent amazement until Brunetti said, speaking to Vianello, 'It seems some people can still slip through the net.'

'But it's impossible,' said a scandalized Vianello. 'We should be able to find him.'

Brunetti refrained from comment, and Pucetti spoke. 'I looked everywhere, Commissario, even in our arrest files, but he's not there. Nothing. I even went down to the archives, but there's no file on him.' Then, hesitantly, as if afraid he might have gone too far, Pucetti continued, 'I did find a Cavanella in the files, sir.'

Vianello turned to face the young officer, and Brunetti said, 'Good. Did you bring it?'

'Yes, sir,' he said, taking a discoloured Manila folder from a larger one that lay on his lap and handing both across the desk to Brunetti. 'Cavanella, Ana,' was written on the file; handwritten, Brunetti was surprised to note. The Manila cover had once been light blue, but the years, exposure to light, and the penetrating humidity of the archive had turned it a sickly grey and rendered the cover unpleasant to the touch.

'Have you looked in it?' Brunetti asked.

'No, sir,' Pucetti said. Then, risking a small smile, he confessed 'But I'd like to.'

'Then let's,' Brunetti said and opened it. He discovered an outdated form with the elaborate seal of the Ministry of the Interior stamped on the top, taking up almost a quarter of the page, and below it two typewritten paragraphs. '*Mirabile visu*,' Brunetti said and held up the page to show them.

'Wow!' Pucetti said in the English that had now become international.

'Never seen typing before?' Vianello asked, smiling, but not joking.

'Of course I've seen it,' said an embarrassed Pucetti.

Brunetti, reading the report, barely heard them. '6/9/68,' he read aloud. 'Suspect apprehended in Standa, carrying four unopened parcels of women's stockings, two unused lipsticks, and brassiere (size 3) with price tag still attached, in her bag. At the police station at San Marcuola, she presented her *carta d'identità*, which stated that she was born in 1952.

'Her employer, with whom she lives, sent her secretary. This woman identified her as Ana Cavanella, showed a copy of a contract of employment signed by the girl's mother, and took the girl home. Because of her age, no charges will be brought, though a report of this incident has been sent to the social services.'

He looked at the others, who had become a silent audience.

'Nice touch, the size of the bra,' Vianello said.

'Nineteen sixty-eight,' Pucetti said, speaking of it as though it were light years away, as in many ways it was, at least for him.

'And Davide bore her name, not his father's,' Brunetti said, putting the paper inside and closing the file. He opened the file and looked for the name of the woman who took her away, but it was not given. An address in Dorsoduro was, however.

He slid the paper across the table to Pucetti, saying,

'This is the address given for them. Have a look at the Anagrafe files and see who lived there.'

'You think they've put things on line?' Pucetti asked. 'That far back, I mean.'

Though Brunetti was only a child then, he hardly thought of it as 'far back', but he did not pass on this observation to Pucetti. Instead, he said, 'I don't know. If you call them, they should be able to tell you. If not, go over and see if they still have paper files.'

'Why do you want to know?' Vianello took the liberty of asking.

Brunetti thought about his very brief meeting with the woman. In his experience, the motive that most often drove people to distance themselves from horror or tragedy was guilt. Were they her pills, the pills that Davide had swallowed? Had she made him hot chocolate and given him some biscuits, and had he, stomach full and a ring of chocolate around his mouth, found her sleeping pills and taken them, perhaps having seen her take them before bed and thinking that he should, too?

Guilt made sense; it fitted with what he had observed of her behaviour. How better to keep it at bay than by refusing to discuss or even accept what had happened?

'Well?' Vianello asked. Pucetti watched his two superiors, silent.

'Let's go and talk to her,' Brunetti said and got to his feet.

10

Brunetti decided it would be better for all three of them to go. He and Vianello represented, he thought, the serious aspect of the law: men of a certain age and sobriety of bearing. Pucetti, looking more like a student, with the fresh-faced eagerness of a boy just in from the countryside, might clothe the law in less fearful garb. Pucetti had – rare in a man so young – the uncanny ability to induce people to confide in him. He had not learned it or studied it, any more than a cat studies how to make people scratch its neck. He smiled, he looked them in the eye, curious to know about them, and they spoke to him.

Foa, who was idling in the cabin of the police launch, took them over to San Polo, commenting on the freshening wind as they went up the Grand Canal, convinced that this was a sign of approaching rain, and lots of it. Brunetti was glad to hear it: it had been an unusually dry summer, a fact that Chiara had drummed into their heads with relentless frequency; the arrival of rain, especially heavy rain, would put an end to her sermons about Armageddon, at least for a while.

When they were still two bridges from the Cavanella address, Brunetti told Foa to stop and let them out. The arrival of three men, one of them an officer in uniform, would be sufficiently unsettling for Signora Cavanella: no need to pull up in a police launch and attract the attention of the entire neighbourhood.

Seeing that it was almost six, he sent Foa back to the Questura. The three of them could go home directly after the visit.

He rang the bell, and after a full minute he heard the window above him open. Ana Cavanella stood there. 'You again?' she said. 'What do you want now?'

'There are some things I'd like to tell you, Signora. About your son. And there's some information we have to get. For our files.' This was certainly true. Behind him, he heard the sound of a window being opened, but when he turned to look at the house opposite he saw no one, nor any sign of motion at the windows.

When he looked back at Signora Cavanella, her attention had moved to the house opposite and to the windows on the floor above hers. She said something, but Brunetti heard only the last word, ' . . . cow'. Then, looking down at them, she said, 'I'm coming.' Almost as an afterthought, she added, 'But only one of you can come in.'

The men moved closer to the door. Brunetti told Pucetti to position himself so that he would be the first person she saw when she opened it. Without consultation, Vianello moved behind them, allowing most of his bulk to be hidden by Brunetti's body.

The door opened. Just as she became visible, Pucetti raised his hand to his head and removed his uniform hat in a gesture he turned into one of great deference. He did not bow his head, but he did lower his eyes before her gaze. Chiara had once shown Brunetti a book about dog behaviour, and what he sensed of Pucetti's made him want to shout out, 'Beta Dog, Beta Dog!'

Remaining a careful distance from the door, Pucetti said. 'Excuse me, Signora', his nervousness audible in his voice and evident in the way he moved his hat around in his hands. His glance was fleeting and he pulled his eyes away as soon as hers met them. And then, as though unable to contain his desire to speak, he asked, 'Did your son play soccer in San Polo?'

Her eyes grew sharp. 'What?'

'Did he play soccer? In San Polo?'

'How do you know that?' the woman demanded, as though he had told in public some shameful family secret.

He locked his eyes on his hat while he answered. 'My friends and I try to play there in the afternoons, Signora. When we're free. And I thought I remembered your son playing with us a couple of times.' His grasp grew more nervous, and suddenly he was crushing the fabric of the hat, bending the stiff brim until it made a creaking noise they all could hear. Then, pointlessly, he said, 'I'm sorry.'

'You play there?' she demanded.

'When I can, Signora,' Pucetti said, not looking at her.

When Brunetti's eyes moved back to her face, he saw that it had softened in a way that was all but miraculous. Her mouth had relaxed and her lips grown much larger and softer. The hand of ease had smoothed the lines on either side of her eyes, which were directed at Pucetti's. Seeing her face in repose for the first time, Brunetti could reconstruct how attractive she must once have been.

'Sì,' she said to the younger man. 'It made him happy.'

Brunetti remained as motionless as a snake on a stone, leaving the next move to her. She stepped back and, using the plural, invited them in. Brunetti stepped inside and stopped, turning to the other two men, only to discover that Vianello had evaporated. He had barely time to register this before Pucetti, muttering 'Permesso', stepped in beside him.

Signora Cavanella turned and walked towards a dimly lit flight of stairs. They followed, rigorously avoiding any spoken or glanced communication, Pucetti careful to remain two steps behind Brunetti.

At the top of the stairs, she used her key to open the door to her apartment, but even that strange cautiousness did not cause Brunetti and Pucetti to exchange a glance. Inside, she moved along a very narrow corridor that led to what must be the back of the building. Along one windowless wall was a low, glass-fronted cabinet, similar to one Brunetti's grandmother had had in her home. He could see small cardboard boxes stacked inside, or rather stuffed in randomly, for none of the piles were straight, and no concession was made to size. The top was covered by dolls, the sort of cheap souvenirs picked up at kiosks in any city of the world: he saw a flamenco dancer, an Eskimo, a basket-carrying Nubian woman, a man in a large hat who could as easily have been an American Pilgrim as a Dutch farmer. They stood or lay on top of a shabby lace runner that was no longer white, no longer smooth.

She led them into a small sitting room, and again Brunetti had the feeling that a time machine had taken him back to his grandmother's home. There was the same over-plump sofa, covered in green velvet corduroy, the top of all three back cushions protected by small, greying antimacassars. Though neither of the lamps was illuminated, Brunetti noticed that they had faded onion-coloured lampshades, both with woven tassels. A small television with rounded corners was placed directly in front of an overstuffed chair. Over the arm hung a small dark green blanket in some material that made a bad attempt to look like wool. Lodged between the cushion and the side of the chair, were a few decades of a rosary, the crucifix trapped out of sight.

Brunetti glanced out of the single window at the wall of the house on the other side of the *calle*, little more than two metres distant.

The Signora grabbed the chair by both arms and turned it to face the sofa, to which she pointed, and then sat in the chair. Brunetti sat at the right end, Pucetti at the left, as if hoping to give physical evidence of the abyss in sentiment that lay between them.

Brunetti unbuttoned his jacket; Pucetti sat upright, his hat on his thighs, hands carefully folded on top of it. 'Thank you for letting us come in, Signora. I'll try to be as brief as I can,' Brunetti said. He did not waste a smile, letting his face show interest and amiability and nothing else: leave the charm to Pucetti.

'I'd like to ask a few questions about your son,' he said and paused, but she did not ask about that. 'I'm afraid I have to tell you the law requires that someone identify him. It is usually a member of his family, but it doesn't necessarily have to be. His doctor or someone who knew him well can also do this.'

'I'll do it,' she said in an even voice.

'He's at the Ospedale Civile. You can go there any time from eight until five: Dottor Rizzardi or his assistant will be there. The assistant will help you with the paperwork, I'm sure.'

'What paperwork?' she asked. The softness had disappeared from her face, and the lines were back where they had been the first time Brunetti spoke to her.

'They need to notify the Ufficio Anagrafe of any death in the city: the usual process is to take the information from his documents. This way, they can cancel his health card and have his name removed from the various registers in the city.' Brunetti decided not to mention his allowance, which would stop at his death, as would hers for taking care of a handicapped person.

He raised his hands in what he hoped would appear to be a calming gesture. 'It's more or less routine, Signora. All they need is some information and your signature, and they should take care of dealing with the various offices.' This, he knew, was a lie: the bureaucratic clean-up after the death of a family member could sometimes be as bad as the long road to death itself. Death consigned the family to grief and then to the seemingly endless chasing from office to office. Arrange for the Mass and the funeral, the plot in the cemetery, close bank accounts, stop the allowance payments, cancel subscription payments for the television, stop the phone service, close the water, close the gas, stop the postal delivery. Each transaction usually required at least one trip to the appropriate office: many were at the Commune, but others were up at Piazzale Roma or at other far-flung bastions of officialdom in the city. Officials spread misinformation with cavalier disregard for the time it would take the person they were advising to go and find out they were in the wrong office and asking for the wrong certificate or form. Mistaken addresses were dispensed like chocolates to greedy children.

She would learn all of this, if the death of a parent had not already taught her. How many millions of hours were sacrificed every day to the gods of laziness and incompetence? How much was sacrificed each working day on the altar of Eris, goddess of chaos? He thought the Indians, whose bureaucracy, he had heard, made Naples seem like Helsinki, had Kali to stir things round for them.

Pucetti's voice called him back. The young officer was saying, '. . . teams of only four or five players, Signora, so we were all very happy to have him'.

'He knew the rules?' she asked.

'Oh, yes,' Pucetti answered. He lowered his head, as if preparing for confession. 'None of us likes much to be goalie, to be honest. But Davide was very good at stopping the ball and tossing it back to us.' He smiled here and raised his hands, as if imitating the catches her son had made. Then, voice suddenly serious, he said, 'I'm really sorry, Signora. We all liked him. And we'll miss him.'

The compliments worked the same transformation and smoothed away some of the traces of age. Signora Cavanelli's lips moved, and Brunetti was curious to see how a smile would transform her, but she did not smile, only spoke. 'I'll come tomorrow morning.'

'Thank you, Signora,' Brunetti said. 'And it would save a lot of trouble for everyone if you could bring his papers.'

'I can't,' she said suddenly, as if she had just realized the impossibility.

'Why is that, Signora?' Brunetti inquired.

'They were stolen, all of them.'

'I beg your pardon,' was the only thing Brunetti could think of to say.

'Someone broke in here a few months ago and took them.'

Brunetti pulled his notebook from the inside pocket of his jacket, flipped it open, and took out his pen.

'That won't help,' she said brusquely.

'Excuse me?'

'Writing down the date. It won't help. I never told the police.'

Brunetti let his hands fall to his lap and asked, 'Why is that, Signora?'

'No one trusts them,' she said, unaware or unconcerned that he was a member of the police.

That, Brunetti was willing to admit, was probably the truth, but he didn't want to admit it to this woman. Instead, he picked up the notebook and asked, 'What was taken?'

'Everything.'

'I see,' Brunetti said and then, rather than asking her to supply a list, asked: '*Carta d'identità*?'

'Yes.'

'Birth certificate and baptismal certificate?'

Here she moved back in her chair and crossed her legs. She was wearing a dark dress, and the motion pulled the hem to mid-calf; Brunetti could not help noticing that they were shapely and long. 'Oh, I lost those a long time ago. When we moved.' In response to his glance, she said, 'You know how it is.'

Brunetti, who did not know how it was, said, 'Of course,' and made a note of it.

'Where was your son born?' he inquired mildly. 'And when?'

Even though it might have been obvious that his questions had been leading to this one, she seemed surprised. 'In France,' she said. 'I was working there. We were, my husband and I.'

'I see. And the name of the town?'

'I don't know,' she said, her voice calm, even in the face of Brunetti's quizzical stare.

'How is that, Signora?' he asked, lowering the notebook, the better to attend to her answer.

'We were working in a small village near Poitiers, and the doctor told us there were complications with the pregnancy and I should try to have the baby there, in the hospital. Because it was so much better equipped. So when the pains began, my husband and I started to go there. By car. A friend had loaned us his car. But my husband didn't know the way, and we ended up in a small town and the best he could do was find a doctor's office, and I had the baby there.'

'Then the name of that place should have been on the birth certificate, no?' Brunetti asked with an easy smile.

She nodded. 'Yes, but things didn't go well, and I was very sick and in the hospital in Poitiers for a month, and when they let me out, we decided we had had enough of France, so we took Davide and came back to Italy. And that's when we lost the papers.'

'Did you move to Venice?'

She hesitated a long time before she answered. 'No, we went to stay with his family.'

Picking up the notebook again, Brunetti asked, 'And where was that, Signora?'

Voice suddenly obstinate, she demanded, 'Why do you want to know all this?'

'Because it's what they need, Signora. It's not that I'm particularly interested,' he said easily, making it sound as though he actually meant it, 'but the people at the hospital are going to need this information for their system to be able to function.' He smiled and shook his head, as if to suggest that he found this quite as absurd as she must.

'Then I'll tell them,' she said with the same note of truculence he had heard the first time she spoke to him.

As though the words could not remain unspoken, Pucetti said, 'I think the Signora should have to give this information only once, sir.' The tone was meekness itself, yet one sensed the steely resolve that animated him: leave this poor creature alone with her grief. There was nothing of insubordination in what he said, but his manner made it clear that he had declared himself the paladin of this unfortunate mother in her loss and would do his best to protect her from the cold insensitivity of his superior.

'All right,' Brunetti said, pocketed his notebook and got to his feet. 'Then we'll leave the Signora in peace,' he said, managing to suggest that this was not the end of the matter for his inferior officer. He nodded to Signora Cavanella and gave Pucetti a hard look not absent of reprimand and warning.

At the door, he turned to Pucetti and said, voice rich with sarcasm, 'If you'd like to see that the Signora isn't persecuted by the officials at the hospital, as well, perhaps you'd go along to keep an eye on her?'

Pucetti opened his mouth to defend himself but glanced at Signora Cavanella, as if to ask her what she wanted. Then he lowered his head and allowed the moment to pass.

'It would be very kind if he could come with me,' Signora Cavanella said, and Brunetti made no attempt to prevent a look of raw anger from flashing across his face. But he was trapped, and his face showed that he knew it. 'All right, then. If that's what you want.' He turned towards the door, saying, 'I'll leave it to you two to decide what time is best for you,' and left the apartment, not bothering to close the door quietly.

11

Brunetti turned into the first *calle* on the right, irritated that the scene had got beyond his control and he had not thought to ask her about the pills that had killed her son. As he approached the bar on the first corner, Vianello materialized from the doorway. 'Would you like a drink?' he asked.

Brunetti walked up to him, saying, 'Pucetti made a serious mistake joining the police: he could have had a career on the stage.'

Vianello turned back into the bar and went over to a table near the window that provided a clear view down the *calle*, thus explaining his sudden appearance at the door. A glass of white wine stood to the left of that day's *Gazzettino*; Brunetti waved to the barman and pointed to the glass.

As Brunetti pulled out a chair, Vianello closed the paper and set it aside. 'Tell me,' Vianello said.

'When we were still outside,' Brunetti began, 'and you

were pulling your disappearing act, Pucetti – completely out of the blue – asked her if her son used to play soccer in Campo San Polo.' Hearing this, Vianello grimaced and picked up his glass.

The barman arrived and set a second glass of wine in front of Brunetti; he picked it up and took a drink. 'He said he and his friends used to play soccer there and her son was goalie for them sometimes.' Even before Vianello could comment, Brunetti went on, 'I know: he lives down in Castello, so why he'd be playing soccer in San Polo is beyond me.'

'He hates sports,' Vianello said. In response to Brunetti's surprise, Vianello explained. 'One day, I was reading *La Gazzetta dello Sport* in the squad room, and when he saw it he said he hated soccer, was sick of reading about it, hearing people talk about it.' He finished his wine and set the glass on the table. 'So you can forget the idea that he was playing anything – especially soccer – in Campo San Polo.'

Brunetti swirled his wine around for a moment and said, 'Then he's even more clever than I thought he was.'

'And the woman?' Vianello asked.

'A liar. She invented a break-in to explain the lack of papers: apparently, she has nothing, or he had nothing. And the birth and baptismal certificates were lost when they moved back from France. Which is where she said he was born.' He finished his wine and set his glass beside Vianello's.

'Why would she lie about something like that?' Vianello asked. It was not that he thought Brunetti had the answer hidden in his back pocket, but an invitation to joint speculation.

'Maybe she stole him from outside a supermarket because she wanted a baby,' Brunetti said.

'Or raised the baby of a relative,' countered Vianello, adding, 'It's not as if anyone much cares whether women who have children are married or not.'

'That's now,' Brunetti said. 'Her son was born about forty years ago. Things were different then. Think about when we were kids, what our parents said about unmarried women who had children.'

Vianello thought for a moment, then said, 'But the fact that we heard them talk about it means that women were doing it, and enough of them for there to be talk. In front of children, that is.'

Casting his memory back, Brunetti was forced to agree that Vianello was right. He remembered hearing his parents – really, his mother with her friends – talk about other women in the neighbourhood who lived with men without benefit of clergy, had children with them. As far as he could recall , all that seemed to matter to his mother was whether they treated the children well, which meant keeping them clean, raising them to be polite and respectful of their elders, feeding them abundantly, and seeing that they went to school and did well. But that was his mother; he had doubts as to whether her friends shared this elasticity of moral vision.

His speculations were interrupted by the entrance of Pucetti, who had seen them from the street. He approached their table, saying, "I hope you don't mind if I have a drink while I'm in uniform."

'Only if you let me pay for it,' Brunetti said and went over to the bar to get him a glass of white wine. When he came back with it, Pucetti was sitting opposite Vianello and busy telling him about his encounter.

'I'm to go and pick her up at ten tomorrow morning and take her to the hospital,' he said, accepting the glass Brunetti offered him. He took an eager swallow and set it down. Turning to Brunetti, he said, 'I hope you understand I didn't mean any disrespect, sir.'

Brunetti laughed, followed by Vianello, and then by Pucetti himself. Looking at Vianello, Brunetti said, 'You should have heard him: "I think the Signora should be asked to give this information only once," and then just the least little bit of a hesitation before he added, "sir".' He turned to the young officer, whose face had turned red with embarrassment, and said, 'Well done, Pucetti.' Then he gave in to his curiosity and asked, 'How did you know about the soccer?'

Pucetti picked up his glass and swirled his wine around; to give him something to look at while he spoke, Brunetti thought. 'The guys in the squad room were talking about Cavanella, and one of them – Corolla – said he used to play soccer over here, and they would let him – Cavanella, that is – play goalie because they felt sorry for him. He fell down a lot, but he played well enough: besides, no one ever does want to be goalie.'

'He said they all tried to make him feel good,' Pucetti went on. 'Smacking him on the shoulder when he caught the ball or blocked a goal.'

That explained, Brunetti called them back to business by looking at Pucetti and asking, 'What did you make of her story?' Then, to aid him, he added, 'Two possibilities we've come up with, which are that she stole the baby' – he smiled to suggest that this was not to be taken seriously – 'or that she raised the child for a relative. Or it could even have been a friend, I suppose.' Then, in fairness before Pucetti committed himself to either proposition, Brunetti added, 'I don't think either one has any merit.' He had seen, or thought he had seen, the resemblance between their faces and did not doubt for an instant that Signora Cavanella was the mother of the dead man.

'Neither do I,' added Vianello. 'I think the obvious reason is that she wasn't married to the father.'

'What difference does that make?' Pucetti asked. The question, but even more the clear perplexity on his face, showed his age and the generation from which he came.

'It was like that, Roberto,' Vianello assured him. 'Believe me. And when your grandparents were your age, women with illegitimate children were shunned by all decent people; sometimes their children were taken from them and put into orphanages.'

The older men watched Pucetti process this tale, his incomprehension as evident as if he had been told that children in former times went to work at the age of eight. Perhaps because Brunetti's grandparents had lived with the family for the first ten years of his life, he was aware in a visceral, real sense of the way things used to be. Pucetti had grown up in a world of computers and an elastic ethical system, so the thought that a woman would be shunned for being unmarried at the time of the birth of her child would be as bizarre to him as the idea that people would be willing to die in defence of an idea rather than the possession of an object.

The older men seemed to decide at the same moment that persisting in a history lesson was futile. Brunetti asked, 'Did she say anything else?'

Pucetti, also glad to return to the present, said, 'She elaborated a bit on her story about France. It turns out that her husband was French and left her soon after he brought them back to Italy.'

'Where she said his parents were living?' asked a sceptical Brunetti.

Pucetti smiled. 'She told me she felt so threatened by you that she got things all mixed up. It seems they went to his parents in *France*, and then they came back to Italy, though she didn't say where.' His voice was neutral, leaving the other men to believe what they would of the story. 'He stayed with them for only a short time, and then he went back to France and she never heard from him again.'

'She called him her husband?' Vianello asked.

Pucetti shrugged. 'I had the feeling it might have been a courtesy title. And she seemed uncertain about where they were living in France.'

'She mentioned Poitiers,' Brunetti reminded him.

'I know,' Pucetti said with a very sly smile.

Vianello reached across the table and poked Pucetti in the arm. 'Come on, Roberto, what else have you done that makes you look so proud of yourself?'

'I told her I'd been there once, with my parents, when I was a kid, and I loved playing on the beach.'

Vianello propped his elbows on the table and hid his face in his hands. He shook his head, and from behind his hands came his muffled voice, 'Oh, you sly bastard.' Then he asked, looking at him directly, 'What did she say?'

'That with the baby she never had time to go to the beach. But that her husband told her it was very beautiful.' After a brief hesitation, Pucetti said, his regret audible, 'It was too easy, really. I almost felt sorry for her.'

His use of that 'almost' did not go unheard by Brunetti, but he said only, 'So she's never been to Poitiers, but if we ask her about that, she'll just say she had it mixed up with some city that was on the beach. Even if her story's true, there's no way we can check it. The French won't cooperate. I don't believe her story, but if it were true, the baby would be registered under the father's name, and we don't know what that is.'

Pucetti made a small gesture that reminded Brunetti of a student's raising his hand in class. 'If I might ask, Commmissario, why is this so important to you?'

'Because she's telling too many lies,' Brunetti answered without hesitation. 'I want to know what she's lying about.'

He decided to tell them something he had realized after his conversation with Rizzardi. 'He can't be buried until he's identified.'

'Isn't that why I'm going to the hospital with his mother tomorrow morning?' Pucetti asked. 'She'll identify him, surely.'

'That's not enough,' Brunetti said, aware of how cold the statement was.

'Why?' Pucetti asked. Brunetti knew that Vianello understood the reason and wanted Pucetti to learn it in a way that would make him never forget it.

'Because there has to be official proof that the dead person is who he is claimed to be or thought to be. She can say anyone is her son, and that dead man could be anyone. Until she can provide a document that proves he is who she says he is, the state will not accept her word.' To prevent Pucetti from saying something he might later regret, Brunetti added, 'Think about it for a minute. People can't be buried before there's certainty about who they are.' He could think of examples to argue his point – the woman who throws herself off a bridge and whose body is found two hundred kilometres away; the unidentified body found in a field – but he thought it more important to state the principle: the unknown cannot be put underground, not before every effort has been made to find out who they are. It was atavistic, he realized, perhaps linked to magic and taboo. The dead deserve at least to be recognized, and the living deserve at least to know the people they have loved are dead, and not missing.

To Pucetti he said, 'Take her to see Rizzardi.'

Vianello glanced at Pucetti, as if assessing whether to

question Brunetti's authority, or his decisions, in front of a uniformed officer. He must have decided that the young man was sufficiently discreet, for he said, 'You're treating it as though you don't believe it was a natural death, Guido.'

That Vianello should say this in front of the younger man was an indication of his confidence in him, or so Brunetti chose to believe. 'I think it is,' he insisted. 'He probably thought the pills were something to eat, something good because his mother kept them hidden from him.'

What troubled him was not the circumstances of the man's death but the fact that he had managed to live for forty years without leaving any bureaucratic traces that he had lived at all. That mystery, and its sadness, nagged at Brunetti, but he did not want to give voice to this.

12

After dinner, Brunetti told Paola about his conversation with Signora Cavanella and her refusal to divulge any information about her son, and about the lies she had told both him and Pucetti to explain away the missing documents.

'Why would she want to lie about her son?' Paola asked. 'It's not as if she kept him locked up in the attic for forty years, is it?' She sank deeper into the cushions of the ratty old sofa she kept in her study: she spent so much time in that spoon-like posture that he sometimes marvelled she could still stand upright and walk.

'It suggests he isn't her son at all,' she said, but it was speculation, not inquiry.

'I saw him only a few times, like you, but he resembled her,' Brunetti told her.

'I can't place her,' Paola said, closing her eyes and resting her head against the back of the sofa. 'But I might not have noticed her. Sixtyish, badly dyed red hair, good legs, good skin, and still attractive. There are scores of women in this city who fit that description.' Then, after a pause, 'I wonder where she works.'

'Why do you think she works?'

'Because manna from heaven falls only in the Bible, Guido.' He smiled, which encouraged her to continue. 'It's our new duty to work until we drop, remember? By the time you and I get there, they'll have extended the age to eighty.' She paused, then added, 'No, I speak ill of our leaders. They'll have pity on women and let us stop at seventy-eight.'

'I still don't understand why she'd behave so strangely,' Brunetti said, accustomed to her sideswipes at the government, any government, and equally accustomed to ignoring them.

'People are strange, as you never cease to tell me.'

He thought of his conversation that day with Vianello and his insistence that people were too much under the eye and observation, not only of the authorities, but of any business that could find a way to pry into their lives. At the thought of Vianello, Brunetti felt another twinge at the presumptuousness of his having suggested to his friend that Nadia be asked to investigate. 'I don't understand it,' he said, patting Paola's leg and getting to his feet. 'I am taking to my bed with Lucretius.'

She gave him a long look, grinned, and said, 'As your wife, I blanch at the thought that you are going to bed with a man who wants to explain to you The Nature of Things.'

He smiled back, reached out to her with one hand, and said, 'Would you like to try, instead?'

She got to her feet.

The next morning, the rain that Foa had smelled in the air arrived, and Brunetti put on a raincoat and carried an umbrella when he left the house. He decided to take the Number One from San Silvestro to the Zattere, and stopped to pick up that day's *Gazzettino* for the ride. On board, he noticed how few people were reading a newspaper; how few, in fact, were reading anything. Of course, that they were slowly passing the most beautiful sight in the world might have distracted them from the *Gazzettino*'s cursory presentation and mistaken analysis of world events, but he still remained surprised at how few people read. He read, Paola read, the kids read, but he realized how seldom he talked about books or found a person who appeared to take a serious interest in them.

His mind opened to the castigation that was never far from it. Here he was again, assuming that what he thought was what other people must surely think; that his judgements must have universal validity. Lucretius knew that what is food to one man is bitter poison to another, a lesson life had been trying to teach Brunetti for a generation.

As he tugged at this idea, studying the people who sat on the other side of the boat, his newspaper lay forgotten on his lap, making Brunetti yet another of those who sat on the vaporetto, gazing about without apparent purpose.

He got off at San Zaccaria and made his wet way to the Questura. He went up to his office, shook the umbrella until it would have whimpered if it could, hung his coat on the outside of the cupboard, and stamped around until his feet no longer left wet prints on the floor.

He turned on his computer and checked his email, quite unconscious of how automatic this process had become in the last few years. It was no longer necessary for him to stop in Signorina Elettra's office or in the squad room to find out what was happening: most information waited for him in the computer. It was, however, information without nuance, without the unveiled scepticism with which Vianello greeted certain reports and without Signorina Elettra's insights to set things straight.

He found an invitation to a conference in Palermo that would 'enhance coordination between the community and the organizations dedicated to maintaining order in civil society'. He pushed his chair back and stared out the window, allowing the Cloud of Ironic Despair to descend upon his head. Did this mean he was invited to a meeting between the citizens of Palermo and the police, or did the people in charge down there have a sense of humour and it was really meant to be a meeting between local citizens and the Mafia, the only organization well enough led, sufficiently clear in its purposes, and free of infiltrators to go about the business of maintaining order in society so as best to suck from it what little life remained? His first impulse was that of the show-off, to forward the invitation to Vianello and ask if the second possibility were correct, but the habit of leaving no traces was second nature to him and he resisted the temptation.

Among the other emails was one from Pucetti: he was just leaving to accompany Signora Cavanella but wanted to tell Brunetti that his relative would gladly speak to him about that subject. He gave a *telefonino* number, nothing more. Using his own *telefonino*, Brunetti dialled the number.

'Bianchini,' a man's voice answered on the third ring.

'Good morning, Signor Bianchini, this is your cousin Roberto's friend. He suggested I call you.'

'Ah,' the man answered, then said, showing he understood that there was no need to discuss the purpose of the call, 'I thought we could meet for a coffee some time.'

Brunetti looked at his watch. 'I have a very light schedule this morning,' he said, not at all certain of this because he had not read the other emails, 'so we could meet any time you like.'

'As it happens, I'm free this morning as well. How about that bar near the Ponte dei Greci? I think you know it.'

'Yes,' Brunetti said neutrally.

'Eleven?'

'Good,' Brunetti said and ended the call with a polite farewell.

Fast work from Pucetti in convincing his cousin to talk to him, Brunetti reflected. He sat for a few moments and thought back to the strange urgency with which Patta had explained the situation in San Barnaba. Patta cared about his family and his job and was unlikely to ask Brunetti for help unless one of the two was at risk. Or perhaps it was nothing more than Patta's attempt to endear himself to the mayor, as a kind of deposit in the bank of favours.

Was it like this everywhere? Brunetti wondered. Was it all connected, and did power in one place seek automatically to ally itself with power in some other place? And did they protect themselves and one another and to hell with the rest?

Remembering that Rizzardi would have reported on the dead man's teeth, he scrolled down the list of his messages, but there was no report from the pathologist. It had been two days since the autopsy, and the report should have been filed. '"Should have" doesn't mean anything,' he said aloud.

He wrote an email, telling Rizzardi the report had not arrived and asking the pathologist to make sure that information about the teeth was included. He was about to send it, when he thought of Rizzardi's sensibility. He cancelled the last sentence and wrote, instead, that he was particularly interested in whatever had been found about the teeth, for this might end up being the only way to make a physical identification of the dead man. This one he sent. He remembered a friend of his who worked as a musical agent once used the term, 'Diva Dienst' to describe the manner in which he was forced to treat certain singers, male as well as female. It was a combination of deference, adulation, and dedication to anticipating their every whim. And here he was, a police commissario, engaged in 'Doctor Dienst'.

Having read his email, he turned to the papers from his in-box. He was successful with the first three, which he understood, initialled, and placed at the other side of his desk. But the fourth, a report on the increase in pickpocketing, breaking and entering, and mugging caused Brunetti, quite literally, to run his hands through his hair. It was at this point that Claudia Griffoni, the newest of the other commissari, knocked on his door and came in without waiting to be told to do so. Her elegant legs were today partially visible under a dark green woollen skirt, the rest of her covered by a long beige sweater with a high neck.

'Hiding?' she asked.

'From reality,' he admitted. He pointed to the papers. 'I'm just reading about the 28 per cent increase in break-ins in the last six months.'

'Reported break-ins,' she corrected him, reminding him that he had to add to that whatever his own experience suggested might be the correct number of people who no longer bothered to report a crime.

'They had a point, though, when they gave the amnesty,' she said as she came across the room and sat in one of the chairs in front of his desk. 'If the prisons are full, and the European Court of Human Rights is screaming at the government, then they have to let some out, if only to make room for the new ones.'

106

There was nothing he could say. Dockets so full that an appeal case in Venice would have to wait nine years to be heard. Drunk drivers on the mainland who exterminated entire families and were placed under house arrest. Mafia control of the country an ever-expanding curse and, not surprisingly, no government willing to examine the increasing symbiosis between Mafia and politicians.

'Shall we talk about the weather?' he asked.

She smiled, and it lightened his heart to see it. 'I'd love to, but I'm afraid I have to speak about our Black Nemesis.'

'What's he done now?'

'It's not so much what Scarpa does, is it,' she asked, 'as what he makes sure will not be done?'

'For example?'

'Foa's been invited by the Guardia Costiera to spend a week with them, starting the first of the month.'

'To do what?'

'To familiarize them with the coastline and the places where it's possible for small boats to make a landing.'

'What's being landed?'

'Cigarettes,' she said. 'But you know that.'

Brunetti nodded.

'It seems now that they're also landing people. Or so the Guardia Costiera believes.'

'From where?'

'Small boats come across from Albania and Croatia, but it looks like some larger ships are stopping off the coast and putting them on to smaller boats to be brought in.'

'What kind of ships?'

'Freighters, tankers. Some of them are so big, it's easy for them to keep fifty people aboard.'

'Without anyone noticing?' he asked.

She smiled again. 'You think the crew cares what happens? Most of them are illegal, anyway, so they're probably willing to help people they think are in the same situation.'

'And they asked for Foa?'

She nodded. 'The commander did. Foa told me a lot of the men who are assigned here come from the South and don't know the coastline at all. He's Venetian, family's been Venetian since the beginning,' she said. 'So he knows the coast like he knows the inside of his pocket and can show them where the likeliest landing places are.'

'And Scarpa?'

'He refused the request – refused it when it was made and refused it again when the Captain of the Guardia Costiera repeated it.'

'Did he give any explanation?'

'He said that Foa is an employee of the police, not of the Marina, so there is no legal protection for anything he might do if he pilots one of their boats.'

'What does he expect him to do, run a pirate attack on the boat to Chioggia?'

'The Lieutenant did not lower himself to discuss details: he was speaking of general principles.' Disgust filling her voice, she added, 'Scarpa wouldn't recognize a principle if it sat down next to him on the vaporetto and hit him over the head.'

'Not that he'd ever take a vaporetto,' Brunetti said, and hearing himself say that, he understood everything. 'It's because Foa won't chauffeur him around, isn't it?'

Griffoni smiled again. 'Of course. He's one of the few who stand up to him, won't take him anywhere unless there's written authorization from Patta.'

'Nasty little shit, Scarpa,' Brunetti said.

'To say the least,' she agreed. 'Except that he's not little.'

'I was speaking in the moral sense, I suppose,' Brunetti said. She nodded in understanding and agreement. 'So he blocks Foa's request?' Brunetti asked. She nodded. 'Is it important for him?'

'It certainly can't hurt him: collaboration with another service, specifically requested to aid them in . . .' Here Griffoni allowed her voice to take on the metronomic rhythm of politicians . . . 'the fight against illegal immigration.'

'The treasurer of a political party steals thirteen million Euros, and the politicians are hysterical about illegal immigration,' Brunetti said tiredly.

'He offered to give five back,' she said in the voice of careful honesty.

Brunetti pushed his chair at a slant and balanced it on its back legs. He latched his fingers together behind his head. 'I was in a bar last week, and two people in front of me were talking about just that: the thirteen million. And one of them – she was a woman at least a decade older than I am – she put her coffee cup down on the saucer and said only one word. "Bombs".'

He saw that he had caught Griffoni's attention, but he kept his hands behind his head and stared at the ceiling as he spoke. 'The woman with her asked what she meant, and she said that the only way to get rid of them was to bomb Montecitorio and kill them all.'

He lowered his head to see that she was paying attention. 'The woman with her was the same age, carrying her shopping bag and on the way to Rialto. She looked surprised and said, "But that would damage the building, and it's so beautiful."'

He took his hands from behind his head and let his chair fall to the ground. 'So that, Claudia, is what the middle class thinks of our Parliament.'

She shrugged, as if to dismiss the woman's comment or the importance Brunetti saw in it, but after a moment's reflection said, 'I like her concern for the building.' Then, back to business, she asked, 'What can we do about Foa?'

'Patta's asked me to do him a favour. If I can manage it, I'll make the price of it that Foa be assigned to this.'

'You don't want to use it for yourself?'

'You sound as if I'm a squirrel burying a nut for the winter,' he said with a laugh.

His laughter proved contagious. When they stopped, Griffoni said, 'We trade them back and forth: I do this for you; you do that for me.'

'And we all have a list, accurate to the *centesimo*, stored away in our memories.'

'Like the squirrels,' she said, thanked him for his time, and left his office.

13

Though it was just quarter to eleven, Brunetti decided to go down to the bar and wait for Bianchini. He looked out the window and saw that it was still raining, so he took the umbrella. The bar was only down at the bridge, so he didn't bother with his raincoat.

Inside, he said hello and exchanged a few words with Bambola, the tall Senegalese who ran the place most days. Brunetti studied the pastries and, seeing that there was only one of its kind left, told Bambola he'd like the apple and ricotta, but not until the man he was meeting there arrived. Bambola took a pair of metal tongs and placed the pastry on a small plate that he set to the left of the coffee machine. The door was pushed open and smacked against the wall. Two straw-hatted gondolieri, who worked at the boat station on the corner, came in and walked to the bar.

They were, unsurprisingly, loud and vulgar, in the middle of a conversation that consisted of boasts about their sexual conquests of clients. Bambola served them with a kind of exalted deference behind which they were unable to see a contempt so palpable as almost to scream its presence in the room. He never failed to call each of them, 'Signore', and insisted upon using the formal 'Lei' with them, though they called him, unasked, 'tu'. Each man had a glass of white wine and a *tramezzino* and Brunetti was astonished when each of them paid for his own separately. The experience of life had taught him to believe there was a genetic peculiarity in Italian men that prevented them, ever, from letting someone else pay for his drink. But then he remembered that they were gondolieri and thus had an entirely different genetic structure. They remained at the bar, leaning back against it, from which position they could see down the canal to the gondola stop, and they continued their conversation, which he sensed was aimed, somehow, at Bambola.

He moved away from the bar, taking the newspaper with him. He sat at his usual table at the back and opened the paper, looked at the headlines, and thought about what Bianchini might have to tell him.

A man came in, very tall, thin, about Brunetti's age but almost entirely bald. What hair remained was cut short and encircled the back of his head, as if he scorned any attempt to disguise his baldness. Brunetti saw the look he gave the gondolieri but they, eyes alert for business at the dock at the end of the canal, did not. He approached Bambola, nodded to him. The African made a graceful gesture towards Brunetti; the man nodded again in thanks and turned away.

'One of them was a Black American, ass as big as a horse,' Brunetti overheard. 'But hot; this one was hot, the way the Blacks are.'

Bianchini stopped and stood perfectly still for a slow

count of five, then turned back towards them. With a motion neither of the gondolieri missed, he unbuttoned his jacket and planted his feet solidly. 'Excuse me,' he said in a normal speaking voice, and then after a pause, 'Signori.' They turned to look at him, and Brunetti could read the astonishment in their faces.

'I think it might be time you went back to your boats.' His voice was very deep, calm, utterly devoid of emotion.

The taller of the two gondolieri lifted a foot as if to take a step towards the stranger, but his companion – older, wiser, quicker – placed a hand on his arm and swung him around until they were facing one another. Keeping his hand on his companion's arm, he gave a small shake of his head and turned towards the door. He had to pull at the other's arm, then he lowered his head and said something to him. The younger one turned his head to look at Bianchini and then followed his companion out of the bar.

Bianchini looked at the barman, who met his gaze with a smile. 'Would you like your coffee now, Commissario?' he called to Brunetti.

'Yes, please,' Brunetti said, face blank as though he had just dragged his attention away from the newspaper.

The man walked over to him, and Brunetti slipped his legs from under the table to stand. 'Bianchini, Sandro,' the man said as he extended his hand. His grasp was firm, but it was only a handshake, not a test of male dominance.

Bianchini was taller than Brunetti, though much thinner, wiry. The skin on his forehead showed the old scars of acne; his light beard was perhaps an attempt to disguise the same marks on his cheeks. His dark eyes were set deep below heavy brows, but his full-lipped mouth and easy smile countered any suggestion of roughness one might see in them.

'Thank you for coming,' Brunetti said and sat. Bianchini sat opposite.

Bambola was suddenly there. He set the plate and pastry before Brunetti and a coffee in front of each man. There were also two small glasses of water, which he put down silently before he went back to his place behind the bar.

'My cousin said you were curious about the vigili,' Bianchini said, wasting no time. Then, after a pause, 'He's a good man, Roberto.'

'Yes, he is,' Brunetti agreed. He poured an envelope of sugar into his coffee and swirled it around, then used his spoon to cut the pastry in half.

'Did he tell you what it was about?' Brunetti asked.

'That mask shop in San Barnaba.'

Brunetti nodded. He picked up a piece of pastry with one of the napkins on the plate and took a bite. 'Would you like the other half?' he asked.

'No, thanks,' Bianchini said with an easy smile. 'I can't eat things like that.' In response to Brunetti's furrowed brow, he added, 'Diabetes.' Saying that, he took a tube of artificial sweetener from the inside pocket of his jacket and dropped two tiny white pills into his coffee.

Brunetti took a sip of coffee, then said, having decided this was not a man with whom one wasted time, 'I've been told that the vigili are being paid to ignore the tables in front of the shop.' Hearing himself say this filled Brunetti with sudden embarrassment. Was he, like Scarpa, Patta's creature, obliged to do his bidding at every turn? 'The licence holder is the fiancée of the mayor's son, so there's a possibility of scandal if this becomes public. The Vice-Questore wants to avoid that.' He stopped speaking and finished his coffee. He no longer wanted the rest of the pastry and pushed the plate aside.

'Is that all?' Bianchini asked, making no attempt to disguise the surprise in his voice and on his face.

'I think so. What I'm supposed to do is safeguard the mayor's reputation.'

'My, my, my,' Bianchini said with a smile, 'how very delicate our politicians are becoming. Next thing you know, they'll be committing hara-kiri if they're caught with their hands in the till.'

'I think that's only in Japan,' Brunetti said drily, 'and nowadays even they don't do it as often as they should.'

'Pity,' Bianchini said, 'I've always thought it was a fine example.'

'It's not "Made in Japan" any more,' Brunetti said. 'Now it's "Made in China", and standards have fallen.'

Again Bianchini couldn't hide his surprise. 'So you know about what's going on?' he asked.

Brunetti didn't, at least not specifically to do with this subject, but that didn't stop him from saying, 'It's hard not to know, isn't it?'

Bianchini shook his head and let a long time pass. 'We don't have to go into it, but you can be sure there'll be no trouble for the mayor.'

'Would you be willing to tell me more?' Brunetti asked.

Bianchini looked away, out the window of the bar, down towards the place where the gondolieri were now standing by their boats. He sat silent, sipping at his water, then placed the glass back on the table.

Brunetti sat still, waiting.

'People are fed up with the Chinese,' Bianchini said, with no introduction. 'They buy stores and no one asks them where the cash comes from. Their shops are filled with Chinese workers, and no one ever bothers to ask for their work permits or residence permits. The Guardia di Finanza never goes in to check their receipts.' He waited to see what Brunetti would say, and when he said nothing, Bianchini added, 'Everyone leaves them alone and lets them go about their business.'

Brunetti's experience as a policeman had given him a strong suspicion of urban myths, but that same experience had proven to him that some of them were true.

'And so?' he asked.

Bianchini finished his water. 'And so we've sort of decided to even up the odds. There are some violations we don't see and aren't going to see.' He met Brunetti's glance, then went on, 'And if we're given something in return for this, then there's no Venetian who'll think it's wrong.' He spoke with conviction, including himself among those Venetians.

Bianchini drank the last of his coffee, set his cup down and said, 'The mayor doesn't have to worry about any consequences.' He spoke with such finality that there was no doubting him.

Bianchini slid to the end of the bench and got to his feet. He reached his hand behind him for his wallet.

'No, no,' Brunetti said, thinking of the way he had driven the gondolieri from the bar. 'Bambola won't take your money.' He pushed the plate and saucer forward and got to his feet. Standing beside Bianchini, he felt the difference in their heights: he was a tall man, looking at Bianchini's chin.

Brunetti went to the door, made a rolling sign with his hand to tell Bambola he would pay him later, and walked outside with the other man.

Both men looked down to the end of the embankment, where one of the gondolieri was talking to a pair of young Japanese tourists. As they watched, he led them to his gondola and helped them down into it, then jumped aboard. With one foot, he pushed the boat away from the *riva* and bent in a graceful gesture to pick up his oar. The boat disappeared to the right. Bianchini turned towards San Marco, and Brunetti, after thanking him for his time, opened his umbrella and headed back to the Questura.

He stopped in the officers' squad room on the way to his office, but there was no sign of Pucetti. Upstairs, he checked his email and found the report from the ambulance squad that had answered the call to the Cavanella home. 'Time of call: 6.13; time of arrival: 7.37; name of person who let them into the house: Ana Cavanella; condition of subject: deceased; condition of deceased: in bed, in pyjamas, signs of vomiting: arrival at morgue: 8.46.' And that was all.

There was also one from Rizzardi, attached to which he found the rough draft of his autopsy report. Brunetti scrolled down, past the height and weight and probable age, past the chocolate drink and biscuits, to the parts of the body, and thus to the teeth. There were two amalgam fillings and signs that a wisdom tooth on the upper left had been removed. None of the work appeared to be recent and all, 'conformed to the standards and style of Italian dentistry'.

'Such as they are,' Brunetti, who went to a Dutch dentist on Lido, said under his breath.

He wrote back to Rizzardi and explained that they might need dental evidence to prove the boy's identity and asked him to take X-rays of the work. He went downstairs to talk to Signorina Elettra.

She considered the problem for a few minutes and said she would have to get a list of the email addresses of the dentists registered with the union of dentists in the province of Venezia and send them the X-rays, along with a photo of the dead man and a description of his disability.

Thus, if Davide's dentist worked in the province of Venice, they might discover more about him. 'Assuming that the work wasn't done in some other province,' she said.

'His mother doesn't seem like the sort of person who would take him to a specialist out the province,' Brunetti said, but then decided to exhaust other possibilities before attempting this.

Signorina Elettra ran the fingers of her left hand through her hair and said, 'How strange all of this is.'

'What?'

'That you refer to Signora Cavanella as his mother while you're still trying to identify him.'

Brunetti nodded in swift agreement. 'I'm not in any doubt about who he is. But it's not enough that she looks like him or that she calls him her son. Not legally.'

She put her elbows on her desk and rested her face in her hands. He noticed the way her skin was pulled tighter by her hands, removing a number of years: he didn't like having to admit that he noticed the difference.

'You'd think, in this world where we're all registered from the time we're born – from even before, with prenatal tests – that something like this would be impossible,' she said, her confusion evident in her voice. 'If he were a foreigner, I'd understand: check the hotels, find out where his shoes and clothing come from, put a photo in the papers, contact the embassies. That's all pretty standard.'

She looked at Brunetti, but he had no suggestions to offer.

'You've got his body. You've got his mother. He was taken out of the house where he was living. And you can't *identify* him.' He knew she had no personal stake in any of this, so the best he could assume was that the patent disorder of it offended her. 'A person can't live somewhere all his life and not leave any traces. It just can't happen.'

Brunetti agreed, and for some reason his mind moved away from the dead man to his mother; he wondered if the same would be true of her. There had to be a reason for the obstacles she was placing in the way of the identification of her son; in that case, she was certainly not going to tell them what it was. But traces there had to be. 'Let me go and get something,' he said.

Back in his office he shifted through the files and loose papers that had accumulated on his desk, telling himself, as he always did when searching for something, that he had to be more orderly with documents and files, and just think of the time tossed away looking for things, when, if he'd only think to . . .

He found her file and still disliked the sensation of his hand on the bleached, warped paper. He opened it and found the address, took the copy of *Calli, Campielli e Canali* from his drawer and looked for the building. And there it was, an enormous beige rectangle on the opposite side of the canal from Campiello degli Incurabili and looking quite enormous. He tried to run his memory over the area, but it was decades since he had been there, and he had no clear image of it.

He took the book downstairs, keeping the page open with his finger, and in Signorina Elettra's office opened it on the desk beside her computer. 'Look,' he said, 'it's in Dorsoduro.'

'What is?' she asked in honest confusion.

'The place where Ana Cavanella lived in 1968, when she was arrested for shoplifting.'

'How old was she?'

'Sixteen,' Brunetti answered.

'What happened?'

'Nothing. She was underage. Her employer sent someone to get her, and that was the end of it.' Seeing

119

that she was not satisfied with this, he added, 'Pucetti couldn't find anything about the son, but there was an old file on her down in the archives, so he brought it up.'

He angled the book towards her and she ran her finger across the bridges and down the *calli* leading to 616. She picked it up and flipped to the end and then forward again until she found the pages with the names of the various buildings. He watched her finger run down the list of buildings until it stopped and she read aloud, 'Palazzo Lembo.' She looked at Brunetti. 'That mean anything to you?'

'The King of Copper,' he said.

'I beg your pardon,' Signorina Elettra answered.

Brunetti smiled. 'It was before your time. Lembo – I don't remember his first name – the King of Copper. His family had mines somewhere; Africa, I think, or maybe South America. But way back, at the beginning of the last century. There was some other mineral, but I can't remember which one it was. Tin, maybe. But copper was the main business.'

'I was at school with a girl named Lembo. Margherita. But they were from Torino, I think.'

'No, no, these Lembos have been here since the crusades,' Brunetti said. The Brunettis had been, too, he knew, but that sort of thing seemed to matter only in the case of nobility or wealth. Poor people had grandparents; the rich had ancestors.

'The *palazzo* was probably broken up into separate apartments,' Signorina Elettra suggested.

'Only one way to find out,' Brunetti said.

She gave him a very quizzical look. 'You're really taken with this, aren't you, Commissario?'

From her tone, he could not tell whether she approved

or not. The silence around Davide Cavanella could be an example of bureaucratic oversight, but it might be something else. 'I think I'll ask Foa to take me over to have a look at the *palazzo*.'

14

Foa, glad of the chance to go for what Brunetti did not tell him was little more than a joyride, gave him a hand getting on to the boat. Over to Dorsoduro to look at a building: this made as much sense to Foa as taking the Vice-Questore to lunch and was certainly much more fun because Brunetti at least stood on deck and enjoyed the ride rather than sitting in the cabin talking on his *telefonino*. Brunetti learned all of this indirectly, just as he learned much of what he knew. Foa never criticized their superior openly, but perhaps because they were speaking in Veneziano, he could make use of a wide range of references and expressions that were virtually untranslatable.

Foa took the Canale della Giudecca, rather than the Grand Canal because the more direct route was around the back, he said. He knew the building, of course: was there a water door in the city he had not taken a boat past in the last twenty years? They turned into Rio delle Toresele, Foa slowing to make the turn. He slowed down even more as they approached Calle Capuzzi on the left. 'That's it,' Foa said, pointing to a high-arched dark green door that stood at the top of three moss-covered steps leading down to the water.

Brunetti had never noticed the door, but who would notice a door that looked exactly like thousands in the city? 'You know anything about the place?' Brunetti asked.

Foa pulled the boat up at the entrance to the next *calle* and switched the motor to idle. 'Some rich people used to live there. I remember because there was a very nice boat they used to tie up here.'

'When was this?'

'Must have been twenty years ago. Maybe more.' Then, after a moment's reflection, Foa added, 'Boat hasn't been there for years.'

'Can you get in a little closer to the *riva*?' Brunetti asked. 'I'd like to go around and take a look at the place.'

Foa pulled the boat up beside the *riva*. Luckily, it was high tide, so Brunetti could avoid the slippery stairs and step directly on to the pavement of the *riva*. He walked down the narrow *calle* to the door of 616, a ponderous oak slab varnished dark brown and divided into four high rectangles by thick, bevelled strips of the same colour. There was a modern brass lock, dulled nearly green by the humidity.

To the left was a tarnished brass plaque with the name 'Lembo' incised below the single bell. The Copper King, or was it tin? Brunetti stepped back and studied the façade of the *palazzo*. Narrow, it rose four floors: the grey plaster had flaked away in many places, exposing the brick beneath. Two simple arched windows stood to the left of the door and one to the right, all three of them heavily grilled with iron bars that were not free of the rust of neglect. The *quadrifora* of the first floor was blackened at the top, as though smoke had leaked out of the four narrow windows for centuries and stained the carved marble above them, which might well have been the case.

The windows of the floor above appeared almost twice as tall as those on the floor below, making them seem curiously etiolated in relation to the building. The frames and glass were obviously modern and the marble pilasters dividing them were a shocking white, smooth and almost entirely devoid of ornamentation, unlike the worn fluted columns of the windows below.

Brunetti took another step back and leaned against the building opposite. Above the windows he saw a row of small *barbacani* supporting a marble drain, though the much later addition of a low top floor had turned the drain into a mere ornamental motif. The real drain, metal and jarringly noticeable, corroded in more than one place, ran under the tiled roof and leaked two dark feathers of mould and rust down the façade.

Brunetti turned to his right, out to the *fondamenta* and down to the bridge at San Vio. He crossed it and went into the bar on the left, where he had often stopped for a coffee and was familiar with the people working there without knowing their names. He asked for a glass of white wine, glanced around at the people at the tables, looking for someone he knew, but he recognized no one.

When the barman brought the wine, Brunetti thanked him. Nodding at the *calle* with his chin, he asked, careful to speak Veneziano, 'Does the Lembo family still live in that *palazzo*?' The man, who was short, stocky, balding, with a thick nose and the rugged skin of a drinker, set the glass on the counter and took a small step back, as if to put a greater distance between himself and the question.

There followed a process Brunetti had been observing

for decades. The barman might not know his rank or branch of service, but he was certain to know, however vaguely, that Brunetti, a client for decades, was involved with the police. Thus his question was not innocent, nor was it idle. This meant that the man had to weigh up his sense of duty to the state (which one could probably estimate as zero) with his accumulated memories of Brunetti's behaviour over time, and then against that he had to weigh any obligation he might have to the Lembo family. This calculation was immediate, and Brunetti was probably more conscious of it than was the man engaged in it.

'The daughters still live there,' he said after a hesitation so short most people would not have noticed it. He turned and switched on the coffee grinder next to the coffee machine, though the plastic container was well more than half full.

Brunetti took a sip of his wine, waited out the noise, and when it stopped, asked for a tuna and artichoke *tramezzino*. It came wrapped in a paper napkin and on a plate.

'Ana Cavanella used to live there, didn't she?' Brunetti asked and took a bite of the sandwich. Too much mayonnaise, as was increasingly the case all over the city, he didn't know why.

'Is this about her son?' the barman asked.

'Yes,' Brunetti answered, seeing no reason to lie.

'What happened?'

'He took sleeping pills, vomited, and choked to death,' Brunetti said.

The man's hand rose protectively to his throat; he left it there while he said, 'Oh, the poor woman.'

'You knew her?' Brunetti asked quite naturally, as though they were old friends and the subject had come up in conversation.

'Years ago,' the man said. 'Must be forty. Even more.' Then, 'How old was he?'

'In his forties,' Brunetti answered and took another sip of his wine. Then, very casually, 'She's still an attractive woman. Must have had him when she was young.'

The man shot him a suspicious look; Brunetti countered it by taking another bite of his sandwich and nodding his appreciation. 'I spoke to her three days ago, just after he died. Terrible, terrible.'

The man's curiosity got the better of him. 'How'd that happen? I always thought the boy was retarded. You think she'd be careful with pills and things like that.'

Brunetti sighed and said, 'I don't think we can be careful all the time.'

Two men came into the bar and asked for coffees. The barman served them and was quickly back in front of Brunetti. He picked up a glass and wiped at it with a towel.

'What was it people called Lembo?' Brunetti asked, as if the name were dangling just at the edge of his memory, in need only of some help from a person with a better one. 'The Duke of Something?'

'King,' the barman said, pleased to have found it first. 'The King of Copper.'

Brunetti smiled in approval. 'Of course. Thanks.' Then, the way people did, he repeated the name, 'The King of Copper', shaking his head at the outlandishness of it. He finished his *tramezzino* and did not order another one because he did not want the barman to move away.

'My father,' Brunetti lied, 'used to talk about him.' Then, as if allowing memory to seep back, he continued, 'He had a boat – my father – and he would take him . . .' He broke off and allowed a look of great confusion to cross his face. 'I don't remember whether it was fishing or to Piazzale Roma.' He shook his head: age takes away so many memories. 'He used to talk about his daughters. One of them was about my age, and he'd tell me I should be more like her; quieter, more obedient.'

'That must have been Lucrezia,' the barman said.

Delight flashed from Brunetti's eyes. 'Yes, of course. That was her name.' He caught the barman's eyes in his glance and said, 'I never met her, but I have to confess there were times when I wanted to go on the boat with my father and throw her off.' He chuckled, looked down at his feet, and shook his head.

'Why?'

With a smile that displayed his pleasure that this man should be curious about his family memories, Brunetti said, 'Because my father talked about her so much. Said she was like this and like that: all the things I wasn't.'

'Is your father still alive?' the barman surprised him by asking.

'No. Why?'

'Because, if he were, you could tell him that he was wrong.'

Confused smile. 'I'm afraid I don't understand.'

'You're a respectable man. A policeman, aren't you?' he asked.

'Yes to the policeman,' Brunetti said. 'I don't know about the respectable.'

'Well, Lucrezia isn't.'

Once more Brunetti looked confused and, he attempted, faintly concerned. 'What happened?'

'Men. Alcohol. Trouble with her children. Divorce.'

'I'm sorry to hear that,' Brunetti said, speaking as though he'd just had bad news about an old friend. Then, deciding to risk it, 'I'm glad my father never had to hear this.'

'No one likes to hear bad things about people they like, do they?' the barman asked.

'No, not at all,' Brunetti said, shaking his head and deciding to meet cliché with cliché: 'But life's a funny thing: it tells us things we don't want to hear.' He shook his head and then, deciding it would be best not to ask more questions, he reached into his pocket and took out some change. He asked how much he owed, left more than that on the counter, thanked the man for his time, and left the bar.

Foa was on the deck, bent over a copy of *La Gazzetta dello Sport*, giving the impression that he wanted to eat it, rather than read it. He heard Brunetti's footsteps and reached a hand across the open space to help him on to the boat.

'Latest scandal?' Brunetti asked, pointing to the screaming headlines.

Foa folded the paper closed and stuffed it under the control panel. 'It's strange, Commissario,' he said as he moved past Brunetti to unmoor the boat. 'We all know it's fake, that the games are all fixed, but you'd think they'd be more clever about keeping what they're doing secret.' He reached down and slapped the paper with the back of his fingers. 'They're blabbing about it on the phone all the time, sending emails back and forth, talking about how much they want to be paid to lose the game, giving the names of the players who will help.' He turned the key, revved the engine, and pulled away from the *riva*, heading for the Grand Canal.

They turned right, back towards the Questura. Foa seemed to have exhausted his comments on soccer and sportsmanship, but Brunetti wondered if he might still be interested in blabbing.

'That *palazzo* belongs to a family called Lembo,' he began. 'You ever hear of them?'

A taxi was making straight for them, the driver busy

on his *telefonino*. Keeping one hand on the tiller, Foa gave a sharp blast of their siren. The driver looked up and saw them, dropped his *telefonino* and pulled his boat skittering to the right. 'Stupid bastard,' Foa said as the two boats passed.

Then, taxi forgotten, he said, 'Yes.'

'Much?'

'Enough. Give me a day, sir, and I'll know a lot more.' He turned and smiled at Brunetti, unable to disguise his pleasure at being treated like a real policeman.

Brunetti was content to stand and watch the buildings and the light, entranced, as he so often was, by the casual, unending beauty of it. Stone, sky, gold, marble, space, proportion, chaos, disorder, glory.

They glided to the dock. Foa switched off the engine and tossed the mooring rope effortlessly over the stanchion, jumped to the dock and held out a hand to Brunetti. It was the second time that day the younger man had offered him a hand: Brunetti put his lightly on the outstretched arm and jumped to the *riva*.

He decided it was time to throw Signorina Elettra some fresh meat and went to her office. She was not at her desk, but the door to Patta's office was open and he could hear voices, one of them hers, from inside. He could have stood by the door to hear what they were saying, but the idea displeased him: next, he'd be scrolling through her computer files, using the skills she had taught him.

Instead he went to the window and looked down at the waters of the canal; he thought about the man in the bar and what he had told him. 'Daughters.' After some time, he heard footsteps and then the closing of the door to Patta's office. Signorina Elettra came across the room and gave him a smile. She sat behind her computer and said, without asking him what he had found in Dorsoduro, 'I am a saint.'

'You are a saint,' Brunetti repeated. 'You are probably also a martyr.'

'I am a martyr.'

'What does he want?'

'This office,' she surprised him by saying.

'What?' he asked and then, as the obvious dawned, he changed that to the even more obvious, 'For whom?'

'Lieutenant Scarpa,' she said, as if this could be the only answer. As it certainly was.

'But why?'

'So their symbiosis can grow even stronger, I imagine,' she said angrily. Brunetti wondered when he had ever seen her really angry, to the extent that her face was red and her voice tight, as was the case now.

'Can't you stop it?' Brunetti asked, realizing how tentative his voice sounded.

'Of course I can,' she said. 'But I don't want to.'

'Why?' he asked, unable to hide his astonishment.

'Because I don't want to have to leave.'

His heart stopped. Brunetti was not given to excessive reactions, nor to excessive language, but he felt his heart stop, well, at least miss a few beats and then begin again with a faster rhythm.

'But you can't even think about that,' he bleated before he could adjust the tone. 'I mean, if you're going to leave, then you should have a better reason for it than that.' He thought about offering her his office but knew Patta would never accept that. He felt as though he had walked into a wall.

'I don't mean *leave* leave, I mean leave this floor.'

'For where?' Brunetti asked, disguising his relief and running his mind through the building.

'All I have to do is change a few offices around,' she said, her anger subsiding.

There was something in the ease with which she said this, as if the task were no more complicated than prising the cork from a bottle of prosecco, that jangled Brunetti's nerves. He sent his memory through the building again, seeking out the offices that might be suitable to her and the names of the persons who currently used those offices. And there it was, on the same floor as his but on the other side of the building, a much smaller room with a view of the garden in the back. The room was currently crowded with two enormous cupboards no one had thought to move when the desk was put in and the office was given to Claudia Griffoni.

He stopped himself from slapping his palm to his forehead and crying out 'Aha!' but that did not dull the clarity of his revelation. Signorina Elettra felt little *simpatia* for her: it was as simple as that. Brunetti had no idea of the reason: he did not want to attribute it to feminine jealousy and, to avoid discussion of that, he had chosen never to talk to Paola about it.

His wiser self told him to stay out of this, to make no comment, and to pretend it did not concern or interest him, so long as she found an office. 'Well,' he said idly, 'I hope you can work it out.' He tried to think of a quid pro quo he could offer Patta. The consequences of non-intervention here, he knew, would not be peace in our time.

Careful to make it clear that what he was about to offer was much more interesting than any talk of offices and who would move into them, he said, 'I have a name for you.'

'For?'

'For you to have a look at.' Seeing that this had caught her attention, he said, 'I went over to Dorsoduro to have a look at the *palazzo*.' In an attempt to relax things further, he added, 'And I came back with a name.'

'Which is?' she said, turning the computer screen to face her.

'Lucrezia Lembo.'

'The wife of the Copper King?'

'The daughter. There are at least two, and they apparently still live at that address.'

Signorina Elettra smiled a real smile, relaxed and easy, and he watched tension and anger seep away from her. 'I'll see what I can find,' she said.

'The person who gave me her name said she's had a troubled life: men, trouble with her kids, divorce, alcohol.'

She pulled her lips together. 'That's more than enough for anyone.'

'I'd like anything you can find about either of the sisters: I don't know the name of the other one,' he said. He had a vague memory that both of the parents had died.

She hit a few keys, then a few more; she read for a moment, hit some more keys, and when Brunetti saw her begin to smile again he wondered if it was at the thought of being back at work or at the prospect of being able to access the data banks of the various institutions of the city without having to bother about pesky things like warrants or permissions or orders from magistrates.

He thanked her and started back to his office, proud of having returned an angry, petulant woman to her rightful place as a buccaneer utterly without respect for rules or regulations.

15

At the bottom of the flight of steps that would take him to his office, Brunetti glanced at his watch and saw that it was after two. It was likely to be one of the last temperate days of the year, and he felt himself entitled, after what he chose to think of as his morning's work, to lunch with his wife. Paola had told him that the kids would not be there, so he could be as late as he pleased, and he decided to take her at her word.

As he made his way towards Rialto, he played at something he told himself resembled that three-dimensional oriental chess game he had read about but not understood and that might be called Go. He had no idea of the rules and so invented his own: he assumed that the people he shifted to another office on another floor would go without complaint and without rancour, emulating the man in the Bible who picked up his bed and walked away.

Scarpa to Signorina Elettra's, Signorina Elettra to Claudia Griffoni's. The large cabinets to the archive, where their high shelves would save some papers from the effects of mildew and time. And where was Griffoni supposed to go? Into the converted cupboard which had been Lieutenant Scarpa's office for years?

He said nothing about the problem of Signorina Elettra's office during the meal, finding the *calamaretti con piselli* more interesting than the territorial disputes of his colleagues. He waited until he was standing beside Paola, drying the dishes and putting them back in the cabinet, but drying them very slowly and not paying attention to what he was doing. He continued to dry a wine glass until she reached out with a wet hand, took the glass from him and set it on the counter. 'What's bothering you?' she asked.

'Women.'

It was seldom that Brunetti managed to stop Paola in her tracks, so her expression gave him a certain satisfaction. 'In general? Or specifically?' she asked. She rinsed her hands and took the towel from him to dry them.

'Specifically,' Brunetti answered.

Appearing to ignore him, she said, 'How nice it would be to live on the first floor.'

'With damp and no light?' Brunetti asked, thinking of the ground-floor offices in the Questura; he had not even dared to consider moving any of the players in his game to them.

'With only one flight of steps if we want to go out to get a coffee in a bar,' she corrected. She reached up for the *caffetiera*, added water, put in the coffee, screwed the top on tightly, and set it on the stove. Paola was certain to return to the subject of women, so he went back into the living room and stood at the window. The clouds had grown heavier during lunch, and a light rain was falling.

She came in with two cups, sugar already added. She

handed him one, stood stirring hers, and asked, 'Which ones, specifically?'

'Signorina Elettra and Claudia Griffoni,' he answered.

'They've come to blows?' she asked.

He sipped at his coffee, finished it, and set the cup on a table. 'You always talk about feminine jealousy.'

'When I'm not speaking about male jealousy,' she reminded him. She went and sat on the edge of the sofa, waiting.

'It's about an office,' he began. 'But that's just a pretext. Elettra has never taken to her. It's evident every time I mention her.'

'And Griffoni's feelings?'

Brunetti had never considered this. 'I'm not sure that she's noticed.'

She waved a hand in the air. 'Earth to Guido, Planet Earth to Guido. Are you there?'

'What's that mean?'

'It means that if Elettra doesn't like someone, there is no way that the person would not notice it.'

He thought of Signorina Elettra's perpetual, and public, goading of Lieutenant Scarpa, so different from the gentle, almost affectionate, pokes she took at Vice-Questore Patta. One man disgusted her, the other caused only irritation. With Griffoni, however, she had been assiduously polite, as she was with no one else at the Questura.

When he explained this to Paola, she said, 'How does Griffoni behave?'

'The same way. It's as if she's addressing a head of state.'

'Well, she is, isn't she?'

'What?'

'Signorina Elettra, at least from what you've told me,

runs the place. Or she certainly runs Patta, which comes to the same thing.'

'And so?'

'So Griffoni's formality could be nothing more than deference to her position.' Before Brunetti could object, she said, 'Remember, she's a Sicilian, and they're far more hierarchical in their thinking than we are. If they come of good families, the impulse towards politeness is even stronger.'

'It's been three years.'

'They'll work things out. It sounds to me as if each is simply waiting for the other one to show some sign of informality.'

Brunetti, refusing to believe this, asked, 'What do I do? Stay out of it and break it up when they're rolling around on the floor with their hands on each other's throat?'

'You said something about an office,' Paola reminded him. 'Is it about who gets one?'

'Yes.'

'Who makes that decision?'

'Patta.'

'Is there some way you can blackmail him into averting hostilities?'

Of course, after decades at the university, she would think of the most underhand way to deal with a problem. He had so far forgotten to tell Patta that there was no risk to the mayor's son because of the bribes being paid to the Polizia Municipale. Patta, however, need not be told how easy it had been to discover that. Let him think that Brunetti had had to call in favours from the forces of order, ask old friends to turn a blind eye, risk his own reputation in defence of the mayor's son and his re-election campaign, his political future.

If he made his efforts sound sufficiently Herculean, he

might also add a request that Foa be temporarily assigned to the Guardia Costiera.

He bent down and kissed her. 'I tremble to think of what you've been learning all these years from those novels you read,' he said and went back to the Questura.

The rain grew heavier while he was still on the way as a serious shower turned into the first full pounding-down of the autumn. Glad that he had worn his light raincoat, Brunetti did not try to stop and wait it out; although he quickened his pace for the last ten minutes, he still arrived at the Questura with his head and shoulders soaked.

He rubbed his hair with both hands, wiped them on his handkerchief, then used it to swipe at his hair. Upstairs, he hung his coat on the door of the cupboard and decided to go down to speak to Signorina Elettra.

Once again, when he entered she was not at her desk. The door to Patta's office was again ajar, and he could hear his superior's voice from behind it, though he could not make out what he was saying. He went and stood by the window, removing himself from temptation, but when he looked down at the *riva* he saw Signorina Elettra stepping into a police launch, Foa holding her hand to steady her on the slippery deck.

Brunetti moved closer to the door.

'I realize the seriousness of the situation, Signore,' Patta said in a placatory voice. 'I've got one of my best men looking into it, you can be sure.' There followed a long pause. 'Yes, he's Venetian, sir.'

Brunetti, one of Patta's best men, moved silently across the office and went back upstairs to his own.

His phone started to ring when he was still a few metres from the room. Quickening his steps, he picked it up on the seventh ring. 'Brunetti,' he said.

'Guido, it's Ettore,' he heard Rizzardi say.

'What is it?'

'A strange thing's happened, and I thought I should tell you.'

'What?'

'You sent one of your men over here with the mother of that man who died, didn't you?'

'Yes. What happened?'

'Oh, she identified him. The young man couldn't have been kinder to her.'

'Is that why you're calling?'

'No, she's back: that's why.'

'Back where?'

'Back in the hospital.'

'With you?'

'No. In the Emergency Room.'

'How do you know that?'

'Favaro,' he said, naming one of his assistants. 'He saw her when she came to identify her son, and he recognized her when she was brought in by the ambulance, so he came to tell me.'

'What happened?'

'I don't know. I haven't seen her.'

'Did he say anything about her?'

'Yes. He said it looked like someone beat her up.'

16

He called the officers' squad room, only to be told that Pucetti was out on patrol. He asked for the young man's *telefonino* number, entered it into his own, and called. Pucetti answered, said he was in San Marco, watching the pigeons and the tourists avoid the rain.

Brunetti told him about Rizzardi's call and was surprised by the force of the young man's response. 'What happened? Is she badly hurt?'

Brunetti repeated that all he knew was what Rizzardi had told him: she was in the Emergency Room, and it looked as if she'd been attacked.

'Can I meet you there, Commissario?' Pucetti asked.

'That's why I'm calling,' Brunetti said, surprised that Pucetti hadn't assumed that. 'I'm leaving now. Rizzardi will meet us there.' He looked at his watch. 'Fifteen minutes.' The young man broke the connection before he did.

He looked out the window: no sign of Foa or his boat.

He put on his raincoat, took his umbrella from the bottom of the cupboard, and left the Questura, telling the man at the door that he was going to the hospital to talk to a witness.

The rain had intensified while he was inside, and his shoes were soon soaked at the toe and then along the sides. The rain had cleaned the pavement and had cleared the streets: although he saw few people on the way to the hospital, inside there was the usual back and forth of visitors, doctors and nurses, and bathrobed and slippered patients.

The automatic doors slid open as he approached them, and he walked into the waiting area of the Pronto Soccorso. He walked past the reception window and into the first corridor, intent on finding either Rizzardi or Pucetti.

'Signore,' a voice behind him called out. 'You have to register.' He took out his warrant card and went back to the door of the small cubicle where the receptionist sat behind his computer. He was an owl-like man with sparse hair who looked perfectly at home inside his glass-fronted box.

Brunetti held up his warrant card and said, 'I'm looking for Dottor Rizzardi.'

Disgruntled, needing to score even this small point, the man behind the desk said, 'You have to show me before you go in.'

Brunetti was about to snap back at him when he recalled the mantra Paola had been beating into his head for two decades: 'This is the only power this man has, and it is the only power he will ever have in his life. Either you show him that you respect it, or he will cause you more trouble than it's worth.'

'Ah, sorry,' Brunetti said, putting his card back in his wallet. 'I forgot.'

The man nodded, apparently mollified. 'She's in the third room on the left.'

'One of our men in uniform should be here soon. Would you send him down to us?' Brunetti asked and then, invoking the wisdom of Paola, added, 'Please.'

The man raised his hand, glad now to help. 'Of course, Signore.'

Brunetti knocked at the door, waited a few seconds, and went in. Rizzardi was standing at the foot of the bed, reading a form attached to a thick plastic clipboard. How strange, Brunetti thought, to see Rizzardi with a live patient; but then he remembered that he was, after all, a doctor.

Rizzardi glanced at Brunetti and used the clipboard to wave him forward.

Brunetti approached. Rizzardi held up the clipboard to indicate it was the source of whatever he could tell him. Speaking softly, the doctor said, 'She might have a concussion, but very slight, a lot of bruising on her face, a cut over her left eye. Two fingers on her left hand are crushed, and there's a hairline fracture to one of her ribs.'

Brunetti looked at the woman in the bed and was shocked to see how much smaller she had grown. She hardly seemed as long as she had been tall; the sheet dipped down at her shrunken waist. She was asleep; her eyes were curiously deep-set, a reddish-grey halo already in place around the left one. Her cheeks seemed to have collapsed into her mouth, or perhaps it was a trick of light that played the clear skin of her cheeks against the darker skin around and under her eyes. He recognized her chiefly by her hair, the only thing that had not changed.

Her left hand lay outside the covers, two fingers splinted and taped.

'What happened?' Brunetti asked.

Rizzardi lowered the clipboard and returned it to its place at the foot of the bed. 'I don't know,' he said. 'All I've seen is this.' He tapped the paper. Taking Brunetti by the arm, he moved him away from the bed.

'Favaro said it looked as if she had been beaten. Her injuries are consistent with that idea.' His voice was soft, cool, instructive.

Brunetti glanced across the room and took another look at the woman's face and hand. 'And if I said it, too?' he asked, having seen the results of many beatings in his career.

Rizzardi gave a relaxed shrug and said, voice warming in response to Brunetti's question, 'I'd agree with you.'

Before Brunetti could add anything, the door opened and Pucetti came in. He looked at the two men, at the woman, then back at Rizzardi. The doctor nodded to him, reminding Brunetti they had met that morning, when Pucetti had accompanied Signora Cavanella to the morgue.

'What happened, Dottore?' the young officer asked, voice lowered. 'Is she all right?' His concern could not have been more audible.

'The ambulance crew brought her in three hours ago. She might have a concussion: she hit her head. You see her fingers: they've been crushed. And she hit her face,' Rizzardi said. 'She might have fallen.' Brunetti was interested in the description he gave, which was utterly devoid of reference to human agency of any sort.

'*Oddio*,' Pucetti said. He remained motionless, just inside the door. Then, with a shake, as if bringing himself back to normal, he asked Brunetti, 'Should I go and talk to the crew?'

'Good idea,' Brunetti said, then to Rizzardi, 'Is she all right alone?'

'Of course,' Rizzardi said, with that complete confidence with which doctors comment on uncertain things.

Realizing it would be difficult to talk in the same room as the woman, Brunetti said, 'Let's get a coffee,' then, to Pucetti, 'Come and find us in the bar after you talk to them, all right?'

'Yes, sir,' Pucetti said and, with one more glance in the woman's direction, was gone as hurriedly as he had entered.

Both men left the room very quietly, as people always do when they are in a hospital. As they went along the hallway, back towards the bar in the entrance corridor, Brunetti asked, his voice returned to normal volume, 'What do you think happened?' Rizzardi said nothing for a while until Brunetti added, 'Between us, that is.'

Rizzardi smiled and answered, 'I don't mind telling you. I'm thinking about the possibilities, not about the risk of giving an opinion.' He paused when they reached the courtyard, where the rain had grown even heavier.

The trees were still fully leaved; the rain had not succeeded in bringing down many of them. It occurred to Brunetti that the leaves should all be on the ground by this time of year.

'I suppose you've seen similar cases,' Rizzardi said, standing with his hands in his pockets and watching two cats sleeping on the low stone wall. 'They could be defence wounds, or perhaps she hurt her fingers trying to break her fall. There's the blow to the head, but it could be that her head hit the wall, or a step, when she fell. There are the wounds on her face: on the left side, which means they came from a right-handed person – if someone did hit her – but that sort of bruising is common in a fall.'

One of the cats opened its eyes, stood, and arched its back before lying down again and lapsing instantly into profound sleep. 'There might be some other explanation. The ambulance crew might know something, or she might tell us when she wakes up.' Turning to Brunetti, he asked, 'What's it look like to you?'

Brunetti ran his right hand through his hair and found it still damp. He wiped his hand on his trousers and continued towards the bar. 'I've seen enough of them, usually women who get beaten by their boyfriends or husbands. This could be one of scores of cases. It's got all the signs: the head, the face, the fingers.'

In the bar he ordered two coffees without having to ask Rizzardi what he wanted.

When the coffee came, Rizzardi took a sip, then said, 'I hit a man once. Once in my life. But I can't imagine hitting a woman.'

'Why'd you hit him?' Brunetti asked.

'Oh, it was just a thing,' Rizzardi said.

Brunetti turned and stared at him. 'Everything's a *thing*, Ettore. Why'd you hit him?'

'I was on a vaporetto,' Rizzardi began. He picked up his coffee, studied what was left in the cup, swirled it around a few times, and finished it. 'There was a man standing to my left. And in front of him was a little girl. Well, maybe not so little. She was maybe thirteen, so, yes, she was still a little girl. When he thought no one was looking, he leaned sideways and put his hand on her ass and squeezed it. And he left his hand there. I watched her, pretty little girl, wearing a dress. It was summer, so it was a light dress.'

Rizzardi set his cup back in the saucer and turned to look at Brunetti. 'The girl looked at him, but he kept his hand there and smiled at her. She was terrified, embarrassed, ashamed.' He turned to the barman and asked for a glass of mineral water, then turned back to Brunetti. 'So I hit him. Made a fist and hit him in the stomach. I'm a doctor, so I didn't want to risk hitting his head or his face: didn't want to break anything, or my hand, so I guess I didn't hit him very hard. But hard enough.'

The water came. Rizzardi picked it up and drank half. 'He doubled over, and when his head was about the level of my knees, I bent down and said, "You ever do that again, I'll kill you."' He sighed. 'I never did anything like that in my life, let myself lose control.'

'What did he do?' Brunetti asked.

'He got off at the next stop. I never saw him again.'

'And the girl?'

Rizzardi's face lit up. 'She said, "Thank you, Signore" and smiled at me.' Rizzardi's face was transformed by a smile. 'I've never been so proud of myself in my entire life.' He waited a few seconds before adding, 'I know I should be ashamed, but I'm not.'

'Would you do it again?' Brunetti asked.

'In a heartbeat,' Rizzardi answered and laughed.

Pucetti arrived just then and stood amazed: like Brunetti, in all these years, he had never heard Rizzardi laugh.

Glad of the chance to move away from what Rizzardi had told him, Brunetti asked, 'What did they say?'

'The call came from a man who passed her on the street, over near the Zattere. He said there was a woman sitting on the steps of a building, with blood on her face. He tried to talk to her, but she didn't seem to understand him, so he called for the ambulance.'

'Do they have his name?'

'Yes, sir. He stayed there until they came.'

'Did he tell them anything else?'

'Nothing. Just that he was on his way home, and he saw this woman.'

'Did she say anything?'

'She told them she fell down.'

'If I had ten Euros for every time I've heard that one, I

145

could retire,' Rizzardi interrupted to say and asked Pucetti if he'd like a coffee.

Pucetti stared at Rizzardi and did not answer, then said he didn't want a coffee.

Brunetti paid and they left the bar, walked past the courtyard, and back to Pronto Soccorso. This time, Brunetti raised his hand to the man behind the window, who waved back and smiled.

Brunetti opened the door to the room and saw that the woman's eyes were open. But by the time the three men were near the bed, they were closed again.

'Signora,' Brunetti said. There was no response.

Rizzardi, obviously deciding to stay out of this, said nothing.

Pucetti leaned down and said softly, 'Signora Ana. It's me, Roberto.' He placed his right hand on her upper arm. 'Signora, can you hear me?'

Slowly, she opened her eyes and, seeing his face so close to hers, smiled.

'Don't try to talk, Signora. Everything's all right, every-thing's going to be all right.'

'Could you ask her . . .' Brunetti began.

Pucetti stood upright and turned to Brunetti. 'I think she's had enough, Commissario. Don't you?' Then, including Rizzardi, he said, 'I think we all ought to get out of here and let her rest.'

Brunetti backed away from him and raised his hands, palms open; in the voice of a man struggling to save face or reputation, he added, 'She's had too much. You're right.' He turned and headed for the door. As he passed Rizzardi, he said, 'Come on, Ettore. Pucetti's right.'

The two men went and stood by the door. Pucetti bent down and placed his hand on the woman's arm again. 'Try to get some sleep now, Signora. I'll come back when

I can.' When she started to speak, he held up one finger, as if he wanted to place it gently on her lips, and said, 'No, not now. Everything can wait. Just sleep now. And get better.' He gave her arm the gentlest of squeezes and moved away from the bed, very slowly, turning at the door as if to see that she was still all right.

The three men left the room; Pucetti was careful to pull the door closed very quietly.

17

Brunetti didn't know whether to laugh or to turn away from the young man. He had certainly deceived witnesses during his own career, but he had seldom been this good at it, though he wasn't sure that was the adjective to describe what he had seen Pucetti do. The young man had a genius for deceit, the way another person had a gift for music or golf or knitting. The comparisons left him uncomfortable, if only because those other pursuits were neutral, whereas deceit was not. If this deceit led to an understanding of the circumstances of Signora Cavanella's son's death, it would surely help, and thus it was good. Oh, how very Jesuitical he had become.

He looked at the unlined face of the young officer and wondered where Dante would put him. Among the Evil Counsellors? The Evil Impersonators? Was Pucetti to be enveloped in a tongue of flame or preyed upon and rent to pieces by others like him?

Rizzardi saved him from the need to comment by saying,

'You had me convinced.' Then he added, 'I saw you together this morning, and you were very good to her then.'

Pucetti looked at the floor, pressed his lips together, and said, 'I'm not sure I like being able to do it, Dottore.' He raised his eyes to watch a white-coated woman doctor approach and pass them by, then looked at Rizzardi. 'Most people want so much to believe in what others say that it makes it too easy.' Then, earnestly, 'I'm not just saying this, you know. I really don't like that it's so easy.' He paused, then added, 'And it's not easy to do it with her. He was her only child.'

Listening to Pucetti say this, Brunetti realized how much he wanted to believe him. His thoughts turned to Paola, as deceitful and duplicitous a person as one could hope to find, yet who remained one of the only truly honest people he had ever known.

Rizzardi interrupted. 'I've got to get back. I'll let you pick over this poor woman's bones.' Leaving them with that, he turned and walked away.

Brunetti and Pucetti continued towards the exit. Pucetti took this opportunity to tell Brunetti that the *parocco* had told him he had been at the parish only six months and had never heard of Signora Cavanella. At the front door, they looked out across the *campo*. The rain had stopped and the sky was clearing, so Brunetti would not need the umbrella. He realized then that he had left it somewhere, either at the entrance to Pronto Soccorso or in Signora Cavanella's room, or in the bar. Where did they go, he wondered, all of those umbrellas he had forgotten on trains, in boats, in offices and stores during all of these decades?

He walked out into the cooler air: autumn had arrived. 'Tell me what happened this morning,' he asked Pucetti. Standing there, feeling the refreshed air, seeing the clouds scuttle west, he had no desire to return to the Questura.

149

He started towards the bridge, heading for home and pulling Pucetti in his wake.

As they walked in front of the school, Pucetti caught up with him and began to explain what had happened. He had arrived on time at Signora Cavanella's home and been careful to be formal and polite, nothing more. But at the second bridge, when she paused before starting up it, he slipped his arm under hers, careful to release it when they reached the other side. Because she had decided to walk, there were many more bridges, and by the time they got to the last one, the one in front of the hospital that he and Brunetti had just crossed, the habit was established that he would help her cross them.

It was she who asked Rizzardi if the young officer could come into the morgue with her, and it was Pucetti who held her arm and kept her from falling when Rizzardi pulled back the sheet that covered her son's face.

Later, he had helped her fill in the forms and had all but sequestered an ambulance to take her home. Brunetti was curious about the reasons for Pucetti's behaviour, but he didn't know how to phrase the question. Without being asked, the young man said, just as they came out into Campo San Bortolo, 'At first, I thought it would be a good idea to win her confidence any way I could, but I ended up feeling sorry for her, Commissario. His death's destroyed her. No one can fake that.'

Brunetti stopped beneath the statue of the ever-dapper Goldoni; he resisted the impulse to point out to Pucetti that he himself had faked a strong emotion, and quite convincingly. Instead, he told the young man he had done well and could call it a day if he wished. But Pucetti decided he'd go back to the Questura. Brunetti raised a hand in an informal farewell and turned right towards home.

*

The next morning, Brunetti made a special point of arriving at the Questura on time, not that anyone paid any particular attention to when he got there. He had called the hospital from home just after eight and spoken to the nurse in charge of Ana Cavanella's ward. The signora had passed a quiet night; the doctor who examined her had decided to keep her one more day and night before sending her home. The nurse did not know if she had had any visitors, only that another woman had been moved into her room.

Signorina Elettra was in her office, standing at the cabinet beside the door, slipping a file back into place. Seeing her wearing cashmere – a rusty orange cardigan – after the long pause of the summer, Brunetti had confirmation that autumn had arrived.

'Ah, Commissario, come and I shall tell you mysterious things.'

He followed her back to her desk. Instead of turning on her computer, she pulled out the small *chiavetta* protruding from the side. 'Shall we use your computer, Signore?' she asked. A quick glance showed him that Patta's door was open, suggesting that he had not yet arrived. Yes, better that Patta's day should not begin with the sight of him in confabulation with Signorina Elettra and her computer.

Upstairs, he left it to her to insert the *chiavetta* and turn on the computer while he hung his raincoat and scarf in the cupboard. 'Please,' he called over to her; she sat in his chair and ran an affectionate hand over the keys of the computer she had procured for him a year ago. He did not want to know what she had done in order to achieve that, nor how many police offices in Bari were without basic equipment because he had this top-of-the-line computer that was the envy of the younger staff and a source of witless pride to himself. To have somehow had the Ministry of the Interior buy him a Maserati would have been no greater example of conspicuous, and wasted, consumption.

From her smile, it was evident how much she appreciated the machine she was using, which caused him, not for the first time, to wonder why she had had it consigned to him and not to herself. He walked to the desk and pulled one of the guest's chairs around behind it.

'Look,' she said, pointing to the screen. He recognized the double-faced document he saw before him: front and back cover and then the inside pages of a *carta d'identità*, issued six years before by the Comune di Venezia. The woman's age was given as 53, birthplace Venice, and residence the address in San Polo. Her civil status was *'nubile'*, not *'sposata'*, and her profession *'casalinga'*, a housewife or woman who kept house. She received the minimum state pension.

Signorina Elettra hit a key, and the identity card was replaced by a report from Ulss that gave the woman's name and the same address, and the name of the doctor who had her under his care. His address was in San Polo, as well.

Another key, and Brunetti saw the list of and reasons for her medical visits as well as the diagnoses and prescriptions that resulted from them, at least for the last seventeen years, since the records began to be computerized. Running his eye down them, he saw that she was another of those people who would, as was said of his mother for most of her life, put the doctors out of business. She had visited the doctor six times in the last twelve years, twice for influenza, once for a bladder infection, and twice to get a referral for her Pap test. A year ago, she had received a prescription for a common sleeping pill.

'And the son?' Brunetti asked.

She shook her head. 'Nothing. He doesn't exist. He wasn't born, didn't go to school, never saw a doctor or went to the hospital.' She glanced up at him and said, 'It's the same thing Pucetti found. Or didn't find.'

She typed in 'Davide Cavanella', and the screen showed the name on a document and, across from it, rows of XXXXXXXXXs in place of information. He was never arrested, or issued a hunting or a driver's licence, had no passport, no *carta d'identitá*, never worked for the state or paid into a pension. Nor did he receive a disability allowance. Then, as an afterthought or to show that she had checked every possible category, Signorina Elettra went back to the previous screen and tapped at the listing: 'No carer's allowance for the mother.'

In a country filled with fake blind people, with others collecting the pensions of relatives who had died a decade before, of people declared to be 100 per cent incapacitated who played golf and tennis, here was a genuinely disabled person who had never made any claim on the state.

'Nothing?' he asked, certain that she had looked in other places and not bothered to tell him.

'Nothing. For all the official evidence there is, he does not exist and never has.'

For some time, they sat quietly, looking at the screen. She pushed another key, and it went blank, as if in illustration of Davide Cavanella's life: Brunetti considered the gesture melodramatic, but he kept this opinion to himself.

'And Lucrezia Lembo?' he asked for want of any other possibility.

Signora Elettra's hands returned to the keyboard, and she brought up the files and highlighted one of them. She opened it to show another *carta d'identità* with a black and white photo of a woman of a certain age looking severely at the camera, as if suspicious of its intentions. Her eyes were light, which suggested that her dark colouring was the result of sun rather than nature, and she appeared to be wearing little or no makeup, so it was impossible to disguise those wary eyes and a tightly closed mouth. He looked at the inner pages, where he read her date of birth: two years before Ana Cavanella, her parents resident in Dorsoduro. Her height was given as 1.74 metres, her civil state as *'sposata'*, her hair *'bionda'*, her current profession *'Direttrice'*, which, without an indication of what it was she was the director of, could mean just about anything.

'What else?' he asked.

Silently, she showed him Lucrezia Lembo's health records for the last fifteen years, which made heavy reading. She had developed diabetes in her fifties, yet apparently kept it under control with pills; she had been hospitalized twice with pneumonia, and according to her doctor's notes, continued to smoke heavily, which the same doctor noted as a factor exacerbating not only the pneumonia, but the diabetes. There was little evidence that she had yearly tests of any sort: she had apparently never had a PAP test or a mammogram, though her doctor's notes were filled with recommendations that she do so.

She took Avandia for her diabetes, Tavor for anxiety, Zoloft for depression, and in the past had been given Antabuse, a drug he knew was given to alcoholics that made them violently ill if they consumed any alcohol. That prescription had been filled once six years ago, then four years ago, but not since then. Brunetti cast his eye down a long list of the medicines which had been prescribed to her with some regularity and noticed a number of common antibiotics; the others were unfamiliar to him.

She had a passport and over the years had always kept it renewed. There was no indication of where she went with it.

Three years before, she had started to receive a state pension, having worked for twenty-seven years as the Director of Products of Lembo Minerals.

'What does Lembo Minerals do?' he asked.

'They extract ore – chiefly copper – from mines all over the world and ship it to factories in other countries.'

'That's all?'

'In essence, yes,' Signorina Elettra said. 'At least, from the public information available.'

'Then what would their products be?'

'Large and small pieces of earth, I'd guess, with quantities of metal stuck in or to them.'

'She was Director of Products,' he said, pointing to the words on the form displayed on the screen.

'It was her father's company,' Signorina Elettra suggested.

'Meaning?'

'Meaning we should be glad he gave her a job and she paid taxes and contributed to her pension. Otherwise, he could just have handed it to her, and that was that, and no taxes paid on it.'

'I hadn't thought of it that way,' Brunetti admitted.

Ignoring that, or pretending to, she said, 'Look at this.' She hit a few keys, and the screen exploded in colour. When his eyes adjusted to the change, he saw that he was looking at the cover of a Spanish scandal magazine. The photo showed a Junoesque woman in a bikini she really should not have dared to wear, not any more, with one hand raised to shield her perma-tanned face from the sun. The background was the standard turquoise-floored swimming pool, palm trees everywhere. Beside the pool, a gloriously handsome young man in equally skimpy bathing attire he could wear with panache handed a cigarette to the woman while another much younger couple in thick white cotton beach robes perched, knees pressed

155

together, on the edge of dazzling white plastic chairs, doing their best to look as though they had no idea who those other two people were.

The Spanish caption was easy enough to translate into: 'Lucrezia, the Princess of Copper, and her new companion, enjoy themselves at the home of friends in Ibiza.' Signorina Elettra flicked the pages with a touch of a key: Brunetti was impressed by the way they turned as if in response to the motions of a human hand. The magazine opened to two inner pages containing further photos of all four people. The page on the left had more bathing suit photos, a very unfortunate one of Lucrezia Lembo from the back, not only because of the sad sagging that had begun to assail the flesh at the top of her thighs, but for the sight of the young man's hand slipped under the elastic of her bikini bottom. The captions on the opposite page explained that the two white-clad young people – who remained fully covered in every picture in which they appeared – were her son and daughter, Loredano and Letizia.

'They seem to like the letter,' Signorina Elettra said.

Ignoring this and pointing at the screen, Brunetti asked, 'How many years ago was this?'

She flicked the screen back to the magazine cover and let him read: twelve years before. Lucrezia would have been fifty, with a face that appeared to have been kept behind for a decade or so. Her children looked in their late teens, so they'd be approaching or in their early thirties now.

'The young man?' he asked.

'Her husband, you mean,' Signorina Elettra said, and Brunetti felt a wave of pathos sweep across him, as if he'd heard of the illness or death of a friend.

Not wanting Signorina Elettra to accuse him of judging people rashly, nor of that equal crime of throwing his compassion around with too liberal a hand, he said nothing, but he did take another look at the face and posture of the young man. His body bristled with confidence: was there a desire that had not been answered? Was there something he still longed to have?

Brunetti forced himself to look away from the photo, troubled that his feelings against this unknown man could be so unreasonably strong. He told himself to stop behaving like a teenage Sir Galahad and said, 'What about the other sister, or sisters?'

'There were three altogether,' she answered. 'Lavinia and Lorenza, and Lucrezia.'

'They were stretching a bit with Lorenza,' Brunetti said, relieved to have so easily rediscovered his ironic tone.

'As it happens, she died.'

'What happened?'

'According to the reports I read, she drowned in their swimming pool,' Signorina Elettra answered. Brunetti's memory fled to the first photo.

'Where?'

'No,' she said, 'not there.' Then quickly, 'I should have explained. They had a ranch in Chile, some kind of *finca*, it sounds like, and she was found there.' Before he could ask, she said, 'Eight years ago.' Then, soberly, 'She was the baby of the family, only twenty when it happened.'

Brunetti had been busy working out the dates and, when he had finished, he asked, 'Same mother?'

'No. He left the first one after thirty-four years and set up a household with – are you ready? – the physical therapist who took care of him after he broke his shoulder in a skiing accident. Lorenza was their daughter.'

'How old was he?'

'When he left?'

'Yes.'

'Sixty.'

It was a common enough story and certainly none of his business. It had usually happened to his friends when they were about forty: all Lembo had done was wait a generation. 'He died last year, didn't he?' Brunetti asked. He had a vague memory of reading about his death, but what he remembered most was his surprise that the newspapers would engage in so much hand-wringing over the death of another dinosaur.

'Yes. They were here, but not living in the *palazzo*.'

'Where? They?'

'He was living on the Giudecca. Not with the physical therapist: she left him after the daughter died. He had a companion and people who came to clean and cook. He wasn't married to the companion.'

Brunetti had the strange sensation that he had just played another round of the backward plot game with his family. Wealthy blonde marries gigolo young enough to be her son. Wealthy man unable to produce a male heir, leaves wife for younger woman, only to have another daughter. Daughter dies. 'And the other daughter? Lavinia?'

Signorina Elettra made no move towards the keys. 'She studied abroad and lives abroad. She's fifty-one now.'

'Where is she?'

'Ireland. Teaching mathematics at Trinity College, Dublin.' Before he could ask, she said, 'She's been to her classes this week.'

Brunetti felt relief pass over him at this suggestion that one of the daughters had turned out well. He returned his attention to Lucrezia and asked, 'Could you go back and show me the name of her doctor again?'

'Whose?' she asked, surprised.

'Signora Cavanella's.'

She quickly brought up the medical records, and he wrote down the name, address, and phone number of the doctor. The name seemed familiar, Luca Proni. Hadn't he been at school with Umberto Proni? Surely there could not be more than one family in the city with that name.

He pulled out his phone and dialled the number of the doctor's office. A recorded message told him the doctor's office hours were 9–13 and 16–19, Monday to Friday. For emergencies, patients could reach him on his *telefonino*. Brunetti was astonished to hear such a message from a family doctor, and even more so when it was followed by the number. He wrote down the number and immediately dialled it.

After three rings, a deep voice answered with, 'Proni.'

'Dottor Proni,' Brunetti said, deciding not to waste time and not to deceive. 'This is Guido Brunetti. I was at school with Umberto.'

'You're the one who became a policeman, aren't you?' he asked in an entirely neutral voice.

'Yes.'

'Umberto's often spoken of you.' From the way he said it, there was no way of gauging what Umberto might have said.

'Spoken well, I hope,' Brunetti said lightly, trying to remember anything Umberto might have told him, all those years ago, about his older brother. Nothing came.

'Always.' Then, 'How may I help you, Commissario?'

'You're listed as Ana Cavanella's doctor.'

There was a brief hesitation. 'Yes, I am.'

'Then you've been told, Dottore?' Brunetti asked. He was her doctor, so the hospital would have called him.

'About what?' Proni asked in a voice somewhere between curiosity and concern, but nowhere near alarm.

'Signora Cavanella's in the hospital.'

'What?' the doctor asked.

'I'm sorry, Dottore. I thought they would have called you.'

'No. What happened?'

'She was found over on the Zattere yesterday. She told the man who found her that she'd fallen down.' Brunetti spoke neutrally, merely repeating a piece of information. When Proni said nothing, Brunetti continued, 'She may have a concussion, two fingers are crushed, and her face is badly bruised. But the doctor who examined her says she's not in any danger.' Proni still said nothing.

'I'd like to speak to you,' Brunetti added.

'You realize I'm her doctor,' he said, this time using that fact to construct a barrier to information.

'I understand that, Dottore.' Brunetti abandoned any idea of asking about Davide: all he wanted was the chance to talk to Proni directly. 'I know what it means in terms of your professional responsibility.'

'But still you want to talk to me?'

Brunetti decided to tell him the truth. 'Yes, I do. There are things about her I don't understand. And about her son.'

'You mean his death?'

'Yes.'

'It was an accident,' Proni said.

'I believe that, Dottore. But I'd like to understand how it was possible.'

'This sounds like nothing more than personal curiosity, Commissario.'

Brunetti let out a small puff of air, exasperated at how transparent he had become. 'I suppose it is.'

'In that case, I'll speak to you,' Proni surprised him by saying.

Brunetti glanced at his watch. 'I could be at your office in twenty minutes, Dottore.'

'All right.' Brunetti heard the click of the phone as the doctor replaced it.

18

Brunetti went to the window, leaned out and saw Foa on the *fondamenta*, talking to the guard at the door. Brunetti called the pilot's name and shouted down that he had to go over to San Polo; Foa raised an arm in assent. As he went down the stairs, Brunetti was conscious of the dim view Chiara would take of his crossing the entire city in a police boat when he could just as easily have used public transportation, even though the Number Two would take more than twenty minutes to get him there. 'People have to learn to wait,' was her current mantra.

He stepped on to the boat, ignoring the pilot's outstretched hand. Foa turned the key, revved the motor, and pulled them away from the dock towards the *bacino*. 'Last days for standing around outside, I'm afraid, sir,' the pilot said amiably.

'For the likes of me, it certainly is,' Brunetti said. 'Until the first sign of springtime, I'll leave being out in the weather to you.'

Foa heard the friendliness and smiled. 'I called a couple of people I know, sir. About the Lembo family, like you asked me to. To see what else I could learn.'

'Very good,' Brunetti said. 'What did they have to tell you?'

'Well, sir,' Foa said, turning right in a broad sweep that would take them up the Grand Canal, 'It's *una famiglia sfigata*.' It was the language of the streets, but from the little Brunetti had heard, it *did* sound as if the whole family was screwed.

'What did they tell you?'

'Well, there's the daughter that died. In Brazil, I think. There's another one in Ireland or some place like that, but it seems she turned out all right. And then there's the one who had the kids, Lucrezia.' He gave a little puff of exasperation with the name. 'Who'd do that to a kid, give her a name like that?'

'She named her own children Loredano and Letizia.'

Foa made another exasperated noise. 'I suppose that was to keep in good with her parents. From what my friends said, they ran a tight ship.' Then, after a moment's reflection, Foa said, 'Though a couple of them said it was the mother. A real tiger. And a religious one at that.'

'What does that mean?' Brunetti looked up to the top of the bell tower of San Giorgio just at the instant when the angel chose to shift in the wind and wave his wings at Brunetti.

'She was a friend of the Patriarch, always wore a black veil when she went to Mass, the worst sort of *basabanchi*.' Then, after a pause, 'Got it from her family, I'm told.'

Brunetti smiled, in love with his own language. He'd seen them as a boy, those veiled women in black, bending forward as if to kiss the top of the pew in front of them. *Baciare il banco*. Only the dialect of anti-clerical – proudly, historically anti-clerical – Venice could transform the word, and the act, and the idea, with such acid contempt. *Basabanchi.*

'The mother had a nun living in the *palazzo* and governesses to turn the girls into ladies. Her father – the mother's father, that is, so the girls' grandfather – had some sort of title, but it was one that the Savoias gave him, so it was really just a piece of shit.'

Well, there's a bit of vox pop to tell Paola about, Brunetti reflected. He hoped she would pass the remark on to her father: because his own title was several centuries older, he was sure to appreciate it. Foa paused and looked aside at Brunetti, who nodded in agreement. 'This is all gossip, sir,' the pilot went on. 'You know what it's like when people sit around in the bars and talk about other people.'

'Who aren't there to defend themselves?' Brunetti asked with a laugh. He did not add that it also helped if the person under discussion was rich or successful, or both.

'Exactly. Besides, it sounds as if the family always – well, the grandfather, they told me – was always quick to go to law with everyone, and no one likes that. Cross him in a deal, try to buy a property he wanted, and you'd find six lawyers at breakfast the next morning. I asked my father, and he said he never heard a good word about him.'

Brunetti stopped himself from observing that the list of the people about whom he himself had never heard a good word was longer than Leporello's list of Don Giovanni's conquests, but, instead, he asked, 'Did you ever meet any of the daughters?'

'Me, no. But my best friend Gregorio told me he had an affair with Lucrezia. A long time ago, before they were married. Wasn't anything important, really.' Brunetti did not have to strain to understand that they did not marry one another. 'Gregorio always thought she did it to spite her mother.'

'What sort of reputation did she have?' Brunetti asked. 'When she was a girl, that is.'

'Oh, you know what it's like, Signore,' Foa said and cut to the left and into Rio de la Madoneta. 'Once a woman goes with a man, everyone's going to say he's had her, too.' Brunetti put this nugget in a side pocket in his memory to pull out the next time someone spoke to him of human progress.

Then, as if to make up for what he had said, Foa added, 'Gregorio said she was a nice girl. They remained friends for a long time.'

'But not now?'

'Not on your life, sir. He married a girl from Giudecca, and she keeps him on a short lead. If she found out he even telephoned another woman, she'd have the cross up in the garden, and she'd send him out to get the nails.'

'Would he go?'

'I'm afraid so, sir.' Foa brought the boat to a smooth stop on the right side of the canal.

'No need to wait for me, Foa,' Brunetti said.

'Thank you, sir. I'll have a coffee and go back to the Questura. If you change your mind, call me and I'll come get you.'

Brunetti said he would, though he trembled at the thought of Chiara's reaction should she learn that he had had a boat travel twice all the way across the city, and the second time when there was no urgency. She'd probably send him out for the nails, too.

He had checked the address in *Calli, Campielli e Canali*, and so found it easily, an undistinguished building with a dark green double door. The doctor's name was on one of the bells, and the door opened soon after Brunetti rang. The entrance hall smelled of damp; no surprise after the previous day's rain. At the very end of the hallway, facing the entrance, a door stood open. Brunetti entered and found the standard chair-lined walls of a doctor's waiting room, though here the chairs were separate, wooden, antique, and beautiful. More surprisingly, the walls displayed, not the usual sentimental portraits of dogs and children, but three fine-lined drawings that drew his eye. At first, he thought they were surreal cityscapes, with abstract towers and cupolas, until closer examination showed that it was his eyes, and not the lines, that created the illusion of a city. The lines were so close together that the background of the drawing seemed grey: Brunetti wondered what technique the artist had used to put them so flawlessly close, for nowhere did one line touch another.

Brunetti took his reading glasses from his pocket and put them on, the better to study these magical lines that drew the gaze of the viewer with the force of an electromagnet. The second drawing suggested a beach, though here again it was the viewer who imposed this reality on the drawing, where the varied spaces between horizontal lines of different widths and lengths suggested the variation in surface and texture between sand and sea.

The third had to be the facades of the buildings on the eastern side of Campo San Polo, but only a Venetian would see that, just as only a Venetian would recognize Palazzo Soranzo and Palazzo Maffetti-Tiepolo. Or perhaps not. When Brunetti stepped back from the drawing, the distance transformed it into mere lines, closely drawn but utterly abstract and devoid of meaning. He swept his eyes along the three drawings and was very relieved to see that they were covered with glass. Then he moved closer to the third one again, and the magic repeated itself: the *palazzi* materialized among the lines. Enough to move back forty centimetres, and again they dissolved.

'Commissario?' a man's voice said behind him.

He turned, removed his reading glasses, and saw a short, thickset man a decade younger than himself. Though the doctor wore glasses, Brunetti saw that one eye was slightly larger than the other, or angled differently in his face. Yet when he looked for similar imperfection in his mouth, he found it was perfectly proportioned. He searched for a resemblance to Umberto and found it in the general square-ness of the face: ears tight to the head, jawbone prominent and almost as wide as the cheekbones.

Brunetti extended his hand. 'Thank you for letting me come,' he said. He had learned, when greeting people who had agreed to speak to him, to say only that and to say nothing at first that would remind them that he was there to ask them questions. He returned his glasses to his pocket.

'Do you like the drawings?' the doctor asked.

'More than that, I'd say.' Brunetti turned back to them and, from this distance, saw that all three had turned into entirely different images. 'Where did you get them?'

'Here,' Proni said. 'A local artist.' Then he turned, saying, 'Perhaps we'd be more comfortable in my office.'

He held the door open for Brunetti, who passed through what must be the nurse's reception room and then into the doctor's, in which there was a desk that held a computer and a small bouquet of orange tulips. Two more of the antique chairs stood in front of the desk, and Brunetti went over to one of them, leaving the doctor to take his seat behind the desk. Being questioned by the police was so alien an experience for most people that it was best to make the circumstances as comfortable and close to normal as possible.

Brunetti sat and glanced around the room. The windows were heavily barred, standard practice in any doctor's office where drugs might be, or be thought to be. A glass-doored cabinet between the windows, its shelves stacked with unruly piles of boxes of medicine, was exactly what addicts hoped to see: cocktail time. Brunetti was pleased to see another of the drawings on the wall opposite the windows. Had he not seen those in the waiting room, Brunetti would have taken it for an abstract watercolour in different tones of grey, but he now realized that the colour resulted from the closeness of the lines: there could not be a millimetre between them.

Proni called back Brunetti's attention by saying, 'I called the hospital and spoke to the doctor in charge of her ward. He says he wants to keep her there for at least another day. The concussion is very slight, but they want to be careful.'

'Did she tell him what happened?' Brunetti asked, though he was certain he knew what the answer would be.

'Just what she told the man who found her: she fell down the steps.' After saying that, Proni kept his eyes on Brunetti's.

'Let's hope that's what happened,' was his response.

'What does that mean, Commissario?'

'Exactly what I said, Dottore: I hope that's what happened.'

'Instead of?'

'Instead of an attempt to harm her.'

'Who would want to do that?' the Doctor asked, seeming honestly puzzled.

Brunetti allowed himself a small smile. 'You'd have a better idea of that than I would, Dottore.'

Proni was immediately indignant. 'If I might repeat myself, what does that mean?'

Brunetti held up one hand and gave a soft answer, to turn away wrath. 'You're her doctor, so you'd know more about her life than I do. All I know is that she is the mother of a man who died, Davide Cavanello.' He knew more than that, but little of it was of substance, and none of any help.

'What sort of thing do you expect me to know, Commissario?' Proni asked, careful to use the polite form of address.

Brunetti responded with equal formality. 'I'd like to know anything you can tell me about the relationship between Signora Cavanella and her son.'

'She was his mother.'

Try as he might, Brunetti found no sarcasm there, so he responded quite naturally. 'Was she a good mother?'

Proni's face remained unchanged. 'That's an entirely subjective judgement, one I'm not qualified to make.' There was no apology in his voice, only explanation. 'She took care of his physical needs to the best of her ability, if that's the sort of information you're looking for.'

It wasn't, but it was still information Brunetti had not had before and was glad to have. He did, however, find it interesting that the doctor specified physical needs and did not describe her ability.

Brunetti had no intention of telling him that he had seen Ana Cavanella's medical records: no doctor should know how easily they were available to anyone skilled enough to look for them. 'Could you give me a general idea of her health?'

The doctor's eyes contracted, as if he had been awaiting a question about the son and not the mother. He appeared to give the question some thought and then answered, 'I'd say that, for a woman of her age, she's healthy. She doesn't smoke and never has, drinks moderately – not even that – and to the best of my knowledge has never taken drugs.'

'Did you prescribe the sleeping pills, Dottore?'

This question could not have surprised him, yet the doctor failed to disguise his nervousness in answering it. He pulled his eyes away from Brunetti's and looked at the drawing on the far wall, then said, eyes still on the drawing, 'Yes, I did.'

'You seem troubled by the question, Dottore. Why is that?'

'Because I don't like being in any way responsible for Davide's death.' He looked at Brunetti as he said this.

Brunetti shook his head. His failure to understand was not feigned. 'That's too hard a judgement, don't you think, Dottore?'

'It's hard, but it's not too hard,' Proni said. 'She had never needed them before: she's always been a patient who takes very few medicines. I should have told her to try drinking something hot before she went to bed, or going for a walk in the evening.' He scratched idly at a point just above the middle of his glasses and then rubbed the tips of his fingers up and down his forehead. 'I should have thought.'

'Thought what?'

'That they come in bright colours and have a slick, sweet covering, like candies. They would be very appealing to someone of Davide's mental age.' He scratched again. 'But I didn't. I just wrote her the prescription.'

'What *was* his mental age?' Brunetti asked.

Proni shot him a glance, as though he'd invited him into his home and found him ruffling through the drawers. 'I have no idea.'

'I see,' Brunetti said mildly. Then, 'Did you ever treat him as a patient, Dottore?'

'Do I have to answer this question?'

'It would save a lot of time.'

'What does that mean?'

'That, eventually – but only by our going through channels and getting an order from a magistrate and spending days of work – yes, you can be required to answer that question.'

Proni pushed his chair back from the desk: its legs made an ugly, scraping sound on the tile floor. He rubbed at his forehead again. 'I went to their home once when he had flu and another time when he had terrible diarrhoea. The first time all I could do was to tell her to keep him in bed and warm and see that he drank lots of liquids. The second time I wrote a prescription. I don't remember what I prescribed: this was years ago.'

'Was this done officially?'

'What do you mean?' Proni asked, obviously confused.

'Was the prescription written for him?'

'Of course it was written for him. He was the one who was sick.'

'I'm sorry, Dottore. I wasn't clear enough. Was the prescription written in his name?'

Proni stared at Brunetti as though he had suddenly noticed smoke coming from his ears. 'I told you this was years ago, Commissario. I don't remember what I prescribed and I don't remember whom I prescribed it for. He had symptoms, I wrote a prescription, and that was that.'

There was nothing to lose in being truthful, Brunetti thought. 'Dottore, I see your irritation, and I think I understand it.' Embarrassed by having no tool left but honesty, he went on. 'I saw him for years. He worked in the dry cleaner's where my wife and I take our clothes. And I'd see him on the street sometimes. He always looked so . . .

I don't know the right word. Vulnerable, perhaps.' He paused, but Proni said nothing. Some inner sense of propriety or decency kept Brunetti from inventing a lie similar to Pucetti's and telling the doctor that his son had known and played soccer with Davide.

'What was wrong with him, Dottore?' Before Proni could answer, he said, 'I don't care if you saw him other times or treated him for other things. I just want to know that: what was wrong with him?'

Proni leaned forward and said, 'He was born to a stupid woman. He was born to a woman who saw whatever was wrong with him as a curse from God, as though she were living in a hut in a forest and believed in witches. Like most Christians, she knew everything about guilt and nothing about charity, so she kept it hidden – remember, it was a curse – and made no attempt to get him trained or taught, and God knows how she raised him. That's why he looked so vulnerable: that's why he seemed so lost and alien.'

'Did she tell you this, Dottore?'

Proni's face flushed, because of either the story he was telling or the fact that Brunetti should question it. His mouth tightened and the difference between his eyes grew more marked. 'She didn't have to tell me, Commissario,' he added in a calmer voice. 'It was implicit in the way she treated him and in everything she said about him.'

Abruptly, Proni got to his feet. 'That's all I have to say, Commissario.'

Brunetti stood and leaned over the desk to offer his hand. Proni did not hesitate to take it.

'Let him rest in peace,' the doctor said. 'He had so little of it when he was alive.'

Sensing that there was nothing to be gained by asking anything else, Brunetti turned towards the door. In the

172

waiting room, he paused and nodded at the three drawings, which had changed again to suit the greater distance from which he was seeing them. 'You said he's a local artist,' Brunetti said, pointing at the drawings. 'Would I recognize his name?'

'Probably,' Proni said with a smile that shaved years off his face.

'What is it?' Brunetti asked, thinking he was being asked to do so.

'Davide Cavanella,' Proni said, moving past him. 'That should explain my anger at his mother.' He held the door open, and Brunetti left.

19

Because he was so close to home, Brunetti decided to go there instead of returning to the Questura. The kids would not be there for lunch; he had told Paola he would not be back, either, but his conversation with Dottor Proni had left him wanting to talk to her.

He found her where he thought he would: lying on the sofa, reading. She looked up when he came in, not at all surprised, and he was prompted to ask, 'What if I had been the axe murderer?'

She picked up a piece of paper on her chest and stuck it back in the book, tossed the book to the foot of the sofa, and said, 'The axe murderer had your footsteps on the stairs, and his keys jingled the same way yours do.'

'You can hear that well?' he asked, his surprise audible to both of them.

'You mean at my advanced age or after having lived through years of the music choices of two teenaged children?' she inquired.

He smiled and hung his jacket on the back of a chair, moved the book aside and sat down. 'Did you really hear me coming up?'

'Yes.'

'And you can tell my keys?'

She hesitated, the way she always did when considering the usefulness of telling a lie. 'No.' He smiled; she shrugged. 'But I did hear keys, and thieves – or axe murderers, for all I know – don't make a noise when they're trying to come in.'

She swung her feet around and put them on the floor. 'Hungry?'

Brunetti couldn't answer; he didn't know. Davide Cavanella had come home with him, filling his thoughts, driving out all else. 'I want to ask you something.'

'What about?'

'Noise,' he said. 'That is, sound.'

'What about it?'

'I wonder what it's like to be deaf.'

She gave him a long look but said nothing.

'How do they learn?' he asked.

'Learn what?'

He waved his hand in the air. 'Everything. How to eat or sit in a chair.'

'I suppose they learn it the same way Raffi and Chiara did.'

'Which was?' he asked, not because he didn't remember but because he didn't know if Paola would have the same memories.

'By watching us do it, I'd say, though with eating we had to guide their hands with the spoon, and then the fork.'

'And sitting?' he asked, having given no conscious thought to the choice of actions.

175

'They sat in highchairs to eat at first because we put them there, and then when they were big enough to climb on to chairs, they copied what they saw us doing.' After a moment's thought, she added, 'And I suppose they figured out that sitting's more comfortable than standing.'

'You get hungry, so you put food in your mouth,' Brunetti said. 'You don't want to stand or sit on the floor, so you sit in a chair. They're practical solutions to real problems.' He paused, but Paola said nothing. 'Why would they brush their teeth? Even if they saw us do it, it wouldn't make sense to a kid. They don't see it as a problem.'

'We told them it was good for them, I suppose,' she said, less interested now.

'That's just it,' Brunetti said.

'Just what?'

'We told them. How do you tell a deaf child?'

Before she could answer, he said, 'I spoke to his mother's doctor. He told me she never had him helped.'

'Helped how?' she asked, her whole face alert.

'I don't know. He didn't say. He told me she never told anyone there was anything wrong with him.' Even as he said it, Brunetti was struck by how terrible that phrase sounded. 'So he grew up without any special training.' And then, 'The doctor couldn't hide his anger when he told me.'

He saw understanding cross her face and leave her features dull with shock. He saw her begin to understand the consequences. 'But people could see there was something wrong with him,' she said. Then, an instant later, 'We did.'

'We thought we did,' Brunetti countered.

Paola moved back on the sofa, accepting with the motion

that there would be no thinking about lunch until this was settled. 'What is it we didn't understand? Tell me.'

'You remember when we first saw him, don't you? What was it, fifteen years? More?' Paola nodded. 'I remember how the woman in the dry cleaner's – with him standing right there, less than a metre from her – told us he was both deaf and retarded. He might as well have been a piece of furniture.' He recalled that there had been no malice in her voice.

He saw that Paola recalled the incident as well as he. 'I remember cringing at it,' she said. '"Deaf and retarded". Sweet Jesus, just like that.' He watched her call up the memory of that scene. 'He didn't react, did he? She could have been talking about the weather for all he understood.'

She rested her head against the back of the sofa and closed her eyes for a minute. Keeping them closed, she asked, 'What are you trying to tell me?'

'I'm not sure,' Brunetti admitted and then, after a long pause, said, 'There are some drawings he did on the wall of the doctor's waiting room. They were extraordinary, unlike anything I've ever seen.'

Paola opened her eyes and smiled. 'That doesn't tell me very much, does it?'

Brunetti acknowledged this with a grin and said, 'They were landscapes created out of hundreds of horizontal lines drawn very close together. Only millimetres apart. Palazzo Soranzo, the Lido, a cityscape. Absolutely accurate, only you don't see it until you're just at the right distance from it. Otherwise, it's just lines.' Realizing how little justice he was doing to the drawings, he stopped.

'And so?' Paola asked.

'So maybe that's what the doctor was talking about. He couldn't control his anger.'

'At what?'

'Maybe he thought that she was ignoring his handicap and that this was making it worse for him, and that he wasn't retarded, only deaf.'

'Is that possible?' Paola asked.

Brunetti latched his hands together than stared at them. 'I don't know. I don't know that much about psychology and how brains develop. But if no one taught him sign, or to read lips, then . . .'

'Then he'd become the way he was?' she asked.

'Possibly. I don't know.'

'But the drawings?'

He unlatched his hands and ran his fingers through his hair. 'I don't know.'

It took Paola a while to answer, and when she did, her uncertainty was audible. 'He never gave a sign that he understood much of what happened. Or had any interest in things.' When Brunetti did not contradict her, she said, 'So I don't know why we would have questioned what we were told.' Then, with every evidence that she was reluctant to show how strong her case was, she added, 'And there was the way he looked, Guido, and the way he walked.' Before he could object, she said, 'I know it's terrible to say these things, but he looked as if there was something wrong with him.'

Working to keep his voice level, Brunetti said, 'We believed what we were told about him and never thought to ask why he was like that.'

Paola leaned aside and placed her hand on his thigh. 'I don't mean to sound heartless, Guido, but I don't think anyone would, especially if a person who knew him said he was deaf and retarded.'

'He learned how to take things home for people, to go with them to their houses,' Brunetti insisted. 'He had to *learn* that. Someone had to *teach* him. Think how difficult that would be if he was both deaf and retarded. We didn't have to teach the kids how to eat or sit: they wanted to. It's been a long time, but I think we had to persuade the kids to brush their teeth and teach them how to do it and then keep at them until they did it on their own. And that's like carrying a parcel to someone's home. It's not something you want to do or do instinctively. You have to be taught. Or trained.'

Paola remained silent, staring at the paintings on the far wall. 'When are you going to tell me why we're talking about this?'

He let his eyes follow hers and studied the paintings: a portrait of a distant ancestor on her mother's side, a not very pretty woman with a beautiful smile; and an unframed wooden panel with the portrait of a man in a naval uniform holding a brown speckled bird that Brunetti had bought with his first pay cheque, decades ago.

'If he – Davide – was both deaf and retarded, and if his mother never got him any help, then how was he taught to do the things he knew how to do?' Brunetti asked, right back at the beginning and thinking of those drawings.

Paola leaned her head back again. Brunetti wondered if he had exhausted her intellectual curiosity or her patience. The man had died an accidental death: there was no question of that. Paola's response forced Brunetti to realize that he could not, even to himself, explain what so disturbed him. This man had passed through life without having left a trace of himself save in the memories of the few people who had seen him: Brunetti couldn't even say they had known him. He thought of that conundrum posed in his first class in logic: if a tree falls in the forest and no one hears it fall, does it make a noise?

Is a human life defined by contacts with other people?

If, as Brunetti believed, people lived on only in the minds of the people who knew them and remembered them, then Davide Cavanella's existence had indeed been a miserable one, and it would cease with his mother's death.

He looked at the portraits again. It had always bothered him that no one knew who the woman was, whether she was an aunt removed by many generations or the mother of someone who had married into the family. The portrait had been in the attic of Palazzo Falier, and Paola had taken it to her room when she was an adolescent but had failed to find anyone in the family who had even the vaguest idea of who the woman might be; nor was there any record of the painting.

Brunetti had also failed with the man he thought of as his naval commander. Even though he wore a uniform jacket, Brunetti had never so much as managed to identify the man's nationality. The bird had finally been identified by an ornithologist friend of Paola's, who told them it was a South American Ruff, whatever that was.

He got to his feet, realizing now how hungry he was and willing to scavenge lunch from whatever he found in the refrigerator.

Hearing him, Paola opened her eyes. 'Is it because we all failed him?' she asked. 'Is that what's bothering you?'

'Probably,' Brunetti answered. 'And now he's dead and there'll be no making up for it.'

Finally, Brunetti tried to shrug it off by asking, 'You think it's still warm enough to eat on the terrace?'

She turned and looked out the windows, studying the angle of the sun: it seemed that things were dry enough. 'Only if we hurry,' she said.

'Good. I'll take the plates out.'

Paola got to her feet, and Brunetti noticed, for the first time, that she used one hand to push herself upright. She passed him and went towards the kitchen, stopped at the door and said, without turning to him, 'It's good that it bothers you, Guido.' She went to see what was in the refrigerator.

20

When Brunetti returned to the Questura, the guard at the door told him that Dottor Patta wanted to see him in his office. This reminded Brunetti that he had, for the last three days, ignored his superior's request that he attend to the problem in San Barnaba. How trivial it had sounded when Patta told him about it, and how much more trivial it sounded now.

This fact, however, in no way affected Brunetti's determination: like any good actor, once he stepped on stage, he never broke role. Well, he told himself, seldom broke role.

Signorina Elettra was not at her desk, so Brunetti faced the meeting with no advance information. He knocked and obeyed Patta's shouted 'Avanti.'

Even though he had resolved the matter with no effort whatsoever, Brunetti pasted a look composed of equal parts of contrition and industry upon his face as he entered. He had taken only two steps into the room before Patta got to his feet and came around his desk towards him. The Vice-Questore's hand was raised, but instead of shaking Brunetti's, Patta placed his hand on Brunetti's upper arm, as if to guide him to a chair. Brunetti set himself adrift in this current of apparent goodwill and allowed himself to be tugged towards his mooring point.

When Brunetti was safely docked, Patta went back to his own berth and smiled across the desk at his subordinate. 'I'm glad you found time to come,' Patta said. Brunetti activated his sensors and swept Patta's tone for sarcasm. Finding none, he adjusted the settings and searched for irony, but there was none of that, either.

'When Garzanti told me you wanted to see me, Dottore, I came right up.' Brunetti smiled, suggesting that the message was the thing he had most been waiting for in these recent days.

'I wanted to talk to you about that situation I asked you to look into,' Patta said with a smile as broad as it was insincere.

'Ah, yes,' Brunetti said, replacing his expression with one of industry and concern. 'I've been very busy.' Then, with apparent reluctance, he was forced to add, 'It wasn't easy, Vice-Questore.'

Patta's smile faded and his tanned face lightened a shade. He opened his mouth to speak, closed it and swallowed, licked his lips, and settled for putting the smile back in place.

Until he saw Patta's unease, Brunetti had been prepared to tell him he had, by Herculean efforts, resolved the problems facing the mayor's son. But now he began to calculate how he could get two for one and see that the Lieutenant neither took possession of Signorina Elettra's office nor prevented Foa from being seconded to the Guardia Costiera.

'That is, Dottore,' Brunetti went on, 'I finally managed to speak to the man in charge of the patrol for that area.'

Patta was all attention.

Brunetti put on his easiest smile. 'Thank God he's a cousin of Foa's,' he began, then, seeing the flash of confusion in Patta's eyes, he said, 'Well, it was Foa who took me over there in the launch, and – as I said – the man in charge of that area is his cousin, so he went in with me and introduced me.' Brunetti paused to give careful thought to something that must just have occurred to him and said, 'I'm sure that helped.'

As if that were an irrelevant detail, he went on. 'When I mentioned the shop to him, he told me that the men on patrol had noticed the way the tables were spreading out and had spoken to the owner about it. But so far there had been no written report.'

'And the pilot? Foa? Was he there, too?'

'I asked him to stay, sir. I thought it would make it easier if he was there.' Then, with relaxed, man-to-man candour, Brunetti added, 'You know how clannish we Venetians can be.'

Patta gave this the consideration it deserved and finally asked, 'What happened?'

Here, Brunetti looked away from Patta, as though embarrassed by his own remarks about Venetians or perhaps about what he was to say next. But he said it, anyway, 'He asked me, sir, why he should help us by ignoring this – that is, help the police – when we're the people . . .' He paused and then said, 'This is what he told me sir.' At Patta's nod, he went on. 'When we refused to help one of our own.'

'I don't understand what you're saying, Brunetti. Or trying to say.'

'Well, sir, I was there with Foa, and this man is his cousin.'

184

'How aren't we helping him?' Patta asked, making no attempt to disguise his exasperation.

'It's about the request from the Guardia Costiera, sir,' Brunetti said.

After a moment, the lights came on in Patta's eyes. Off, then on. Brunetti didn't mind in the least; it might be good to let Patta see just how clannish these Venetians are.

'What else do you want?' Patta asked in a level voice.

With equal lack of emphasis, Brunetti answered, 'Lieutenant Scarpa might be persuaded to remain in his own office.'

Brunetti had to admire the fortitude with which his superior received this request. He did not grimace, nor did he blink. 'I see,' Patta said. He looked down at the surface of his desk for a while, then across at Brunetti, and asked, 'And there will be no more trouble in Campo San Barnaba?'

'None, sir. And the tables can stay where they are.'

Again, his superior consulted the surface of his desk before meeting his eyes. 'I'll speak to the Lieutenant,' he said. Then, 'You can go now, Commissario.'

Brunetti got to his feet, nodded to his superior, and left the office.

Upstairs, Brunetti opened the online pages of *Il Fatto Quotidiano*, a newspaper which often delighted him by its manifest distrust of every political party, every politician, and every religious leader. And there he found it, a story announcing that the officers of the Guardia di Finanza had yesterday arrived at the City Hall of Venice and entered the office charged with the awarding of contracts and financial contributions to encourage start-up businesses and shops. Acting on an order from the magistrates in Mestre, they had carried away files, records, and computers. The newspaper reported that someone close to the investigation said that there had been reports of the involvement of certain politicians in the awarding of these grants and contracts to relatives and friends.

After he finished reading the story, Brunetti allowed himself a smile and addressed the computer directly. 'If the mayor calls, please tell him I'm busy speaking to the magistrates in Mestre,' he said aloud in the imitation of Patta's voice which, over the years, he had honed to something approaching perfection.

'Certainly, Vice-Questore. It's a message I'd be delighted to give him,' Signorina Elettra's voice responded, but when he looked towards the door he had forgotten to close, he saw not her, but Commissario Claudia Griffoni.

'You manage the Venetian cadence very well, Claudia,' he said. 'The nuances of his Sicilian accent have proven too much for me.'

Griffoni smiled and said something to him that, though it was virtually incomprehensible, with only a few words peeping out enough for him to grasp, was an exact imitation of Patta's voice speaking in his native dialect and thus far more accurate than his own imitation had been. She came across the room and sat in the chair in front of his desk. 'He says he's from Palermo, but his accent is pure San Giuseppe Jato,' she said, with the same disapproval a lord would use should his butler attempt to play polo. As ever, she spoke in an Italian the purity of which he envied.

In the years she had worked at the Questura he had learned very little about her private life or background, but he had no doubt that she came from what his maternal grandmother had always referred to as *gente per bene*, with its strong suggestion that the people so defined were not only well intentioned but wealthy.

Beyond this, she was intelligent and cooperative, and the few times they had worked together, he had been impressed by her seriousness and lack of interest in becoming the hero of the investigation, a weakness to which some of his other colleagues were prone. She was also possessed of physical courage, a quality Brunetti admired.

'You know anything about the investigation?' he asked.

'You mean the mayor and the Guardia di Finanza?'

'Yes.'

She shrugged. 'They'll find certain irregularities in the bookkeeping, an enormous amount of money will not have been accounted for, and they will not be able to find it, people will say things and trade accusations, one of the accused will weep for the press, and for a few months the people in the office will be very cautious. And then things will go back to normal.'

Letting the subject of political corruption retreat for the moment, Brunetti gave in to his curiosity at her arrival and asked, 'Can I help you with something?'

'Not at all,' she answered with a quick shake of her head. 'In fact, it's the opposite. I've come up because I'd like to try to help you with something.'

Brunetti lifted his chin in an interrogative gesture. He had no idea what she could mean. For months she had been dealing with a suspicious fire which had gutted a former factory that the owner planned to turn into a luxury hotel. Though the official investigation had declared it an accident, doubts remained, especially after one of Griffoni's informants told her that the son of the expert who had written the report had been hired as manager of a hotel in the chain that was interested in transforming the factory.

How, he asked himself, could her investigation be of help to him? 'Tell me more,' he said, turning from the computer screen to face her directly.

'It's none of my business,' she said, suddenly sounding hesitant.

'What isn't?'

'Your friendship with Vianello.'

Where did that come from? he wondered, and what business of hers was his friendship with Vianello? To give himself time to think about how to respond, he turned back to the computer and closed all of the open windows, then pushed another key and watched the screen grow dark.

He turned back to her. 'But you're choosing to make it your business?' he asked in a voice wiped clean of everything save mild curiosity.

She started to speak, but all she managed to produce was a hesitant vowel sound, perhaps 'a', which could have served for *allora* or *adesso*, or, for all he knew, *amico*.

'He's helped me, you know,' she said. 'With Scarpa. And with the others.'

'Helped you how?' Brunetti asked. Then, because there could be no doubt of the universal desire to help against Lieutenant Scarpa, he added, 'With the others, I mean.'

She studied his face for a long time, as if trying to make up her mind about something, or about him. 'You mean you don't know? You've never noticed the way some people here talk to me?' she asked.

He thought of Signorina Elettra, and his impulse was to lie, and then he started to recall other things he might have noticed or sensed, references and undertones he had chosen not to interpret in a particular way.

Then, to goad him, 'Or about me?'

Books often described how beautiful women became when they were angry: how wrong her face proved that to be. Her mouth was a tight line, her strong nose suddenly sharp and too big. And her eyes lacked all warmth, all willingness to understand.

'Because you're Neapolitan, you mean?'

She made a puffing noise replete with disgust. 'If it were only that,' she said. 'I'm used to being thought of as a *terrone*: every cousin has to be a *Camorrista*, my brother has to be under house arrest; and every investigation I make has to be half-hearted, at best, since my only purpose is to be a spy and see that nothing is ever done to harm the Camorra.' Brunetti had been with her when shots were fired and a man killed, but he had never seen her like this. Her cool dispassion and sense of irony were gone, replaced by an anger he could feel as a force coming across his desk.

He frowned and then asked, 'Do you think you're exaggerating?'

'Of course I'm exaggerating,' she said sharply. But she paused long enough for some of the anger to melt from her face. 'There's no way I can escape it up here. It's in the northern air.'

Confronted with his own hypocrisy and how it would colour anything he chose to say, Brunetti opted for silence. How could he tell this woman she was imagining things when his own distrust of southerners was as strongly rooted as his teeth? Like them, it had been formed in childhood, and he had been equally unconscious of the growth of both.

Had she sensed it in him, too? Brunetti no sooner concluded that, if she had, she would hardly have mentioned the subject to him, than he recalled just how subtle a person she was, and was again uncertain. How strange, prejudice: so comforting until someone noticed it.

He ran his hands over his face and back through his hair as a visual signal of wiping the slate free of a digression. 'Where did Vianello go?' he asked.

'Downstairs. I just spoke with him.'

Brunetti smiled and waved a hand to dismiss her answer. 'No. I mean where did the idea of my friendship with him go?' Seeing the faint relief signalled by her more relaxed posture, he added, 'We were distracted, I think.'

She blushed, she actually blushed, and with it her full beauty flowed back into possession of her, or she of it. 'Sorry, Guido, but you really have no idea.' For a moment, he was afraid she was going to pick it up again, but she said no more.

'Tell me,' he said.

'You asked him to ask Nadia to do some work for you.' Before Brunetti could explain or avoid explanation, she said, 'No, he didn't want to tell me. I could see something was bothering him, so I asked him, and I wouldn't let it go until he told me.' When she saw that Brunetti believed her, she went on. 'All he told me was that you wanted her to ask some people about this man who died.'

'Davide Cavanella,' Brunetti supplied, still not liking the way her original description of his request had sounded.

'And he's afraid he offended you by refusing.'

'He told you, but he didn't tell me,' Brunetti said, hearing the petulance in his voice.

She smiled again. 'He said he doesn't want to let you down. Or hurt your feelings. He'd do anything for you: you know that. But that applies to him, and not to his wife.'

'You make it sound like a conflict of loyalties,' he said, hoping to surprise her.

Ignoring his affronted tone, she said, 'Of course it is. Vianello has his wife and his children, and then he has you.'

After she said this, Griffoni bent down to do something with her shoe, something Brunetti knew to be entirely unnecessary. He marvelled at the grace of women and at their charity.

When she sat up, she asked, 'Why don't we do it?' she asked.

'What?'

'Why don't *we* do it, the two of us? Go over there and ask people – in shops, in bars – about Signora Cavanella and her son. You can be the good cop and I can be the bad cop, if you like.'

'You know about the case?'

'I've read everything you've read: Rizzardi's report and the report from the ambulance squad that answered the original call, and yours about missing documents.' She paused, then added, 'I've asked Signorina Elettra if there are any other documents.'

Brunetti didn't touch this. Instead, he said, 'I spoke to Davide's doctor. Well, to his mother's doctor, who treated him twice.' He folded his hands by interlacing the fingers and tapped on his desk a few times. 'But there was no sign of a medical record.'

'I don't want to say that's impossible,' she began, 'but it's hard to believe. There's got to be some sign of him. Somewhere.'

'There isn't,' Brunetti said, thinking of the drawings in

the doctor's office but not considering them part of the official record.

'Then what do we do?' she asked.

'We play good cop and bad cop and go and talk to people and see if we can find some gossip.'

21

As Foa took them over to San Polo, Brunetti told her about his conversation with the women in the dry cleaner's, his meeting with Ana Cavanella, and the apparent ease with which Pucetti had befriended her.

The wind had driven them into the cabin and they sat side by side on the back cushion, hands braced against the occasional thrust of the waves. 'He's a clever boy,' Griffoni said with a smile of approval. The noun sounded strange coming as it did from lips that could not be a decade older than the 'boy's'. As they passed San Giorgio, she turned to Brunetti and asked, in an entirely normal voice, 'Do you ever get tired of all this beauty?'

His gaze passed beyond her to the clouds scuttling behind the dome. 'Never.' The answer was automatic, unconsidered, true.

'I feel that way about Naples,' she said. Before he could react and perhaps reluctant to return to the subject, she asked, 'Have you met Pucetti's fiancée?'

'The Russian girl,' Brunetti answered. Then, to show that, although she might see him as just another man without interest in people's feelings, he still took the trouble to learn some things about them, added, 'She's a mathematician.'

'She was on the fast track to becoming a full professor in Moscow, and now she's teaching algebra to teenagers in Quarto d'Altino,' Griffoni said and gave the sort of shrug with which Neapolitans acknowledge the truth that life tosses us around like bags of potatoes at the market. Then, too casually, she said, 'I've had a look at her pension.'

'Whose?'

'Ana Cavanella's,' Griffoni answered. 'She worked for the Lembo family from the time she was fifteen until she was seventeen.'

Brunetti wondered where she had found that information but did not ask. Instead, he inquired, 'And then?'

'Then there's a gap when she did not work – at least she did not declare an income – for twelve years. And then she worked for a cleaning company until she retired two years ago.'

'Cleaning what?'

'Offices and shops. The company's in Mestre, but they do a lot of work here. She was legally employed: taxes, health contributions, pension.'

Brunetti saw that she had something else. 'Tell me,' he said. The boat rose up without warning and slapped down with a heavy thump, shaking them both. Brunetti pulled back the curtain and saw that wind was playing on the water, slashing at the white tops of the waves. There was another, lesser, thump and then things quietened down.

'I read about the Lembo family,' she said.

'What?'

'What was available online,' she began, then paused.

194

'And?'

'And I called some friends and asked about them.'

'Friends where?'

'Here. And in Rome.'

'What did you learn?'

'Probably no more than you did. A few people said the mother got what she deserved, but no one explained what they meant. Drugs, sex, and rock and roll for the oldest daughter.'

'Lucrezia,' Brunetti supplied.

She nodded and said, 'There's much less about the next one, Lavinia. It seems she's in Ireland.'

Brunetti nodded, then asked, 'You know that one of them died?' he asked.

'Yes. The baby.' She spoke the word in quotes. 'In Chile. In a swimming pool.'

'Strange place to die,' he said neutrally.

'If you're the one dying, any place must be strange.'

He made an assenting noise.

'What did you find out about Lavinia?' he asked, surprised by his own easy reference to this unknown woman.

'Only official things. School, university, jobs.'

'You can get into those files?' he blurted out, wondering where she could have learned to do that. Surely not from Signorina Elettra.

'Vianello checked for me,' she said. Then, tossing away the line, she added, 'He asked Signorina Elettra for some help with Ireland.'

The motion of the boat softened. He looked out again and saw that they had turned into Rio San Polo, where the wind effectively ceased. Foa pulled up to Campiello Sant'Agostin, slipped the engine into neutral, and jumped up on to the *riva* to moor the boat. Brunetti stepped up

195

beside him, reached back and took Griffoni's hand to help her up. 'I don't know how long we'll be,' he told Foa. 'You might as well go back.'

'Do you mind if I stay, Commissario?' the pilot asked, looking, Brunetti thought, uncomfortable. 'My aunt lives over here, and I never come to see her much any more. So I thought that, being as I'm here . . .' The pilot's voice trailed off. Brunetti glanced at Griffoni, who shrugged and looked at the pavement: this was not her decision.

'How long has your aunt lived here?' Brunetti asked.

'For ever.'

'Ask her about Ana Cavanella, then, would you?' Brunetti said.

'Sure thing, Commissario,' Foa said, jumped back into the boat to retrieve the keys, then vaulted back on to the *riva*.

The two commissari took the bridge and started down towards Campo San Stin, where they went into the only bar. A man stood behind the zinc counter, propped over a newspaper: both looked as tired as the *tramezzini* in a glass case to his left. He glanced at them, then went back to his reading.

Brunetti asked for two coffees; the man turned away to make them. Reading upside down, Brunetti saw that the paper was three days old: he turned it towards them and paged through until he found the article about Davide Cavanella's death. When the man returned with the coffees, Brunetti pointed to the article and asked, 'You know him?'

The man's glance was level, a combination of suspicion and insolence. 'Do I have to answer your question?' he asked.

'No,' Brunetti said. 'You don't have to serve me a coffee, and you don't have to answer my question.'

The barman put the saucers on the counter and turned away. He disappeared into a narrow space to the right of the bar, leaving the red curtain open behind him.

'I don't think there's any sense staying here,' Griffoni said beside him. She put two Euros on the counter and they left. Neither of them had touched the coffee.

They spent another hour in the neighbourhood, going into a hardware store, a grocery, a shop that sold buttons and underwear, a gloomy place that sold food and products for pets, even into a shop that sold handbags, but there the saleswoman was Chinese and spoke no Italian except, it seemed, numbers.

Though they realized early on that no one was going to talk to them, they still persisted. Most people said they did not know Ana Cavanella or her son, but some of them repeated a variation of the response of the man at the bar, a fact that led Brunetti to suspect that phones had been ringing ever since they left the bar.

As they walked out of the last shop, Griffoni said, 'It's just like being at home.'

'Where nobody talks to the police?' Brunetti asked.

'Yes.'

'Why should it be any different?'

She could not disguise her surprise, as if she had never considered the possibility that Venetians, too, might be suspicious of the police and have strict ideas about *omertà*.

Deciding that it was futile to continue, Brunetti dialled Foa's number and asked him if he was still in the area. Sounding relieved to hear his superior's voice, Foa said he was and, without being asked, said he'd be at the boat in ten minutes.

Just as they started walking down the bridge to the side of the canal where the boat was moored, Foa appeared in the *calle* ahead of them, his smile visible even at this distance. The three of them arrived at the boat at the same time. 'I talked to my aunt, Commissario,' he said, his smile now even broader.

'And she knows Ana Cavanella, I assume?' Brunetti said, unable to hide his own smile.

'Yes, sir. Or at least she knows her to see and knows what's said about her.'

'Which is?'

Foa looked around the small *campiello*, as if he had picked up the neighbourhood's nervousness about talking to a policeman. 'Let's go on board,' he suggested, turning towards the boat. He jumped on to the deck, which now lay lower in the water than when they arrived. He held out his hand, first for Griffoni and then for Brunetti, who took it gladly as he stepped down.

Foa switched on the engine and pulled away from the *riva*, then put the motor into reverse and backed up and into the canal on the right to turn back the way they had come. When they emerged into the Grand Canal, he slowed and Brunetti and Griffoni moved up to stand on either side of him.

With no urging, Foa began. 'The story is that the mother moved here ages ago, when Ana was a little girl. The mother rented a house, but then later Ana got hold of it, no one knows how.' How very Venetian, Brunetti thought, to begin a story like this with talk of real estate.

'When she was still a young girl, Ana got a job as a servant somewhere else in the city and went to live there during the week, though she came home to visit her mother when she could. Then after a couple of years she came home to live with her.' Foa paused and said, 'You have to understand, my aunt's almost ninety.' He saw their surprise and added, 'She's my father's aunt, really. But she's still an aunt.' He laughed, 'My father's always said she was his *eredità* from that side of the family, and I guess I've inherited her.'

'And Ana?' Brunetti prodded, not interested in the particulars of Foa's relationship with his great-aunt.

'The story that's told is that she went away on a trip and came back with this son of hers.'

'What?' Griffoni asked.

Foa glanced at her, perhaps relieved to find someone else who found the story strange. 'That's what she told me. She said it's what the local people say: she went away for some time – my aunt didn't know how long – I think they didn't have a lot of friends in the neighbourhood – and came back with the son.'

'How old was he?' Griffoni asked.

'No one knew. Exactly, that is. He wasn't a young child any more, though. Maybe twelve or so. And deaf. That's what my aunt said Ana and her mother told people, but most people thought something else was wrong with him because he was so simple.'

'Wait a minute,' Griffoni said. Foa, confused, slowed the boat. She laughed. 'No, I mean wait a minute with this story. Did she have this boy stuck in a parking lot somewhere, and when he reached a certain age, she went and picked him up?' She shook her head repeatedly. 'It doesn't make any sense.'

'My aunt said she told people he lived with relatives in the country, and then when he was old enough, she brought him home.'

'Old enough for what?' Brunetti asked in a soft voice, as if speaking to himself. The others heard him, but neither had any suggestion to make.

Surprising both men, Griffoni asked, 'Why don't we try the Lembos?' When neither opposed her suggestion, she said, 'She worked for them for years. Lucrezia's a few years older than she is, so she would have been a teenager then, and maybe she remembers her.'

Brunetti glanced at his watch and saw that it was after six. 'You can drop us off there, Foa, if you like, then take the boat back.'

'Do you want to hear what else my aunt said?' Foa asked, failing to disguise how much he was offended by their having cut off his story.

Brunetti put a hand on his arm and said, 'Of course. I'm sorry. What else did she say?'

'That she was a beautiful girl, and all the boys in the neighbourhood were crazy for her. But she never had anything to do with them, like she thought she was too good for them or something.' He reflected on this, then asked, as though the question had no suitable answer, 'She's a girl from San Polo, and she's too good for the local boys?'

'My daughter's a girl from San Polo,' Brunetti said lightly, 'and I certainly think she's better than most of the boys I've seen in the neighbourhood.'

It took a moment, but when Foa understood, he laughed and increased the speed to get them to the Lembo *palazzo*.

22

Foa pulled up at the place where he had taken Brunetti the last time but showed no desire to linger, perhaps still smarting from their apparent lack of interest in his aunt's story. He helped them up from the boat, waved, and proceeded on towards the Canale of the Giudecca.

The wind had dropped, but it had grown colder, and Brunetti wished he had brought a scarf with him or had thought to wear a heavier jacket. Griffoni, he noticed, wore a padded coat that came to just above her knees and seemed not to notice the cold at all.

As they walked up the *calle*, she asked, 'How do we play this?'

'We see what happens and we react to that,' was the only thing he could think of suggesting.

There was no response. A boat was passing in the canal at the end of the *calle*, and he waited to ring the bell again until it passed out of hearing. He pushed and kept his finger on the bell; both of them heard the far-off echo from inside.

If no one comes, he told himself, then that's it, and I'll forget all about it. Let the dead rest. Let them all rest. He allowed a full minute to pass and then rang the bell again, holding his finger there for a long time.

Inside, a door slammed, and Brunetti flushed with relief. Someone was there, and he could go on with this.

Suddenly the door was pulled open. No warning, no sound from inside: it was closed, and then it was open. A tall woman who might have been the older sister of the woman who had been wearing the bikini in the photos Signorina Elettra had shown him stood before them. She wore a grey tracksuit that appeared to have been bought for a thinner person.

Time had passed since the photos had been taken, but more time had passed for her, or harder time. One glance told Brunetti that her face had been lifted, perhaps a number of times, but at some point she had abandoned the attempt or the trouble and had accepted the inevitable. Wrinkles had accumulated under her chin like thick batter poured too slowly from a bowl. Her hair was a rusty red, pulled back in a ponytail, frayed hairs curling away from her head.

Little rivulets, looking like something between a U and a V, hung below her eyes, the flesh above them darker than the skin of her face. She stared, first at the man and then the woman, with eyes devoid of curiosity or interest. '*Sì?*' she asked. Had they been coming to collect the rent or to tell her the house was on fire, her response to their presence would have been the same.

'Signora Lembo?' Brunetti asked.

'*Sì*,' she answered neutrally.

'I'm Commissario Brunetti, and this is Commissario Griffoni. We'd like to speak to you.'

'About what?'

'Ana Cavanella.'

Her eyes changed, came alive, though not in a manner Brunetti found particularly appealing. She looked at Griffoni, and when Brunetti glanced aside at her he saw that his colleague had assumed a slumped posture that took centimetres off her height. Her posture had also managed to become graceless and awkward, her face so reduced in expression or signs of interest as to be almost plain; certainly not attractive.

'What do you want to know about her?' Lucrezia Lembo – for this must be Lucrezia – asked. She moved her hand from behind her and took a deep pull on her cigarette, almost as if she had thought, until then, that she had to hide it. Tilting her head back, she blew a long line of perfect smoke rings into the air. Brunetti could not repress a smile of appreciation, which she saw.

'Come with me,' she said. 'It's cold out here.'

She turned and went across the small courtyard to a door, opened it, and climbed stiffly up a single steep flight of steps. They followed, Brunetti averting his eyes from the sight of her broad buttocks ahead of him on the steps. The hallway they entered was even colder than the court-yard had been. The only sound was their footsteps, his and Griffoni's: when he did look, he saw that the woman wore bedroom slippers. No wonder they had not heard her cross the courtyard.

At the end of the corridor she opened a door that led to another corridor. She left it to them to follow her and close it, which Brunetti did. He thought of how many times he had watched this scene in films, both good and bad: the innocent welcomed into the home of the killer; the killers coming into the home of the innocent.

The woman paused in front of another door long enough to poke her cigarette into a brimming ashtray that stood on a walnut table. This door led to a dimly lit room that must once have been a library. Most of the shelves were empty, and what books remained lay like rectangular drunks, any which way, on the shelves. There was even a rolling wooden ladder attached to the shelves, leading up to the highest, they too almost completely devoid of books.

There was no smell of cigarettes in the room. No dust lingered on the books; the carpet was so freshly vacuumed that their shoes left prints on the pile. What little light remained in the day came effortlessly through the windows, which showed no trace of dirt or grime.

Lucrezia lowered herself into the middle of a plush sofa, her feet flat on the floor in front of her. She motioned them to the chairs which sat opposite. 'What about her?' she asked.

'She worked for your family, didn't she?' Brunetti asked. Griffoni had, to all intents and purposes, become a deaf mute.

'Yes. Many years ago.'

It was only then, hearing the way her voice pounded the words, that Brunetti realized she was drunk or drugged, at least enough for her speech to be affected. She moved her ponderous glance to Griffoni but seemed to find her as inert as Brunetti had. Was this all that was left of drugs, sex, and rock and roll? Surely no one could have imagined this.

'What services did she perform for your family?'

A sudden flash of anger lit Lucrezia's eyes and her hands drew themselves involuntarily into fists. But, within a second, her face was calm and her hands relaxed. 'She was a maid, if that's what you mean,' she said stolidly.

'For your mother?' Brunetti asked, remembering a time when wealthy women had what were called 'ladies' maids'.

Again, that lightning flash, the involuntary motion of her hands followed by the instant calm. 'No. She was the maid for the entire family.'

'She was very young, wasn't she?'

'She was fifteen when she came here,' she said. Her displeasure hit harder on the words this time, again giving voice to whatever she had drunk or used. 'It depends on how young you consider that.' Brunetti thought the age uninteresting; it was her response to it that struck him: why would she remember something like that from half a century ago?

'It's a dangerous age,' Griffoni stunned him by saying, not so much for the words as by the fact that he had all but forgotten about her, sitting there, humble, plain, silent. Waiting.

Lucrezia's eyes swivelled in the direction of the woman next to Brunetti and she studied this suddenly vocal thing. Griffoni was looking at the hands clasped in her lap, but enough of her face was visible for the other woman to see the suddenly furrowed brow and tightened mouth.

'Dangerous,' Lucrezia repeated with no expression at all. It might as easily have been a shoe size she was giving. With no explanation, she got to her feet, crossed the room, and went out, leaving the door open behind her.

Brunetti turned to his colleague with an inquisitive glance, but she, perhaps thinking of Lucrezia's silent feet, held a finger to her lips and shook her head. He looked around the room again, made uncomfortable by the contrast between the spotless cleanliness and the disorderly state of the books.

Griffoni apparently incommunicado, he turned his thoughts to Davide Cavanella. He had no determinable age: he could have been born when Ana Cavanella worked here, or after. The family had watched her grow up, ripen, mature. He recalled, as if he had photographed them, Lucrezia's tight hands, replayed the scene of her slowly relaxing them, forcing them, perhaps, to open and look natural. He recalled the look in her eyes when he asked what Ana's services – such an inopportune choice of word – to the family had been. Who could know if she had been a ladies' maid or a maid of all work, or what she had been? Or what her services were? And for whom?

Lucrezia Lembo came back into the room. Both Brunetti and Griffoni could see the difference: she was calmer, her body relaxed and her walk more fluid. Her hair, Brunetti thought, was the same, as was her body, but she looked refreshed, even younger; certainly happier.

She returned to her place on the sofa and lowered herself into it with another sigh. 'We were saying?' she asked, trying to smile in Brunetti's direction but unable to keep her attention from returning to the silent Griffoni.

'I was asking you about Ana Cavanella, who once worked for your family,' Brunetti reminded her.

'Yes, I think I remember her,' Lucrezia said in a voice that had grown almost languid. 'Pretty girl, wasn't she?'

'I didn't know her then,' Brunetti said, not thinking it expedient to tell her that he had been a child at the time. Then, deciding to lie, he added, 'But my father might have.'

Her eyes turned to him, and only then came into focus. 'How is that?' she asked.

'He ran a boat service, a kind of taxi, but he also transported precious objects for antique dealers.' Brunetti put on his easiest smile, one filled with the remembrance of past times, happier times, in his father's case, times that had never existed. 'He had a delicate touch. That's what the dealers said. So they trusted him to move things.' Again, that smile. 'I remember him speaking of your father.' Given his age at the time, this was highly unlikely, but he doubted she would consider this.

Lucrezia's mouth put on a smile. 'My father bought a lot of things,' she said, listened to the echo of her own words, and smiled again, but this smile, though real, was not pretty. She waved her hands at the almost empty shelves, and Brunetti looked at them admiringly. 'So your father might have worked for him,' she concluded, speaking as though the words were somehow meaningful and related to their previous conversation.

Brunetti repeated the smile that greets good times recalled. 'He said your father was always very generous to him, and to the men who worked with him,' Brunetti invented. Generosity was so appealing that everyone wanted it to be attributed to them, unlike a sense of justice or probity: those unwieldy, uncomfortable virtues.

'Oh, he was very generous, my father,' she said so slyly that Brunetti was left feeling they were not having the same conversation or not talking about the same thing.

'That's dangerous, too,' Griffoni said with sibylline indifference. 'Generosity.' She followed this with a half-mocking snort.

Lucrezia started, as though she had no idea where that voice could be coming from. She turned the vague attention of her eyes towards Griffoni, but she had gone still again. Lucrezia's confusion splashed across her face. Then, surprising them both, she said, 'It was my mother who wasn't generous.' Her eyes moved to the shelves of the bookcase and then, as if the echo of her words had spent time there before coming back to her, suddenly slapped her hand across her mouth. 'No. That's not right. She was good. She made us say the rosary. Every night, before we went to bed, we had to kneel down with her and say the rosary: Monday the Joyful Mysteries, Tuesday the Sorrowful

Mysteries, Wednesday the Glorious Mysteries.' She closed her eyes and brought her hands together, as though holding the beads.

'The Presentation of Jesus in the Temple,' she said in an entirely different voice, solemn, deep, reverent. 'Fruit of the Mystery: Purity. Obedience.' Brunetti watched her hands move as the invisible beads slowly passed through her fingers. Her lips moved. It looked to Brunetti as if she were repeating the last two words.

In the same type of voice, falling into the same rhythmic incantation, Griffoni said, 'Better to think of the Crucifixion, Signora. Fruit of the Mystery: Salvation, Forgiveness.' The hair rose on the back of Brunetti's neck, and he thought of her duplication of Signorina Elettra's voice.

Lucrezia's eyes opened slowly and she looked across at Griffoni, with a softer smile. 'My mother taught us obedience.' Her smile dimmed, and she said, 'She taught it to my father, too.'

She turned her attention to Brunetti and, in an entirely normal voice, said, 'People called him the King of Copper, I know. But it was my mother who ruled, not him.'

Brunetti was overwhelmed by fear of suffocation, trapped in a world of distorted femininity: Griffoni appeared to have taken leave of her senses and fallen into a religious trance, while the Lembo woman summoned up the spirits of her dead parents, and both of them recited the names of the decades of the rosary he had not heard since he was a boy, staying with his grandparents and listening to the old women as they fell to their devotions.

He got to his feet and went to the nearest window and pulled it open. Cold air swept into the room. Lucrezia did not notice, but Griffoni gave him a sharp look and jerked her head to the side, commanding him to close the window. He did so but remained beside it. From there, he could see both of them, but he turned away and looked to the north, where he saw the bell tower of Santo Stefano looking even more crooked than from the ground. 'Everything tilts but nothing falls,' he had heard his fellow Venetians say all his life.

Behind him their voices murmured: Brunetti had no idea whether it was the rosary they were saying or whether one of them was confessing to the other. He had not seen, nor had he heard, anything pass between the two women, but he had felt the moment when the rosary had united them in spirit. The memory of that look from Griffoni, however, sent him cringing away from the fraudulence of whatever union had been struck between them while leaving him eager for any advantage it would provide.

The light had diminished across the city while they had been inside. The tower of Santo Stefano was outlined against darkness only by the lights that glowed up from around it. Luminous and heaven-reaching, the tower was out of true and looked as though it would soon collapse: of how many of us could the same thing be said? Brunetti wondered.

Their voices drifted across him like smoke; Brunetti was unable to turn to look at the women and unwilling to know what they were saying: let them swap the names of the decades back and forth, tell each other what virtues they encouraged, but keep him free of it.

Though he tried to block or filter the words, they continued to float past him: 'Contempt of the World', 'Grace of a Happy Death', 'Desire for Holiness', 'Mortification', 'Purity'. Hadn't they had that one already? Why this obsession with sexual purity? he asked himself. What a distorting way to look at life.

The voices droned on. Finally, unable to endure it,

Brunetti turned and looked at them. Lucrezia Lembo's head was pressed against the back of her chair, her face covered with her hands. Griffoni was leaning forward, speaking to her in a voice so low Brunetti could not hear it.

Something in him snapped at this grotesque religious theatre. 'Griffoni,' he said, so loudly that both women turned to him in alarm. 'That's enough.'

She knew better than to dispute this with him. She got to her feet, leaned down over Lucrezia, who uncovered her eyes and whispered to her. Griffoni nodded and reached out to touch her arm with her right hand.

Brunetti ignored them both and started for the door. He held it open for Griffoni, who gave the back of the other woman's hand a few pats and came obediently to Brunetti's side. Together they left; silently they walked down the stairs and across the courtyard. Brunetti found the handle and opened the door. Together they stepped out into the narrow *calle*.

He resisted the urge to slam the door and turned to the left, toward the Accademia stop. Hearing a muffled noise behind him he turned to see Griffoni standing with her arm pressed against the front of the house on the other side of the *calle*. The night's chill hit him as Griffoni took a step towards him, grabbed his arm, and fell against him. Without thinking, he wrapped his arm around her and tried to hold her upright. But she started to sink away from him, and he stepped up in front of her to wrap his other arm around her. Her head banged against his shoulder, and one arm slapped against his side.

There was a low barred window nearby, and he half carried, half pushed her towards it. He lowered her until she was sitting on the sill, leaning forward, her head against his stomach. He crouched down, one hand bracing her against the bars, the other feeling for her pulse, though he had little idea of what he was supposed to feel there.

Her head fell back and rested against the bars. Her eyes opened, and Brunetti watched her confusion as she saw the wall of the building on the other side of the *calle*. Suddenly she was aware of him and pulled away, backing against the bars. Then she recognized him, and her face relaxed.

'What happened?' she asked and raised a hand to wipe her eyes.

Brunetti relaxed minimally. 'I think you fainted.'

'I never faint,' she said, managing to sound offended.

'Perhaps it was a vision of the Madonna,' Brunetti risked saying.

Her eyes widened, but then she smiled. 'It was too much for me, I think,' she said.

'What was?'

'Doing that to that poor woman.'

'Doing what?'

'Getting her to tell me about her mother and the way she prayed the rosary.' Then, after a moment and with deadly seriousness, 'What a monster.'

'That poor thing?' Brunetti asked, nodding his head back towards the closed door to the *palazzo*.

'No, the mother.'

23

Deciding she needed something to drink, Brunetti helped Griffoni to stand and waited while she steadied herself. At her nod, he latched his arm in hers, and they set off together. They turned to the right, crossed the bridge, then went into the bar. Luckily, a small table at the back was free. 'A chamomile,' she said in response to his look: Brunetti went back to the bar and asked for the tea and a coffee, then changed it to two pots of tea. His mother had said it was good for emergencies, and this seemed close to being one.

He went back to the table. He heard the swish of steam, the clatter of crockery, and soon the waitress brought their teas. He put her teabag into the pot, then did the same with his own. He added two packets of sugar to Griffoni's cup, ignoring her protest that she didn't want any, and two to his own.

Her face was stiff, the way the kids' used to be when they first went walking, then skiing, in the mountains. He decided hers would thaw: it just took time and a warm place.

He picked up his cup and blew at the surface then stirred it a few times, and blew on it again: she mirrored his actions. Finally he chanced it and took a small sip: still hot but no longer boiling. He set the cup down and began to stir it again. When the temperature was right, Brunetti said, 'Tell me.'

She sipped at her tea a few times, then added more to the cup without adding more sugar, as if to show him how she liked it. Another sip. Then she said, '"Purity". That was the word that set her off, I think. Her mother was mad for it. Baths, hand-washing, clean clothing twice a day. They had maids, so they could do that. Then,' she continued, pausing to drink more tea, 'when they got older, she started talking to them about a different type of purity. There was a nun living with them, and priests all over the place.'

Griffoni stopped speaking and finished her cup of tea. With undisguised exasperation, she demanded, 'Why do people make such a mess of everything?'

Brunetti shrugged. He had never found an answer to that one.

'When they got bigger, she sent them to a girls' school in Ireland, but then she got sick – the mother – and Lucrezia had to come back and take care of her.'

'Sick with what?'

'I didn't understand,' she said and glanced at Brunetti, as if weighing how far she could go. 'It sounded like one of those diseases rich women in novels get.'

'And the father during all of this?'

'I don't know, really,' Griffoni said, her confusion audible. 'It's as if he didn't exist.'

'How can you be the King of Copper and not exist?'

'I don't know,' she repeated, her voice tight. 'I asked her about him, but she said he never counted for anything: the company belonged to her mother's family: he was in charge only because he married her. He was always away, working. They had mines everywhere, and he would go off to see them.'

To Brunetti, it sounded like the stories he had heard about the days of La Serenissima Repubblica, when the merchants who sailed with their fleets came home once a year, stayed long enough to unload and reload their cargos and impregnate their wives, and then off again in pursuit of gain.

Colour had returned to her face, and her voice had steadied. First Pucetti befriended Ana Cavanella and now Lucrezia Lembo had confided in Griffoni: was he trapped in a nest of vipers able to worm themselves into people's sympathies? Was he another one?

Brunetti finished his tea and looked towards the bar, hoping to catch the waitress' eye. Griffoni leaned her head back and closed her eyes, much in the manner of Lucrezia Lembo.

Then she opened them, tried to smile, and said, 'I'm sorry, Guido. I just feel so sorry for her. For them all.'

'It shouldn't happen,' Brunetti said, 'that stupidity costs so much.'

This time, it was she who didn't understand: he saw it in her face. 'Her mother and her talk of purity,' he said, and then, with no introduction, added, 'The doctor who treated Ana Cavanella and her son said she never tried to get him any help: no tests, no teaching, nothing.' He saw Griffoni's astonishment. 'He said she was so stupid she was ashamed of the fact that he was deaf. That she saw it as God's punishment for her sin, so she let him grow up like an animal. And die like one.'

'Is any of this enough to make you want to stop?' she asked, waving her hand as if to take in the room, the *palazzo* across the bridge, Ana Cavanella, and her dead son.

'No.'

'What next, then?' The eagerness with which she asked this pleased him.

'We keep looking until we find something, I suppose,' he said.

'Good.'

Brunetti considered going back to the Questura for an hour to begin to hunt through the public record for further traces of the Copper King's family but dismissed the idea. He could not invite Claudia Griffoni back to the house and tell his wife that they would be working on the computer for a while and she should just go about making dinner, perhaps set an extra plate for their guest, could he?

When he saw how exhausted Griffoni looked, he suggested they start the next morning, knowing she would agree. She did and stopped him from offering to take her home by saying she felt much better. 'It was bad, but not terrible, doing that to her,' she said. Then, trying to sound casual about it, she added, 'It's the part I dislike most: getting people to trust you and then using that to get things from them.'

'It's part of the job,' Brunetti added, 'though I don't like it, either.'

They walked slowly towards the *imbarcadero*. She stopped and faced him to say, 'Sometimes, though, with the bad ones, there's satisfaction in it.' When Brunetti remained impassive, she added, 'It's hard at times, especially with the younger officers, to listen to them talk about the way people are victims of society or circumstances or their families.'

'What about Lucrezia Lembo?' Brunetti couldn't stop himself from asking, though there was no evidence that she was bad in any way, just weak and unstable.

She smiled. 'I set myself up for that one, didn't I?'

'Yes.'

She started towards the Accademia stop again. 'I meant the ones who beat up their girlfriends or kill or rob someone and then kick him in the face just to show how tough they are. Those are the ones.'

Brunetti agreed with her but said nothing. They heard her boat approaching and hurried on to the covered dock. He patted her arm a few times and waited while she got on, then turned and went to the other dock to wait for his own boat.

He woke and looked out the window of their bedroom; the moral hangover from the evening before glowered back at him from the grey clouds hanging motionless over the city. He turned aside, but Paola was not there, and when he stretched out a hand under the covers – complimenting himself on his instincts as a policeman – he felt that her place was cold. He looked at the clock: almost nine.

Pyjama-clad, he went into the kitchen but found no one. The only sign of life was a coffee cup in the sink and the Moka still on the stove. Like Paola's place in their bed, it was cold. He rinsed it out, put in water and coffee, and set it back on a low flame. From the window that looked at the far-off Dolomites, he saw that the clouds stretched all the way up there, darkening in the distance.

Was this what it would be like if he were single, if he lived alone and had never married? Paola's grandmother's china would not be in the cabinets, there would be no Canaletto on the wall, nor would the corner of the counter display the herd of ceramic statues of animals that Chiara had been bringing home for years. No yellow duck, no pink elephant, nor giraffe, nor family of penguins. Liberation from these thoughts came from the bubbling noise of the Moka. He took the cup from the sink, poured in the coffee, and added sugar.

An hour later, he and Griffoni sat in front of Brunetti's new computer, a copy of the late King of Copper's *carta d'identità* on the screen before them: Ludovico Fadalti. 'I thought his name was Lembo,' Griffoni said. 'Not Fadalti.' She put her finger on the screen, almost as if she thought Brunetti incapable of reading the name printed there.

'She told you the company was the mother's, didn't she?' Brunetti asked.

'Yes, she did. But the company is called Lembo.'

Brunetti hit a key, and a new *carta d'identità* appeared: same date and place of birth, same photo, but the surname was now 'Lembo'.

'He had it changed,' Brunetti said. He had never heard of anyone actually doing this and was curious about how much the man born Fadalti had been willing to renounce on his path to becoming the King of Copper. 'The children could then be called by the mother's name.'

He looked at the other documents they had accessed: birth and death certificates, driver's licence, marriage certificate, health system registration. Lembo had had no travel pass, as these had been initiated only a few years ago, but perhaps wealthy men in their eighties were not given to taking the vaporetto. His passport had been registered and re-registered up until four years before his death, and his bank accounts and credit cards had been closed only after his death.

On all official documents, beginning soon after the marriage, his name was given as Lembo. He recalled Lucrezia's birth certificate: he could not remember having seen any sign of 'Fadalti' there, so the metamorphosis had been complete before her birth.

He retrieved her birth certificate, then the wedding certificate of her parents. Same year, yes, but only six months apart. He nudged Griffoni and pointed to the two dates.

'*Mamma mia,*' she said. 'Even in dissolute Naples, that sort of thing wasn't common sixty years ago – certainly not among people of their class.'

'Even less so here,' Brunetti added.

Official sources exhausted, he went back to Google and put in the name Ludovico Lembo. Pages of articles appeared, though when he read quickly through the listings, he saw that although in many his name appeared, they didn't centre on him. He began a new search, using Ludovico Fadalti, but there was no reference in the press to a church wedding: no basilica, bride arriving in a white gondola, blessing by the Patriarch. A few subsequent articles reported on the early years of Lucrezia's wild ride through life, listing Ludovico only because he was her father.

They found a few articles about him, when he was still Ludovico Fadalti: son of a Venetian engineer, only child, degree from the University of Padova. There were a number of articles about Lembo Minerals that provided information about the company and its success under the 'dynamic direction' of Ludovico who-knew-when-his-name-had-become-Lembo the engineer whose 'skills and initiative' gave direction to a traditional company while maintaining the 'family-centred concepts' that had propelled its success during the early years of the century.

The earliest of these articles, it seemed, had been written years after the 'dynamic' new path had been set for the company. There was a meagre record of the early years of Lembo's – Brunetti decided he might as well give in and call him that – leadership. There were references to the honours he later received from business and industrial organizations, culminating in his nomination, two years before he left the company, as 'Cavaliere del Lavoro'.

Starting in the mid-1970s, articles began to appear about the women in the family, featuring the haughty Signora Lembo and her two beautiful daughters. Seeing them posed in photo after photo, the mother's arms encircling her teenaged daughters in a gesture redolent of love, Brunetti thought of the Mother of the Gracchi, she too glowing with pride as she displayed her jewels. Signora Lembo, he learned, was distinguished by her intense faith and ceaseless good works in the cause of Holy Mother Church. There was even a photo of her kneeling, unrecognizable in a black veil, head bowed over the extended hand of the Pope.

Then, slowly, during the next decade, the articles disappeared, replaced by articles about the woman, no longer young, whom they had apparently decided to call 'The Princess of Copper'.

He stood to stretch his back, leaving the computer to Griffoni. She continued reading while he walked over to the window, bent to feel the radiator, which was still cold, and began to study the figures in the *campo* on the other side of the canal.

The father, he realized, was yet another disappearing person, though this one had given up only his name. Was it worth it, in order to become King of Copper, and what was the rest of the price? To marry the woman whom the gutter press presented as a saint? His first-born daughter had married a gigolo half her age and was now cushioning her final years with drugs or drink. The second had gone off to God-haunted Ireland to study and work, apparently to settle there. The last-born had died at twenty, and her mother had decamped soon after, leaving the former King of Copper, in his eighties, with a new companion, to die on the Giudecca.

He turned back towards Griffoni and watched her work for a minute or two. She had become enthralled in the search for information: nothing else was. Brunetti was too far away to be able to read the screen, but he could see each page flash up, flash away, only to be replaced by another, and then another.

At last she pulled her hands away from the keys and turned towards him. 'Most of the articles about the parents are public relations nonsense. Worthless. Especially the obituaries.'

'Only saints die,' Brunetti said.

'What?'

'Only saints die. In obituaries, everyone is a saint; everything else is washed away.'

'I'm afraid you're right,' she said and killed the page. 'What do you suggest we do?'

He waved a hand at the computer. 'Why don't we take a look in there for the name of someone who might have known them?'

24

That took some time. Brunetti finally, after explaining that he and Commissario Griffoni needed her help, enlisted Signorina Elettra to access the records of the state pension fund, where she found the names of two former employees of the Lembo family, a maid and a man whose job was listed as 'major-domo'. But the man had arrived after Lucrezia's marriage, so he would know nothing of the early history of either the marriage or the company.

The maid, however, had worked for the Lembo family all the time that Ana Cavanella had been there and had then remained on for another thirty years. Griffoni sat opposite him, with between them some sheets of paper that Signorina Elettra had delivered. Brunetti, while appearing to pay no attention, had been acutely conscious of the way the two women dealt with each other during Signorina Elettra's brief apparition in the room and, like those seeking Signs of Peace from Heaven, had seen them.

'So the maid would have seen it all,' he remarked to Griffoni.

'One trembles at the thought of what *that* might have been,' Griffoni answered.

'Perhaps,' he began, reaching forward and picking up one of the papers, '. . . Maria Annunziata Ghezzi can tell us.'

Maria Annunziata Ghezzi, it turned out, lived down towards the end of Castello, behind San Francesco della Vigna, and was easy to find in the phone book. She answered Brunetti's phone call with her name, and when he spoke to her in Veneziano, answered readily. Yes, she had worked for the Lembo family. No, she was no longer in touch with them, aside from receiving her pension, and that came from the state, not from them.

Brunetti asked her if she would be willing to talk to him. 'It's about that boy who died, isn't it?' she replied.

'Davide Cavanella?' he asked.

'Yes. Ana's boy.'

'Yes, Signora. It is.'

There followed a long silence; Brunetti chose not to break it. Finally she said, 'Then you better come here, and we'll talk.'

He debated, but for only an instant, the wisdom of taking Griffoni with him. Against her failure to speak Veneziano, he weighed her femininity and the ease of her presence. 'Feel like a walk?' he asked.

'Let me go and get my coat.'

On the way there, they talked about her investigation of the fire in the factory. 'No one saw anything. No one heard anything,' Griffoni said.

'You sound as if you don't believe it,' Brunetti said.

She paused at the bottom of the bridge that led to San

Francesco. 'I don't,' she said. 'The fire started inside the factory. It had been broken into years ago, and people used it. I don't want to know what they used it for. It looks as if it started in a room where old paint and rags were stored.'

Years ago, Brunetti would have interjected here, 'or put', but time had taught him to control the impulse to insert trouble where it was not at first found. He had not read the report of the arson squad, and if 'stored' was good enough for them, it was good enough for him. From the very first suggestion, at a city council meeting – it must have been six years ago – that the building was suitable for transformation into a hotel, Brunetti had been interested only in how it would be brought to pass.

They continued towards Signora Grezzi's address. 'I've been thinking,' Griffoni said.

'Always a dangerous thing for a woman,' Brunetti replied flatly.

As if he had not spoken, she said, 'About how we're always being made conscious of our regional differences: dialect, food, customs, even our appearance.' This came from a Neapolitan who was a clear-eyed blonde almost as tall as he.

'And then I think about the way no one is going to bother to investigate this fire or go to the trouble of finding out what might have caused it. If anything did cause it. Deliberately, I mean.'

'And your point?'

'That those differences of dialect and food and customs are all meaningless.'

'Because?'

'Because in the end, we're all the same: beaten down by this system that is never going to change, by the people who are on top and who do exactly what they want to do.' She sounded not in the least angry. If anything, she sounded relieved, but that might be from nothing other than being able, finally, to say this to someone.

Brunetti stopped to try to remember which was Ramo Sagredo or when he had last been near it. His feet suddenly remembered and took him to the left.

He led her through the underpass and stopped at the corner. 'Well?' she asked.

Brunetti gave her a level look. 'It's the twenty-first century, Griffoni. And that's the future.'

'You don't mind?' she asked.

'Of course I mind,' he answered. 'But there's nothing we can do.'

She turned and looked at the slice of *laguna* exposed between the buildings. 'Except talk to Signora Ghezzi?' she finally guessed.

'Exactly.'

The old woman lived on the fourth floor, the windows of her kitchen, where she asked them to come to talk to her, looking out at the *laguna* and the cemetery. Though Brunetti knew from her pension records that she was eighty-four, Signora Ghezzi appeared at least a decade younger. White-haired and round-faced, she had the apple-skin wrinkles he had seen on the faces of his mother's friends. Her expression, however, was that of a younger person, quick and intelligent. She offered them coffee, and both accepted.

Griffoni went and stood at the window, watching the boats and clouds chase one another to the east. 'How beautiful, to stand here,' she said. Signora Ghezzi turned from taking cups and saucers from the cupboard and smiled at her, but Brunetti wondered uneasily if this were simply another attempt to flatter a witness into confiding in them.

The coffee bubbled up and was quickly served. When it was put in front of them – Griffoni having taken her place at the table – Signora Ghezzi asked, 'What is it you'd like to know?'

'We wondered if you could tell us about Ana and about the Lembo family,' Brunetti said, deciding that subterfuge was not likely to work with this woman.

Signora Ghezzi spooned sugar into her coffee; Brunetti noticed the faint tremor in her hand, the grains of sugar on the table and in the saucer. 'Why?' she asked.

'Because I don't like the way Davide lived,' Brunetti surprised himself by saying.

He surprised Signora Ghezzi, too, who asked, 'What do you mean?'

'He was born with physical and mental problems, and his mother never did anything about them – to help him. That's one thing, and it's terrible. But no one else ever did anything to help. No doctor or social worker and no city office. Nothing. No one paid attention, and he grew up the way he did.'

'I never saw him as a baby, you know.'

They were speaking in Veneziano, hers the accent of deepest Castello, the one he loved the most. He glanced at Griffoni, who seemed to be following everything; not that he could stop to ask this, not now. What was it Ana Cavanella had never done? Helped? Cared enough? Had the intelligence to know how to help? Did what he, four decades later, thought she should have done? 'She never tried to get him help,' he repeated.

'How do you know this?' Signora Ghezzi asked.

Brunetti opened his hands in a display of candour. 'We've checked all the city records, and there's no sign of Davide: no health card, and he never went to school, and he had no pension.'

She looked away from Brunetti and out the window, as if only the long view across the water could help relieve her feelings. Neither Brunetti nor Griffoni said anything. 'She must have done it like that,' she said.

Alert to her remark but not wanting her to realize that he was, Brunetti contented himself with saying, 'Would you tell me about her, Signora?'

'There's not much to tell, really.' She took a sip of coffee, reached her spoon towards the sugar bowl, but pulled it back, as if she heard the reproachful voice of her doctor telling her not to use so much sugar.

'Ana was a simple girl. When she came. I don't know how much schooling she'd had: maybe until a year before she came to us.' Absently, she stirred her coffee.

'There was a woman who did the laundry and the ironing – the signora was crazy for having things washed and ironed, and it took this woman three days a week to keep everything looking the way she wanted it.' She took another sip of coffee, then got up and went to the cabinet for a plastic box filled with biscuits. She set them on the table and took one, dipped it into her coffee and bit off the very end of it. Both of them reached in and took a biscuit.

'Where was I?' she asked, looking from one to the other of them.

'The ironing woman,' Griffoni said.

'Ah, of course. She left. No explanation. That happened a lot to the Signora. But before she went she told her that she knew a girl who could do the ironing and clean, too. She said she was a good girl.' She stopped and looked at Brunetti.

'Ana?' he asked and took another biscuit.

'Yes. Her mother brought her round, and she talked to the Signora. I wasn't there. But two days later, Ana moved into a room up on the fourth floor and was in the store-room all day long, ironing. Then she started to help me with the beds and cleaning.' The woman's eyes travelled to that distant past, when she could eat as much sugar as she pleased and had a young girl to help with the heavy work.

'Did you talk to her, Signora?' Griffoni asked. 'She must have been lonely in such a big place,' she added and took another biscuit.

'I think she was. At the beginning. But the signora kept us busy.'

So casually that Brunetti could do nothing but marvel at her skill, Griffoni dipped her biscuit into the coffee, bit off only the damp end, and smiled in continuing delight, then asked, 'What was she like, the Signora?' It was seamless, and Brunetti, if he had been asked, would have told her everything he knew.

'She was very religious,' Signora Ghezzi said, but it was a neutral word, without the least suggestion of approval. She might as well have been saying that the Signora was tall or right-handed. 'There was a relative, a nun, who lived in the *palazzo*. We never saw much of her, but the Signora did. And the girls.' She reached for another biscuit but resisted and settled for finishing her coffee. She looked across at Griffoni. 'Have more of them. My daughter-in-law makes them.'

'They're wonderful,' Griffoni said, taking another. She dipped it into her coffee and ate it with something approaching glee. Griffoni, he knew, hated coffee without milk and disliked sweets or pastries of any sort. She started to dip the stub end of the biscuit into the coffee but stopped herself, holding it up in the air as visual proof of how arrested she was by her own thought. 'It can't have been a very exciting place for young girls,' she began, as though the idea had flashed upon her, then let her voice trail off, looked at Brunetti and said, 'Sorry, Commissario.' Then, to Signora Ghezzi, 'I don't mean to . . .' and let that trail off, too, though this time she managed to blush. To cover that, she finished her coffee.

Signora Ghezzi smiled and leaned forward to pat her arm. 'Don't worry, dear. You're exactly right. And it was religion that made the Signora find out.'

'Excuse me?' Brunetti said for both of them.

'She was away at one of her religious retreats. The Signora. She had another relative – I think it was an aunt – in a convent in Assisi, and she went to stay with her for a week every month. Her confessor was there – she was very close to him – and she told us how she lived with the sisters, following their rules: getting up and going to bed when they did, and eating with them. But not talking. For a week.' She smiled at Brunetti and said, 'We were all very impressed with that at the time, I can tell you.'

'At the time.' Brunetti was struck by Signora Ghezzi's language. He smiled back at her but did not interrupt.

'Well, anyway, this time the Signora was away for ten days, and when she came back, Ana didn't come to work for three days, so when she did, the Signora hadn't seen her for almost two weeks, so she noticed the change in her.' Signora Ghezzi touched the tips of her forefingers together and drew a wide arc above her stomach.

Both Brunetti and Griffoni stared at her.

'You hadn't noticed?' Griffoni asked. Better that she ask, Brunetti thought: this was women's business.

'Well, I knew something was wrong. But I wasn't sure.'

'Did anyone else in the house know?' Griffoni asked.

'Lavinia was away at school, and Lucrezia wasn't paying attention to much of what was happening around her.'

Like so much of what the old woman had said, that

cried out for clarification. Brunetti nodded and waited for her to go on.

'What happened?' Griffoni asked.

Signora Ghezzi shook her head. 'I don't know. The Signora spoke to her, and then she was gone. That's when the Signora got sick. At the time, as I told you,' she repeated, 'I thought it must be because she was so religious.' She stopped speaking and took another biscuit. She put it in her mouth all in one piece and chewed.

Silence fell. From the direction of the *laguna*, they heard the motor of a large boat go past. Neither Brunetti nor Griffoni paid attention to it, not with the interesting sounds that were on offer here.

Few people liked betrayal, he knew. To avoid it or the accusation of it, people would dodge around facts or present them in a way that hid them at the same time as it showed them. '"At the time,"' Signora,' Brunetti repeated in a level voice. When Signora Ghezzi responded with only a glance in his direction, he added, 'We saw Lucrezia yesterday, Signora. She's still not paying much attention to what's going on around her.'

He noticed Griffoni suddenly remove her arms from the table and sit farther back in her chair, as if to create a distance between herself and Signora Ghezzi. The old woman noticed it, too.

'Did Signora Lembo ever mention Ana again?' Brunetti asked.

Surprised, Signora Ghezzi asked, 'Did you know the Signora, then?'

'No, Signora. I never met her.'

'Ah,' she said. She folded her hands on the table in front of her and looked down at her knuckles. Like Ana's hands, hers had spent a great deal of time in cold water and harsh detergents. Like his mother's hands, as well. She looked quickly across the table at him. 'But you've learned enough about her to understand her,' she observed.

'Why do you say that?'

'Because of your question. That was her way: if she didn't like something, she made it not exist any more.' She folded her hands in her lap.

Griffoni interrupted to ask, 'So she made Ana not exist any more?'

The old woman nodded.

'And her baby?' Griffoni asked.

'Oh,' she said in a normal voice, 'She made him not exist, either.'

25

'What does that mean, Signora?' Brunetti asked calmly. The boy had become a man, so there had been no abortion or miscarriage or early death. The woman had, however unknowingly, expressed what had been bothering Brunetti from the moment he first heard about Davide Cavanella's death: his failure ever to exist.

'She never talked about Ana again or allowed anyone to mention her.' She looked into the past and said, 'I can still hear her saying it, when Lucrezia asked where she was: "That person doesn't exist." The girl had been there for more than two years, and suddenly she didn't exist.' She looked at them, first at one, then the other. 'That's exactly what she said. Those were her words. "That person doesn't exist."'

She remained silent for some time, so as to allow them to hear the words and then their echo. When she glanced at Brunetti again, it seemed to him that her face had changed somehow or that her eyes had become sharper and she had ceased being the retired old maidservant and become a younger and stronger woman.

'Why are you asking this?' she asked.

Brunetti realized that, had the woman who had let them into the house and given them biscuits asked that question, he probably would have given her a sweet lie. But this woman would have none of that and, from the look of her, would laugh at him if he tried it.

'I want him to have lived.' He listened to that, unsure why he could not make things clearer.

'Why does it concern you so much?' Signora Ghezzi asked. Griffoni turned and looked at him, as curious as the other woman.

'Because everything I've been told since he died means something different, and everyone I talk to has something to hide or that they don't want me to know.' He remembered the stone-blank faces of the neighbours and their truculent refusal to speak. Solidarity with an unfortunate woman who had lost her only son? Shame at having been part of the even greater silence that had filled the life of the deaf man?

Brunetti shoved his chair back and got to his feet. He took two steps away from the table but turned back and sat down again. He looked across at Signora Ghezzi's lined face, feeling himself reduced to honesty. 'What should I know, Signora?'

Slowly she got to her feet and stood for a moment to steady herself, the way many old people did when standing up after having been sitting for any length of time. She stacked her cup and Brunetti's but, before she could reach for Griffoni's, the younger woman stood and carried her cup to the sink. Taking the plastic box to the counter, she put on the cover and snapped it closed. She took the other cups from Signora Ghezzi, put them in the sink and ran cold water in them. After that she stood by the window, leaving it to the others to decide what was going to happen.

Signora Ghezzi kept one palm flat on the table. 'I think you should find out who owns the house where Ana lives,' she said. 'And I think you should bear in mind that most people don't change as they go through life, and as life goes through them.'

'Do you mean Ana?'

'I mean all of them,' she said. She appeared to consider this, then added, 'Lucrezia is the best of them. Of all the people you'll meet because of this, she's the only honest one.'

'Not Ana?'

'Ana Cavanella is a cold-hearted viper,' she said with no inflection whatsoever. 'But Signora Lembo was worse.'

If this kind-eyed old woman had hurled herself to the floor in a fit of demonic possession and begun to scream obscenities at him and Griffoni, Brunetti could have been no more startled. That would have shocked him only for herself, but her quietly spoken words spurred him to re-examine most of the people he had spoken to or heard about during the last days.

Ana Cavanella was the bereaved mother; Lucrezia was a ruin; Signora Lembo the much-photographed wife, mother, and saint. The King of Copper remained an enigma: powerful, potent, always away on business.

In a voice softer than Brunetti had ever heard her use, Griffoni broke the silence to ask, 'Will you tell us more, Signora?'

Neither woman moved, then Signora Ghezzi lowered herself into her chair, looked at both of them and finally said, 'Most of them are dead, you know. All that's left is the money, and it's never done them any good. Now all they can do is fight over that. No, I don't think I want to tell you any more. Because it doesn't make any difference.'

Brunetti opened his mouth to speak, perhaps to protest, but she raised a hand, and he stopped. 'I'm older than you are, Signore,' she told him and then, with a kind look towards Griffoni, 'and much older than the Signora, and I have my own ideas about this, different from yours.'

There was a ring of liquid on the surface of the table, and she stuck a forefinger into it and rubbed at it until it was gone. She looked at Brunetti and addressed him. 'They all did things because of the way they are, you know, not because they wanted something or because of something special that happened. It's just the way they are. And that doesn't change.'

She leaned forward, as if to push herself to her feet again, but gave up the effort and settled back into her chair. 'You can go now, and thank you for the visit. It's nice for old people to see new faces. It's not good for us always to look at the faces from the past.' She smiled after she said this and waved a hand as a signal of some sort: to brush them out of her house; to wish them well; to sum up the futility of human desires. It could have been any one of these. Or all of them. They left.

'Do we go and talk to her?' Griffoni asked.

It was convenience that decided him. They were less than a hundred metres from the Celestia stop, and he could hear the boat approaching from the right. Instead of answering, he turned away and walked quickly to the *imbarcadero*; she followed in his wake.

As the boat pulled up, Brunetti turned and said, 'Go back and find out who owns the house. Call me as soon as you know. I'll be at the hospital.'

Griffoni was walking away even before he was on the boat for the one-stop trip to the Ospedale. When he asked at the desk in the entrance hall, Brunetti was told that Signora Cavanella had been taken to Geriatria, the only ward with free beds.

Brunetti made his way through the courtyard, decided to take the steps, and heard the ward as soon as he turned into the last flight. A high-pitched voice, no telling its sex, began to climb up the scales, dully repeating 'No, no, no, no,' until it reached the top of its vocal range and fell back down into the lower notes, only to begin again. Brunetti emerged at the nurses' desk and asked where he could find Signora Cavanella.

'Room fifteen,' the nurse said, without glancing up from her magazine.

He passed the room from which the voice was coming, turned right and then left at the end of the corridor, the voice growing fainter, but no less agonized, with each turn. He stopped just before the next to last room in the corridor, not certain how he was going to deal with a woman who had, with a phrase, been transformed from a bereaved mother to a cold-hearted viper. Deciding that he would leave it to events to resolve that, he knocked lightly on the side of the open door and went in.

An old man slept in the bed closest to the door, toothless mouth agape. In the other bed, a long, mountainous form lay under the blankets; Brunetti didn't even have to look at the bearded face to know it was a man and that he'd entered the wrong room. He turned and took one step towards the door and suddenly stopped as he saw a man he knew pass by, coming from the direction of the last room on the ward. Leaving him enough time to get beyond the door, Brunetti moved quickly over and put his head out into the corridor.

He recognized the portly form that moved away, feet splayed to either side, forced there by thick thighs. From his right hand hung the battered brown leather briefcase that had, over the years, become a metaphor for the man: Beni Borsetta, aka Beniamino Cresti, lawyer to the masses, paladin of the lower orders in their endless fight against the myriad injustices of the wealthy and successful. For a mere 50 per cent, it was rumoured in some circles.

As Brunetti watched, Cresti turned right at the end of the corridor, showing in profile the out-thrust paunch that Brunetti had several times seen clear a path from the courtrooms in which Avvocato Cresti had worked in the pursuit of justice.

He glanced at his watch, propped his shoulders against the wall of the corridor, and began to draw up a list of reasons why Beni Borsetta might have taken his briefcase on a visit to the hospital. He could come up with none he liked, but he found all of them interesting. He let a few minutes pass before he went down to the door from which the lawyer had emerged. Standing slightly to the side, he knocked and said, in a normal voice, 'Signora Cavanella?'

He heard a voice answer and went in. She was sitting up in bed today, looking much better, though her face was worse. That is, though she recognized him and seemed fully conscious, the entire left side, from the eye to her hairline and down across her cheekbone and almost to her chin, had turned a light grey-red that Brunetti knew would, in two days, turn almost black.

'Good morning, Signora,' he said.

'You're the policeman, aren't you?' she asked. Her look was calm, lucid, disconcertingly so, at least to someone who was now curious to see how the viper might manifest itself.

He approached the bed, his face taut with a look of

236

concern. He allowed himself a small smile, rich in every sign of relief. 'I'm glad you recognize me, Signora.'

'I recognized you the other time,' she said, annoyed but not angry.

He broadened his smile. 'I'm even happier to learn that, Signora. The doctor was worried about your fall and thought you might have a concussion.' There it was: from the police. A fall.

She did not smile, but her face softened, as if she too felt relief. 'I hit my head.' Then, meaning it as a joke, 'I suppose it was as hard as whatever it hit.'

Brunetti added a nod to his smile, radiating satisfaction at this happy circumstance. 'Have they told you when you can go home?'

'Tomorrow.'

'Good,' Brunetti said and turned, as if preparing to leave the room. What were she and Beni up to? he wondered. She had said nothing about having tripped, so perhaps she was not going to claim negligence on the part of the city, one of Beni's standard cases. And since it was being treated as a fall, Beni was not going to bring a case of assault, as he had over many barroom shoves – even once against the owner of a bicycle over which a man had tripped.

His phone rang and, excusing himself to the woman, he answered it.

'Lucrezia Lembo owns the house,' Griffoni said.

'I see.'

'But Ana Cavanella's son had the legal right to stay in it all of his life, after which it reverts to the owner or her heirs.'

'I see,' he repeated. 'And when did this start?'

'If you mean the contract, it was the the year she left her job at the Lembos'.'

'Ah,' was all Brunetti would permit himself to say. But then he thought of something else and asked, 'And the expenses?'

'Paid by Lucrezia Lembo: tax, gas, light, garbage.' Then, before he could ask, 'We're checking Cavanella's bank account.'

'We?'

'Signorina Elettra and I. She's much better at these things than I am.' True as that might be, Brunetti, who had recognized Signorina Elettra's office telephone as the source of the call, had to admit that Griffoni was no slouch when it came to flattery.

'Good. Let me know.'

'Of course,' Griffoni said and was gone.

'Excuse me, Signora,' he said. 'My wife.'

'Of course,' she said in a warmer voice, as if he had become more human by having a wife.

'If you need any help, Signora, in getting home, I'm sure we could send a launch, and I'm sure Pucetti would be glad to accompany you.'

'He's very kind, Roberto,' she said.

'He's a good boy,' Brunetti answered, meaning it. He was running out of things to say to keep him there long enough for Griffoni to call him again. It came to him. 'I'm afraid there's been no progress, Signora,' he said.

'In what?' She sounded honestly confused.

'In finding any identification for your son. Official, that is.'

Her face hardened. 'I told you. There was a robbery in my house, and they took all of the papers.'

His gaze was so level, his scepticism so palpable, that she said, 'They took them. And my money. And my wedding ring. Everything.' For a moment, it looked as though she were going to attempt to cry, but then she

238

abandoned the idea and settled for putting a hand across her eyes.

His phone rang again. 'Money's been transferred into her account every month for the last forty years,' Griffoni said. 'From Lucrezia Lembo's account.'

'Really? And how much would that be?'

'It started in lire and changed to Euros, but it's always been the equivalent of a monthly salary.'

'For what sort of work?'

'Hardly for a maid. It's now three thousand Euros.'

'I see. Thanks. We can talk about it tomorrow,' he said and replaced his phone in his pocket.

Brunetti waited until Ana Cavanella took her hand from her eyes and looked across at him, when, just as though he were asking her the time, he said, 'What were you blackmailing the Lembo family about, Signora?'

26

Her mouth opened and stayed that way for a long time. Brunetti saw no expression on her face, only her once-beautiful eyes, frozen now, and the grey-red flush on the left side. This woman, he had been told, had once been thought to be a good girl: her patent fear suggested that Signora Ghezzi's assessment might be closer to the truth.

'What are you talking about?'

How many times had he been asked that? Short of a confession, it was as close to an admission of guilt as he had known many people to come. He had heard it said with indignation, incredulity, arrogance, menace; only rarely had he heard it asked in honest confusion: this was not one of those times.

'Money has been transferred into your bank account for the last forty years, Signora. From Lucrezia Lembo.'

'I work for her,' she spat out, trying for indignation.

'Doing what?'

'That's none of your business.'

Brunetti allowed himself a small smile. 'Perhaps not, Signora.' Then, after a slight pause, 'Have you paid taxes on that money?'

He watched the once-beautiful eyes move from him to the window, to the door, as if she were looking for a way out of the room. Failing to find it, she said, 'She pays the tax.'

'I see,' Brunetti said. Then, ever so casually, in the voice of the man who had once seemed genuinely concerned for her welfare, he asked, 'Where are you going to live, Signora?'

This time, her confusion was real. 'What?'

'Where will you live now?'

'What are you talking about?' she asked so timidly that Brunetti had no doubt about her failure to understand.

'It was Davide who had the *usufrutto* for the house.' He saw she didn't recognize the legal term. 'He had the right to stay in it. Not you, Signora. You'll have to leave.'

A friend of Paola's often said her son had married a woman with 'cash-register eyes', but he had never understood the expression until he watched the calculation Ana Cavanella made in response to his statement.

She stared at the window behind him and to his left, and he had the sense that he had disappeared from the room, so far as she was concerned. She pulled her eyebrows together, pursed her lips, and worked at the problem for a long time. He saw the moment when she found her way free of it: her brows relaxed, and she gave a small, satisfied nod.

'That won't matter,' she said, and he heard the steel in her voice and at the same time saw her face snap shut.

'I'm sorry about your son,' he said and left the room.

He walked from the hospital and went directly to Rosa Salva. He had seen the grey-haired woman behind the bar for at least twenty years, if not more. To Brunetti, she looked much the same as she always had, though that was impossible. He wondered if he looked the same to her, but could not ask, not after all these years of polite formality.

He did ask for a glass of white wine and two *panini* with ham, then added a *tramezzino* with ham and artichokes. He avoided looking at himself in the mirror, as he always did in bars.

Ana Cavanella had said it wouldn't matter that she could no longer stay in the house where she and Davide had been living, and she had used the future tense, the grammar of gamblers, or dreamers. But she'd found her answer. Did this mean the blackmail would continue or that Ana Cavanella saw herself as headed for finer things?

He paid and started towards the Questura.

He found Griffoni in Signorina Elettra's office, the two of them sitting behind the computer like friends at a PlayStation. When he came in, Griffoni was saying, 'Could you go back to her will, please?'

She used the familiar *tu*, and Signorina Elettra answered in kind, when she said, 'But you've already seen it.'

'I know, but I want . . .' Griffoni began but stopped when she became aware of Brunetti standing at the door, all traces of paternal approbation wiped from his face. 'Come and look at this,' she said, moving her chair to clear a space between them.

'It's Signora Lembo's will,' she explained, pointing to the monitor. He saw that she had died fifteen years before. 'Her husband and daughters got her interest in the company, and almost all of the rest was divided among them.' He looked at the copy of the will and saw what a considerable 'rest' it was. She tapped at a name, Sister Maria Rosaria Lembo-Malfa, who had received a modest sum. She was probably the nun who lived with them: perhaps nuns didn't need large bequests.

'They were still married?' Brunetti asked. Her husband had left her for the physical therapist, Brunetti recalled, but a man of his wealth was unlikely to complicate his finances with a divorce.

'Of course,' Signorina Elettra answered, and hit a few keys, to display the last will and testament of Ludovico Lembo. Both the company and all of his remaining wealth were divided evenly between Lucrezia and Lavinia. There were no codicils, no other stipulations, just that simple statement of desire prefaced and followed by the usual decoration of legal terminology.

Griffoni moved her chair farther to the side and turned to him. 'What did she tell you?'

'That she worked for Lucrezia Lembo: that's where the money's coming from. The first's a lie.' She nodded her agreement and he went on. 'It took her a while to understand about the *usufrutto*, but when she did, she said it wouldn't matter.'

'Which means?' Signorina Elettra asked.

'That she has a plan of some sort. Or a place to go. She's not troubled in the least.'

'How smart is she?' Griffoni asked.

Brunetti had not thought about Cavanella in these terms, but his answer was immediate: 'Not very.' Seeing that this was insufficient, he went on. 'She doesn't think about the consequences of things. I doubt she plans anything or thinks anything through. Or she thinks she does, but doesn't know how to do it.'

Silence fell as each of them tried to find a way to continue this conversation. Finally Brunetti said, 'Beni Borsetta was in her room.' He used the nickname because it was the more widely known; the lawyer's real name had almost fallen into disuse apart from direct address or by someone meeting him for the first time.

'*Oddio*,' Griffoni exclaimed. 'If we need proof that she's stupid, there it is. Poor woman.'

A more reflective Signorina Elettra asked Brunetti, 'Do you have any idea what he was doing there?'

'Trying to earn money by persuading her to bring a case against someone, I'd guess,' Griffoni interrupted to answer. Neither of the others tried to contradict her, even though she'd been in Venice only a few years.

Brunetti thought about the extent of Beni's creative genius. Would he try to sue the pharmaceutical company for having sold a sleeping pill that was packaged like a sweet? The rescue service for being late? The social services for forty years of negligence?

Beni, he knew, was willing to take chances with his clients: there was no ambulance he would not chase. But he doubted that even a gambler like Beni would waste his time in litigation about any of those claims. No lawyer in his right mind, even one with a better reputation than Beni Borsetta's, would go up against Big Pharma with such a weak case; the rescue services came when they came; and where was Davide's birth certificate to authorize the intervention of the social services?

'While you have that turned on,' he said to Signorina Elettra, his choice of words causing her to close her eyes in momentary distress, 'could you check the register of the lawyers and see if Avvocato Cresti is still listed?' Walking to the Questura, he had recalled a few incidents in Beni's variegated past when he had been threatened with expulsion from the union of lawyers and one time – it must have been ten years ago – when a judge had had him removed from the courtroom by the bailiffs when he refused to stop talking. Beni, in Brunetti's estimation, was not a man who would learn from his mistakes, and certainly change of behaviour was not in his repertory.

He stepped back to give Signorina Elettra better access to the computer; Griffoni leaned to her left, better to see the screen, but did not move her chair. Brunetti folded his arms and studied the screen from behind them. Documents appeared on the monitor but remained there for such a brief time that he had no chance to read them. Griffoni, he noticed, occasionally wrote things in a notebook open on the desk beside her. Once she asked Signorina Elettra to explain something, nodded at her answer, muttering, 'Very nice.'

After ten minutes, Signorina Elettra swivelled around and said, 'If he's practising law, he's also breaking it. He's been barred for three years, and the time isn't up for another twenty-seven months.'

Beni might be a friend of Ana Cavanella's, Brunetti supposed, were it not that Beni didn't have any friends. The fact that his visit had taken place in the hospital made it even more certain that he had been in pursuit of work, not practising one of the Seven Corporal Works of Mercy. If he needed proof of Ana Cavanella's lack of intelligence, the fact that she would have anything to do with Beni Borsetta was more than enough.

With a pleasant nod in the direction of the computer, Brunetti asked, 'You think that thing could find his address and phone number?'

Avvocato Cresti, when Brunetti called him a short time later, sounded not in the least surprised to be contacted by an officer of the law. Indeed, he was vociferous in his expressions of goodwill towards the Commissario, whom he had met on various occasions and remembered well. Eager to be of service to the state, he seemed delighted to learn that all it requested of him was conversation. He asked for a moment to check his calendar and seemed even more delighted to discover that he had a convenient gap in his schedule and could pass by the Questura in an hour. That is, unless it suited the Commissario's convenience that they meet in some other place?

'My office is fine, Avvocato,' Brunetti interrupted the stream of words to say and broke the connection before the lawyer could return to the floodgates. Brunetti had twice been a witness in trials where Beni had appeared for the defence and remembered clearly the feeling he had had, both times, of being suffocated by irrelevant detail. He had been in the courtrooms only briefly, but he had heard enough not to be surprised when both of Beni's clients lost their cases.

Griffoni had opted to remain downstairs with Signorina Elettra, who had started to explain to her the easiest way to access the records of two state agencies which had, until then, proven resistant to all legitimate requests for information on the holding company that owned the company that owned the chain of hotels that had displayed interest in acquiring the gutted factory. As he left the office, the last thing Brunetti had heard was Griffoni, saying, 'It's like one of those Russian dolls, isn't it? There's always something else inside.'

Brunetti went to the window and stared down at the water of the canal and, not for the first time, began to ask himself what in heaven's name he had been doing for the last week. He had not broken any laws, he had not lied to any of the people he had spoken to, he had not subverted the cause of justice in any way. But he had also not learned anything significant about Davide Cavanella. His mother was a liar, his doctor knew more about him than he was willing to say, an old woman knew probably even more but would not say what that was, and the daughter of his mother's former employer lived in a buffered world where she didn't have to know or say anything and was probably paying her way out of having to.

To learn this little, he had avoided his professional responsibilities for a week, and had engaged or commandeered the help of other officers of the state, all in pursuit of what was becoming to seem like nothing more than a whim. And now he was about to drag in another member of the public but one who – unlike everyone else he had spoken to – was knowledgeable enough about the law to realize that his questions were not part of an authorized investigation.

He could easily go downstairs when Borsetta came in and tell him that the question he had wanted to discuss with him had been resolved, thank him for his civic-mindedness, and send him on his way. And he could then decide to forget about those forty and more years of monthly payments to the account of Ana Cavanella and what they might mean. Or he could threaten Beni Borsetta and wring him dry.

'Commissario?' someone asked from the door of his office, and he turned to see Avvocato Cresti, today without his briefcase though most decidedly with his paunch and his air of self-satisfaction.

'Ah, Avvocato,' Brunetti said with an easy smile. 'How exemplary a model of civic duty you present. Do come in and have a seat.'

Made nervous by this effulgent goodwill, Cresti crossed the room towards Brunetti, who stood and leaned across his desk to shake hands. He waved towards a chair and Cresti sat. The chair had armrests, and Cresti fitted easily within them, leading Brunetti to realize that the man was larger front to back than side to side. He smiled and took a closer look at the lawyer: his shoulders were actually quite narrow, narrower than his own. A portrait bust or a painting would show a perfectly normal man in late middle age, with a thinning patch of greyish hair, none too clean and perhaps too long, brushed back from a long, thin face.

He must buy his clothing ready-made – always an error on the part of a man with a paunch as vast as Cresti's, Brunetti thought, for his jacket gaped open at least three hands' breadths and left his paunch free to pull at the buttons of his shirt.

Brunetti gave Cresti his most benign smile but said nothing. Silence apparently made the lawyer nervous: he wrapped his fingers around the armrests of the chair, released them, then grabbed them again. Brunetti, smile nailed to his face, studied the other man. His face was quite thin and looked out of place above that girth: had Cresti's neck been a metre long, he would have looked very much like an ostrich, his head disproportionately small in relation to his body.

The silence proved too much for the lawyer, and he launched himself. 'I'm very glad to be of service to you, Commissario, for whatever's necessary. Lawyers, as I'm sure you know – you studied law, I believe – have a heightened respect for the law. In fact, I'm sure that this bond between us will aid us in establishing a mutually helpful and productive relationship.'

He paused to breathe and Brunetti forgot his smile and asked, 'What have you been telling Signora Cavanella?'

'Who?' Cresti asked, as stupid a mistake as he could have made, and Brunetti knew he would have no trouble wringing him dry.

Brunetti ignored his question. Cresti must have realized he had made a tactical error, for he asked, 'Ah, do you mean Ana Cavanella?' He smiled. It was an automatic smile, utterly humourless, that he could flick on and off, and did, without response to any sort of stimulus.

Brunetti permitted himself a small nod. This conversation was private and could never be introduced as evidence, so he did not have to speak for the tape recorder and could use gestures if he chose.

'Yes. She's an old friend of mine,' Cresti said with another automatic smile.

'I see,' Brunetti said. 'When did you last see her?'

'Before I answer that,' Cresti said, with one of his flashsmiles, 'could you tell me what it is you want to know about her?'

'I want to know when she last saw you.'

Just like Signora Cavanella, though with a great deal more certainty that he could calculate the response to various answers, Cresti prepared an answer. 'I'm not sure. It's been some time.'

'You were seen in the hospital, Avvocato, coming from her room. Only a few hours ago.' He watched Cresti move some pieces around on the board of his mind and volunteered, 'Perhaps you were so troubled by seeing her there that all memory of your visit has been driven from your mind?'

Cresti nodded. 'Yes, that's it exactly. I saw her this morning.'

'And were shocked, I assume.'

'Yes.'

'But you remember what you talked about, I'm sure. After all, you were there as her lawyer.'

Cresti moved uncomfortably in his chair, as if the arms had begun to contract. 'Not exactly as her lawyer, you understand, Commissario. More as a friend who might be able to give her some legal advice.' As if startled by that last word, Cresti jumped a little in his chair and said, too quickly, 'Legal information, that is.'

Brunetti nodded, and the lawyer went on. 'I was there as a friend, please understand: only that. It never occurred to either of us that I would work for her in a professional sense.' Brunetti was suddenly aware that Cresti was speaking for the tape recorder he assumed was running. 'Only out of my affection for the woman, please understand.' He flashed a smile that was meant to show his integrity and goodwill.

'You're also a neighbour, aren't you, Avvocato?' Brunetti asked, having noticed the San Polo address when Signorina Elettra printed out the information he had asked her for.

'Am I?' Cresti asked. 'How very coincidental.'

Now, why should he lie about that? Brunetti asked himself. He remembered the unified silence of her neighbours and began to wonder what information they were all so eager to protect.

'Shall I look in *Calli, Campielli e Canali* and remind you of just how close you live to her, or do you perhaps recall having seen her?' Brunetti's voice echoed his diminishing patience.

'Yes, I do remember seeing her, now that you mention it,' the lawyer said. 'But only occasionally, the way one does.' Brunetti saw that Cresti was holding the arms of the chair as tightly as if he were trying to keep himself from being spilled from his seat in the middle of a storm at sea.

'So you knew her history?'

'Well, everyone in the neighbourhood does,' Cresti said, aiming to sound casual, and failing.

'And if I might inquire into your professional dealings

with Signora Cavanella,' Brunetti began. 'That is, your work for her as her lawyer . . .'

'But I'm not her lawyer,' Cresti said with another strained smile. 'I'm just trying to help the poor woman. She lost her son, you know.' Cresti's voice was rich with an actor's pathos.

'I know. Did she come to you about that?'

'Well,' Cresti began nervously, 'yes and no.' Seeing that Brunetti was not satisfied with this, he continued, 'That is, she came to me before he died.'

'Asking you to work as her lawyer?' Brunetti asked.

'No.' Cresti's lie was adamant. 'She came to me as a neighbour and asked if I could give her some information, being as I was a lawyer.'

'But not then working as one,' Brunetti supplied ruthlessly, to let Cresti understand how much he knew.

'Right, exactly right. I'd never tell a person I could act for them, not until my suspension is over and I'm taken back into the union of lawyers.' Avvocato Cresti, exemplar of justice.

'What did she want to know?'

'About bastards.'

'What, specifically, about bastards?'

'She'd read something in the papers, and she asked me about a new law.'

'Which law?'

'The one from last year, that says bastards are entitled to an equal share of their father's estate.'

27

'Ah,' Brunetti said, fighting to hide his astonishment. Uncertain that he could keep his voice level, he pursed his lips and frowned, as if making note of a detail that might be interesting, or might not be.

'Do you remember when this conversation took place?'

He watched as Cresti worked out the time, assuming a bland look of infinite patience while he waited for the lawyer to answer.

'It must have been in July some time. I remember because I'd gone out to try to find a birthday gift for my mother, and I met Signora Cavanella on the street.'

Brunetti had smiled amiably at Cresti's mention of his mother, as though he'd done something special and virtuous by having one. 'That's when she asked you?'

Cresti nodded a few more times than necessary. 'Yes, she suggested we have a coffee, and she told me she'd read something in the paper a few days before about this law, and she wanted to know what it meant.'

'What did you tell her?' Brunetti asked, now in full possession of his voice and with the conversation where he wanted it to be.

'I told her it was quite simple: if the child could prove his parentage, then he or she had full rights to an equal portion of the estate. Along with the legitimate children.' Cresti flashed a smile at Brunetti.

'That's all?'

'For once, Commissario,' Cresti said, 'it is a law that is quite concise and easy to understand.'

'Did she understand your explanation?'

'I think it would be difficult' – flash, flash – 'for anyone not to understand.'

'Did she ask you anything else?'

Cresti made the mistake of fidgeting in his chair so that he could remove his eyes from Brunetti's and look down as he did so.

'Did she ask you anything else, Signor Cresti?' Brunetti asked again, hoping that his failure to refer to him by his professional title would remind Cresti of what might happen if Brunetti were to alert the union of lawyers to Cresti's visit to the hospital.

'Oh, a few things,' he said, as if allergic to telling a policeman anything important.

'Did she ask you anything else?'

Trapped, Cresti said, 'She asked if it would pass to the heirs of the child.' Then, after another nervous smile, 'You know, if the heir – the bastard, that is – had a child, would that child inherit?'

Calm, calm, calm. Brunetti asked, as if intrigued by the chance to speculate, 'That's an interesting question. Would it, as it were, skip a generation and pass to the next?'

'That's it exactly, phrased perfectly, Commissario: if the bastard had a child – would it pass to that child?'

'What did you tell her?'

'I couldn't tell her anything. I hadn't studied the law, so I didn't know the answer.'

'What did you tell her?'

Cresti smoothed his hair back and left his hand at the base of his skull, as if to encourage his brain to come up with an answer. 'I couldn't answer, could I, since I wasn't sure?'

'What did you tell her?'

Cresti took his hand away and locked his fingers on the arm of his chair. 'I told her that it probably would pass to the child's heirs.'

Stupidity and greed, Brunetti told himself, stupidity and greed, and a willing helper in a lawyer who took advantage of the first to nudge his non-client towards the second.

'I see,' Brunetti said. Then, because he couldn't stop himself, even though he knew there was no sense in doing so, he asked, 'What did you think when her son died?'

Cresti flashed another smile, but this one was meant to show his surprise at Brunetti's question. 'I thought how unfortunate she was.' His voice deepened into the solemnity so often used to give voice to grief and the tragedies to which the world exposes us, poor, frail humans that we are. 'The poor woman, to lose her only child like that.'

'And she his only relative,' Brunetti could not stop himself from answering. He got to his feet. 'Thank you for coming in, Signor Cresti. I'll call you if we need any further information.'

Cresti's face went blank with genuine surprise. He was being let go. He had said what he had said, and this man was letting him leave. He started to push himself to his feet, but one of the pockets of his jacket hooked itself on the arm of the chair. His upward motion pulled the chair from the floor, then the pocket ripped free. Cresti lost his footing for a moment, flailed his arms in the air, and regained his balance.

Brunetti stood behind his desk, unwilling to help, nodded when Cresti said goodbye, and watched the lawyer leave the room.

He picked up his phone and dialled Signorina Elettra's number. When she answered, he said, 'Could you have a look at Signora Cavanella's bank statements again and tell me the date when those payments arrive?'

Responding to the tone of his voice, she said only 'One moment.' He looked at his watch and saw that today was the fifth.

She was back. 'It usually arrives on the first of the month, Commissario.'

'Has it come this month?'

A few seconds' delay, and then she said, 'No, it hasn't.'

He thanked her and replaced the phone.

All that remained was to talk to Lucrezia Lembo again, but this time he wanted to do it himself: no rosary, no Madonna, no religious excess of any sort. He wanted numbers and dates and facts, and she would be able to give them to him.

He walked. It was late afternoon, the day was drawing down, and it looked as if it was coming on to rain. As he passed the *campi* and buildings between the Questura and the Accademia Bridge, which was the only place where he could cross the Grand Canal and backtrack to her home, Brunetti constructed a narrative based on random facts and even more random possibilities. When he checked the report from the crew that took Signora Cavanella to the hospital, he had seen, but not then noted, that she had been found on the steps of a house only a few minutes from the Lembo *palazzo*. The payment into her account had not arrived this month. Ana Cavanella had ceased working for the Lembo family four decades ago and had received a monthly payment since that time. She lived in a house owned by a member of the Lembo family in which her child had the right to remain for the duration of his lifetime. The King of Copper had left his wife of thirty-four years for a younger woman, by whom he had a child, another girl, only to have the woman leave him soon after the death of that child.

Lucrezia was the only one left: her parents were dead, her half-sister had drowned, and her other sister had moved to a foreign country. Signora Ghezzi had said all she was going to say, Ana Cavanella was not to be trusted to tell the truth, and poor silent Davide couldn't tell it, even if he had known what truth was.

Brunetti heard the rain before he saw it, heard it in the squelching of his feet on the pavement. He heard it, he saw it, and when he put his hands to his head, he felt it. Sure enough, at the bottom of the Accademia Bridge he found three Tamil umbrella sellers – he often wondered if they were freeze-dried and popped back to life at the first drop of rain, their hands laden with five-Euro umbrellas. He committed a crime by buying an umbrella from one of them, gave the man ten Euros and told him to keep the change, then turned down towards the Salute. In Campo San Vio he turned right, and then into the *calle*.

He rang the bell, keeping his finger on it until he heard it bleating away inside. He removed it. Silence. He pushed it again, shifted his feet to make himself more comfortable while leaning against it. The noise went on for a very long time. At last he heard a sound from the courtyard, released his finger, and the noise turned into the sound of footsteps approaching the door.

A woman's voice said something from inside, and Brunetti ignored it. The door was pulled open by Lucrezia

Lembo, who seemed not at all surprised to see him there. 'You've come for me, then?' she asked, sounding far more lucid than she had the last time he spoke to her.

'I've come to talk to you, Signora,' he declared; a statement, not a request.

Without protest, she turned away, leaving the door open, and he stepped into the courtyard. She led him back towards the entrance, then upstairs, but this time to the kitchen, a room with windows on the canal; like the other room, this one was spotlessly clean. Brunetti stopped just inside the door.

She could have been a different person. Her hair was clean, and she was dressed in a very conservative skirt, sweater, and light woollen jacket. Her low pumps were the sort, and of the same high quality, Paola wore when she went to teach. She was no longer fat, only robust.

She went to the counter in front of the row of windows that looked across the canal to the shuttered windows of the building opposite. She turned and leaned back against the counter. 'Sit if you please, Signore.'

Brunetti approached the table, hearing the noise his shoes made on the marble floor. She took his umbrella and placed it in the sink behind her. Because it would give her the advantage, Brunetti pulled out a chair and lowered himself into it.

'Have you come to arrest me?' she asked.

'For what, Signora?'

It looked as though she had had a good night's sleep. He reminded himself that she might just as easily have found the right combination of alcohol or drugs, but it did not seem that way to him.

'To the best of my knowledge, there is no reason to arrest you, Signora.' He saw her eyes widen, and then her face relaxed even more. 'Nor is it my desire, Signora.'

'Then why are you here?'

'To talk about your father.'

'Father?' She lowered her head and shook it, and when she raised it again, she was smiling at him, as if at his innocence in saying such a thing.

'Ludovico Lembo, once Fadalti, also known as the King of Copper,' Brunetti said.

'What do you want to know about him, Signore?'

'Is he the father of Ana Cavanalla's son?'

'Davide?'

'Yes.'

'Yes, he is. Or was.'

'Have you been paying for Davide's upkeep?'

'Yes.'

'Is the house in San Polo where he lived yours?'

'Yes, it is. It was left to me by the same man.'

'Ludovico Lembo?'

'Once called Fadalti. Yes.'

'And Davide had the *usufrutto* of that house?'

'Until his death. Yes.'

All of these things, Brunetti knew, save for the first, were matters of public record. 'Was Ana Cavanella black-mailing you, Signora?'

'What?' she asked with honest surprise.

'Was she blackmailing you?'

'About what?'

'The name of Davide's father?'

'Why should she do that?' Lucrezia asked.

'To keep other people – your mother, perhaps – from finding out.'

This time she shook her head, as if he had told her something too ridiculous to believe but was afraid of hurting his feelings if she laughed.

'Finding out what?'

'I don't know,' Brunetti said honestly. With this family, no possibility could be excluded. Then, not admitting to himself that he was irritated by her air of knowing something he did not, he said, 'I know your mother learned about her pregnancy.'

She turned away, but it was only to open a cabinet behind her and lift down a glass, then another one. She turned on the water in the sink and filled them both, placed one in front of him and drank half of her own. She kept her glass in her hands; Brunetti pulled his closer to him but did not drink.

'Tell me your name again, please. I'm afraid I wasn't myself the last time you were here.'

'Brunetti,' he said, relieved to learn that she remembered the other visit.

'And the name of your rather excitable colleague?' she asked.

'Griffoni.'

'Ah. Yes.' And then, 'Signor Brunetti, I think you and I have some of the same information. But it means different things to us.' She sipped at her water.

When Brunetti judged that she was not going to say anything else, he said, 'The payments to her, from your account. If they are not blackmail, what are they?'

'Just what you said, money for his upkeep. Enough to let the two of them live.'

'And the use of the house they were living in?'

'The same. The attempt on the part of a very decent man to see that his son did not live in misery.'

'You mean your father?'

'Ludovico Lembo, formerly Fadalti.'

Her tone told him. 'Who is or who is not your father?' Brunetti asked.

'Who is not my father, nor my sister Lavinia's father,

259

but was the father of his companion's daughter Ludovica and of Davide, Ana Cavanella's son.'

'You say that very lightly, Signora,' Brunetti risked observing.

'You're sadly mistaken, Signor Brunetti,' she said. 'I say it with more pain than you will ever be able to understand.' Another sip of water. 'But we were raised in a very hard school, my sister and I, and we are not much given to lamentation or complaint.'

'Raised by whom?'

'By my mother and her cousin.'

'Sister Maria Rosaria Lembo-Malfa?' Brunetti inquired, unable to stop himself from showing off.

'Exactly. She and my mother. Cousins united in their service and devotion to Christ. Except . . .'

'Except what, Signora?'

'Except that my mother's devotion was perhaps not characterized by the same purity as was her cousin's.'

Brunetti was suddenly tired of her and her posturing and her speaking in allusion and riddles. He almost preferred her drunken excesses. 'Could you speak more clearly, Signora? It would save us both time and effort.'

He saw her surprise, but then her amusement. 'How refreshing, to be spoken to directly. I thank you for it, Signore. I've seen very little of it in my life.'

He believed her. 'Then tell me, but don't tell it slant.'

'My mother did not like my father, and my father did not like my mother. That is, the man I've spent my life calling my father did not like my mother, and my mother did not like the man I've spent my life calling my father.'

'But he married her?'

'He married her because she was pregnant and asked him to marry her.'

'Pregnant by him or some other man?'

'Good heavens: a man like my father would never have had sex before marriage – not with the woman he hoped to marry. It was not done: not if you're an upstart engineer and the girl is the daughter of your boss, and the company is one of the biggest in the country.'

'So he married her to get the business?'

'My father was a businessman before he was anything else. He loved it, loved making things work and loved making money from that.'

'You automatically call him your father,' Brunetti pointed out.

'I loved him. He was a good man and very kind to the two of us. I've never met our real father – at least not knowingly – and so he was the man I loved as my father. Lavinia, too.'

'She wasn't his daughter, either?'

'Haven't I just said that?' she asked and turned to fill her glass.

'Of course, of course,' Brunetti assured her when she was again facing him.

'But were they never . . .' he didn't know how to say it, not while speaking to a lady. 'Were they never really husband and wife?'

'I have no idea of that, and I don't want to know,' she said heatedly, speaking quickly, the faster to have it said. 'They always had separate rooms and separate lives. And my mother went off to see her cousin in the convent every month, didn't she?' she asked, leaving Brunetti to make of that whatever he pleased.

'And then Ana Cavanella came into the *palazzo*,' he said.

'Indeed. She was our age. That is, near to our age. I'm sure the psychiatrists would have a wonderful time with that: talking about his hidden lusts for us. None of which either of us ever detected.'

'How did she behave?'

'I don't know. That is, I don't remember. I was at an age when I found life difficult and revolting.' Then, with a shrug, she added, 'I suppose I still do to a certain degree,' and Brunetti realized he was beginning to like her.

'Does your sister remember?'

'She was at school. In Ireland. With the sisters.'

'I see,' Brunetti said, though he didn't.

'And then Ana became pregnant?' he asked.

'Yes. And my mother went wild. I'd never seen her like that.'

'Jealousy?'

She laughed. 'Hardly. She raged on about the insult to her honour, to her family.'

'What happened?'

'Ana left.'

'And the house and the payments?'

'My father bought the house in my name. I was nineteen then, and he asked me if I'd do it for him: allow for the *usufrutto* and allow the payments to go in my name. I signed the papers: he was a good man.'

Brunetti picked up the glass and drank some of the water. He could not reconcile this conservatively dressed and clearly spoken woman with the raving wreck they had met the day before. He had a growing suspicion that this woman had outwitted them, and the victim of deceit had been Griffoni.

'Why did you think I was here to arrest you, Signora?'

'Because of what I did to Ana Cavanella.'

'You mean hitting her?'

'Is that what she says?' she asked, unable to hide her surprise.

'No. Would you tell me what happened?'

'She came here two days ago, and I let her in. I didn't

recognize her: forty years is a long time. She had to tell me who she was. That's when I let her in.'

'What happened?'

'She told me that her son was dead. And I told her I knew that.

'She came because she'd received a letter from my lawyer, telling her that the death of her son Davide changed the nature of our existing fiscal relationship. She came to ask me what that meant.'

'Did you explain it to her?'

With something close to irritation, Lucrezia said, 'I don't know why lawyers can't say things clearly. Just tell her there would be no more money. And she'd have to leave the house.' She looked across at Brunetti. 'I tried to explain it to her, but I don't think she understood. Or didn't want to. I told her my obligation was to Davide, not to her.'

Curious as he was at her use of the word, 'obligation', Brunetti said nothing.

'She got angry and said the family couldn't lie about him any more, or about her.' She followed that with a puff of incredulity and went on. 'I told her she was nothing to me and told her to leave, but she said Davide was my half-brother and was entitled to a third of my father's estate.'

She made a shivering motion. 'She'd read something about the law that was passed last year, and she said there was proof.'

'Proof of what?'

'That my father – that is, my mother's husband – was also Davide's father. And then when I told her there could be no proof, she said something about what she called DNU. I didn't understand at first what she was talking about, and then she said it was the proof in the body, in the blood, that people were related.'

'DNA,' Brunetti whispered and breathed a silent prayer to be delivered from the hands of the ignorant.

'Yes. DNA. God knows where she got the information. She didn't understand anything, but she kept talking about the DNU test and that it would prove he was Davide's father. I told her to go ahead and try to prove it.'

'Did you tell her anything else?'

'No. She wouldn't stop talking, and then she was shouting. We were still standing at the door. I opened it and told her to get out: we'd been talking in the courtyard all this time. I didn't want her in the house. She kept shouting that she deserved to be helped, and I told her all she deserved was to be put away in jail or an institution.' Lucrezia's emotions overcame her, and she stopped, breathing heavily.

'I raised my hand to her. It frightened her. I grabbed her shoulders, shoved her out into the *calle* and slammed the door in her face before she could come back in. Then I went into the house.' She smiled then, speaking to Brunetti as though he were an old friend. 'I have to confess I've never enjoyed anything so much in my life.'

'In her face?'

'I meant it figuratively,' she said. 'She stood out there, howling like a hyena. It must have been ten minutes. But then it stopped. She went away.'

She finished her glass of water and placed it behind her on the counter.

'What did you mean about her belonging in prison or in an institution?'

In that same, easy voice, still speaking to a friend, she said, 'For what she did to Davide.'

'What did she do?'

Her eyes widened. 'You mean you don't know? I thought everyone in the neighbourhood knew.'

'I don't know what you're talking about, Signora.'

'Really?'

'Really.'

'About the room?'

'What room?'

'Oh my God,' she said, honestly stricken. 'I swear by my father's memory I thought you knew, that you'd found out from the people in the neighbourhood.'

'I don't know anything, Signora,' Brunetti said, feeling the profound truth of this.

She leaned forward and put her palms flat on the table, thumbs barely touching, and she looked at them as she spoke. It took her a long time to find the energy to continue speaking. 'When my father told her she had to leave our home, she refused, and when he said he'd make sure she and the baby were taken care of, all she said was that she'd take care of the baby.' She stopped, and swallowed twice. Then she pulled out a chair and sat, facing him.

'We didn't know what she meant. At first she went and lived in the house, but then she disappeared. Later, she came back to live with her mother. And she got some sort of job, but I think that was only to keep her out of the house.'

'And the mother?'

'She helped her.'

'With what?'

Her hands gave the only indication, beyond her voice, of her emotions. The fingers contracted into fists, and the veins on the back of her hands stood out.

'They didn't talk.'

'What do you mean?'

'They didn't talk to the baby. To the boy. He was there. Maybe she even had him there and no one ever knew.

He lived in a room, and they fed him and cleaned him – I suppose. But they didn't talk to him. That's what she meant when she said she'd take care of the baby.'

She looked up then. 'Don't think she's crazy, Signore. She's not. She's bad. They both were.'

'How long did this go on?'

'Years, a decade or more. Then the old woman left or died or disappeared. I don't know. I was busy making a ruin of my own life: I had no time to pay attention to hers. Theirs.'

'How did you learn all of this?'

'Signora Ghezzi. But not until years later.' Brunetti fabricated a confused shake of his head. 'My mother's maid. She had friends in that neighbourhood, and she heard the talk. Nothing certain, only rumours. No one wanted to get involved. No one had the courage to interfere in what she was doing. No one trusted the police.'

She pushed herself to her feet, then sat down again. 'And one day the old woman was gone and the boy was there, her son, her disabled and retarded son. She told people he had been raised by relatives in the country; even then no one dared to ask questions.'

'And you kept paying?'

'My father did. Through my account. When he died, I kept paying. I'd promised him that.'

'Did he know about the boy?'

'What she did to him?'

Unable to say the word, Brunetti nodded.

'No one ever had the courage. He had moved to the Giudecca by then.' She paused and gazed into the middle distance. 'He might have killed her if he had known. Davide was his only son, you know.'

She met his gaze. 'If you do the research, you'll find

out that's what happens. If you don't talk to them, that is. They're like animals. Like Davide.'

Then she rose to her feet, saying, 'I think that's enough, don't you?'

He did. He left.

28

Brunetti let himself out, being especially careful to close the door to the apartment very quietly, descend the steps with the silence of a wraith, cross the courtyard and emerge into the *calle* with thief-like care. It was still raining, but he did not notice until he was back at the Accademia, when he bought another umbrella from another Tamil.

Since his shoes were soaked through, he decided to walk. Plod, more like, but he thought of it as walking. Not talked to, not spoken to, no language, no contact, no words, no communication, no meaning, no sense to anything, no words to think in, no names for things. Nothing more terrible. No way to sort it all out; no way to distinguish between the sound of a dog and the words of a lullaby; 'yes' sounding the same as 'no', and both words the same as 'upside down'.

He stopped at the door to their building. His pocket was sodden, the keys colder than he had ever known them to be. Tonight there were three hundred steps to the apartment. He closed the umbrella and dropped it outside the door, let himself in, kicked off his shoes, and bent to put them out on the landing. There were sounds from the kitchen: words, phrases: 'he's such a good . . .' 'she never says what . . .', 'five more minutes'. They all meant something, those snatches. Those words created the possibility for larger categories or for larger, more encompassing ideas. Praise, criticism, time.

He went into the bathroom and shed his clothing, socks first, draping them all, sodden and dark, on the edge of the bathtub. He wanted to take a shower, but resisted the desire and merely wiped at his hair with a towel, draping that next to his shirt. He put on his terry-cloth robe and went down the hall to their room. He found an old pair of woollen slacks he had refused for years to allow Paola to throw away. He took comfort from their familiar, shapeless softness. He pulled on a T-shirt and an old green cashmere sweater he had saved time and time again from her discarding impulses. He pulled on socks and slipped his feet into leather slippers.

He went down the corridor and into the kitchen. At his entrance, Chiara said, 'Your hair's a mess, *Papà*. Come over here and let me fix it for you.' She hopped to her feet and Brunetti sat in her chair, amazed at the way 'fix' was just right for this sentence, even though hair couldn't be fixed, probably because it couldn't be broken, but when hair was a mess, it could be set right again by being fixed, just as though it were broken, and wasn't that an amazingly flexible thing to do with words?

Chiara spread her fingers and ran them through his still-wet hair, brushing at it repeatedly until she had it looking more or less the way it was supposed to look. When he didn't say anything, she snaked her way around his shoulders and pulled her face close to his. 'What's the matter, cat got your tongue?' she asked in English.

How remarkable that it happened in different languages, too, and that phrases could have two meanings. Obviously, there was no cat biting his tongue, but it was a wonderful metaphor for a motionless tongue. Like Davide's.

'Just thinking,' he said and smiled round at them all.

'What about?' Paola asked. Raffi was interested, but he was more interested in his risotto.

'About a joke my mother told me when I was a kid. I wouldn't eat carrots one night, and she told me that carrots were good for my eyes.'

Chiara slapped her hands over her ears, knowing what was coming. Paola sighed; Raffi ate.

'When I asked her how she knew that, she asked me if . . .' and he paused to give them time to join in the chorus, as they did every time he told this story . . . 'I'd ever seen a rabbit wearing glasses.' Sure enough, they all joined in with his mother's question, her mother-in-law's question, their grandmother's question, and Brunetti was left marvelling that his mother could have all those different names.

He ate the rest of the dinner, though he didn't know what it was he was eating. He drank a glass of wine, left the second one unfinished, drunk with the words that crossed the table, their different meanings, the fact that they indicated time: future and past; that they indicated whether something had been done or was still to do; that they expressed people's feelings: anger was not a blow, regret was not tears. At one point, Paola expressed a wish and used the subjunctive, and Brunetti felt himself close to tears at the beauty of the intellectual complexity of it: she could speak about what was not, could invent an alternative reality.

He began to return to the real world with dessert, helped

in the descent by a cake topped with red plums. As Paola cut a second slice and put it on his plate, he asked her, 'Do you think God is language?'

Raffi was having none of this. He held up a forkful of cake. 'God is plum cake,' he said and took communion.

Later, he sprawled on the sofa in Paola's study and told her all about it, every detail, starting with his first conversation with Ana Cavanella and finishing with his quiet exit from the Lembo *palazzo*.

Paola sat in stunned silence for a long time and then did what she could to fight her way back to human understanding: she talked about what she had read. 'There's Kaspar Hauser, and there's that girl in the United States. I've read about them, and I've read a bit of the theory.'

She looked his way, and he nodded. 'They're pretty much agreed – the people who write about this – that if you don't learn language by about twelve, then the wiring is formed in your brain without language and you've missed the chance, and you'll never get it, never understand how it works.'

'Talking?' he asked.

'Language. The concept of it. That a noise can equal a thing, or an action.'

'Or an idea,' Brunetti added. 'Or a colour.'

'She would have been less a monster if she had poked out his eyes,' Paola said with sudden ferocity. 'He would still have been human.'

'Don't you think he was?'

'Of course he was,' she said. 'But he wasn't like us.'

'Is that rhetorical exaggeration?'

'I suppose so,' she admitted. 'But he really wasn't. He'd never understand what we do. Or what anything meant.'

'You think he understood other things?' Brunetti asked,

not knowing fully what he meant by that, but thinking of those drawings.

'Of course.' She ran her hands across her face and through her hair. 'It's so hard to talk about this without sounding like the worst sort of eugenic monster, placing different values on different people.'

'Or defining what people are by what they can do?' Brunetti suggested.

'Can we go to bed now?' she asked like a petulant child.

'I think we'd better. We can't answer any of these questions.'

'Neither of us was asking questions,' she said.

For a moment, Brunetti thought he'd contest that, but he was too tired for it. Instead, he said, 'Besides, there aren't any answers.'

They went to bed, and the next day dawned bright, but much colder.

Well, he'd gone this far, animated by nothing more noble than curiosity, he told himself as he studied the face of the man in the mirror, pushing his collar down over his neatly knotted tie. The man's mind slipped into English: The cat's got your tongue. Curiosity killed the cat. To stay in vein, the man in the mirror gave a Cheshire smile, and Brunetti left the house.

He could have gone anywhere. Because he was a commissario and there was little crime in the city at the moment, he probably could have got on a boat and gone out to the Lido to walk on the beach, but he walked the same old, familiar old, *calli* to the hospital and went to Geriatria, where his mother – she too having lost her mooring to language during her long descent – had once spent some months. Things looked cleaner, but the smell was the same.

He went in without knocking and found Ana Cavanella sitting in an orange plastic chair, staring out the window. A woman attached to a number of plastic tubes, like a ship unloading liquid cargo while taking on fuel at the same time, lay in the other bed, sailing on some other sea, not docked there with them.

Cavanella looked up at him, face impassive and unfriendly. The left side was almost black, darkest at the point on her forehead where the closing door had hit her.

Brunetti went and stood with his back to the window so at least what little light there was would shine on her face and into her eyes. 'I've spoken to Lucrezia Lembo,' he said.

'About me?' she asked.

'The Signora and I have nothing else in common.'

'You're a policeman: what interest can you have in me?'

'I'm curious about how you plan to prove it.'

'Prove what?' she asked, but her eyes slid across to the sleeping woman.

'That Ludovico Lembo was Davide's father.'

She was silent for a long time, and he watched her search for a way to answer him.

He watched her fight the desire to show him that she was clever, too. She lost. 'There's that test. DNU.' She still hadn't learned, yet she allowed herself the self-satisfied smile of the dullest student who believed she knew something the others didn't.

'And what will that prove?'

'That he is. The father. Because of his other children. They can match them. It's scientific.'

He decided not to tell her yet and, instead, asked, 'And if no judge will order the test? After all, anyone can make that claim about any rich man, can't they?' To himself at least, his question sounded entirely reasonable.

She gave it long thought, consulted with the somnolent woman in the bed, with the tops of the pine trees that rose up from the courtyard below. 'Really?' she asked, just as though she believed she could ask him to work in her best interests and suggest some other outcome.

'You need stronger evidence.'

She tried, and failed, to repress a smile. He marvelled that he had ever seen signs of beauty in this face. 'I have a letter,' she said.

'From him.'

'His lawyer wrote to tell me about the house and about the money.' To show her expertise, she added, 'It's dated, too,' and could not repress a smile. Then, her voice a mixture of anger and self-satisfaction, 'Any judge would believe that. People don't give money away unless you force them.'

He'd let her go on believing for a while yet. 'And you're Davide's heir, aren't you?' he asked as if the thought had just come to him.

'Yes.'

'First it goes to his estate, and then it passes to you?'

'Yes.' She was incapable of disguising how excited she was by this possibility, which to her was a fact. The right side of her face flushed pink at the thought: the other side remained close to black.

'And the house and the money in the bank?'

'That doesn't matter now, does it?' she asked, speaking with what life had taught her was the arrogance of wealth. A house with no rent to pay, three thousand Euros a month: these had suddenly become small change to the likes of Ana Cavanella, soon to be the heiress to one third of an immense inheritance. What did such paltry things mean to the mother of the son and heir of the King of Copper?

'His death was very unfortunate,' Brunetti said.

It was clear that she didn't know who Brunetti was talking about, her son or her son's father. But her face soon found a pious expression that suited both, and she said, 'Yes. Very.'

'But fortunate, in a way,' Brunetti encouraged her. 'Davide never would have appreciated all that money.'

She tried to suppress her smile and managed it after only an instant, but the sight of her teeth had been enough to seize Brunetti with the desire to strike her. He took a small step back, but it was to distance himself from her physically, not from the temptation of violence, which had only flashed through him, leaving him shocked.

'I could have bought him so many things,' she said with falsity so palpable Brunetti was amazed the woman in the other bed didn't wake up screaming.

'A radio, for instance,' Brunetti suggested.

'But he was deaf.'

'Was he, Signora?'

'What do you mean?'

There it was again, that question that was really an answer. 'I mean there was nothing wrong with his ears. With his hearing, that is. The autopsy showed that.'

'I don't understand.'

'Everyone in the neighbourhood understands, Signora.'

He watched her move from idea to idea, excuse to excuse, pose to pose. She couldn't ask him again what he meant, so she settled on an angry noise instead of words.

'They know, Signora.'

'They don't know anything,' she hissed.

'And once you make your claim to the inheritance, they'll know about what happened to Davide, too. And if it comes to law, they'll learn about the hot chocolate and biscuits he had, along with the little yellow candies.'

This time, one half of her face went white while the

other remained suffused with the signs of the blow. She tried to speak, to give voice to the indignation she knew she was supposed to show, but she failed, tried again, choking with rage. Choking. He was conscious of that. Finally she managed to spit it out: 'It doesn't matter. Let them think what they want.'

A loud noise came from behind him; when Brunetti turned, he saw an immensely tall building crane slam a metal ball into the remaining wall of one of the old hospital buildings alongside the *laguna*. A piece of wall crumbled to the pile of rubble below, and an enormous cloud of white dust climbed up the wall that remained. Through the new opening, Brunetti saw, across the water, the wall of the cemetery and the tower of the church behind it, the tips of the peaceful cypress trees.

Brunetti decided not to tell her. Let her follow Beni Borsetta's advice and demand a 'DNU' test. And please let some compassionate judge grant it to her, and let Lucrezia and – if she ever appeared – Lavinia give a sample of their DNU, and let the test show that their father was not the father of Ana Cavanella's child. And let her live with that: with no home and no monthly cheque and with former neighbours, he hoped, pushed past the point of tolerance and the acceptance of what can't be proven and needing a way to punish someone for their own guilt. And without her son. Though nothing he had seen so far suggested that this would bother her much.

Wasting no more words on her Brunetti left the hospital to go and get the boat to the Lido to go for a walk on the beach.

Read on for the first chapter of Donna Leon's next
Commissario Guido Brunetti mystery
ISBN: 978-0-8021-2264-3

On Sale April 1, 2014

1

It had been a tedious Monday, much of it spent with the written witness statements about a fight between two taxi drivers that had sent one of them to the hospital with concussion and a broken right arm. The statements had been made by the American couple who had asked the concierge of their hotel to call a water taxi to take them to the airport; the concierge, who said he had called one of the taxi drivers the hotel always used; the porter, who said he had done nothing more than his job, which was to put the Americans' luggage into the taxi that had pulled up to the dock; and the two taxi drivers, one of whom had been questioned in the hospital. From what Brunetti could make of the various stories, the driver from the usual company was nearby when he received the call from the concierge, but when he arrived at the hotel, another taxi was docked at the landing. He pulled up, called out the name of the Americans, which the concierge had given him, and said he was to take them to the airport. The other driver said the porter had waved to him as he was passing, so it was his fare. The porter denied this and insisted he was simply helping with the luggage. The driver into whose taxi the porter had put the luggage had somehow found himself on the deck of the other taxi. The Americans were enraged that they had missed their flight.

Brunetti knew, but could not prove, what had happened: the porter had waved to a passing taxi so that he, instead of the concierge, would get a percentage of the fare. The consequences were evident: no one would tell the truth, and the Americans would not understand what had happened.

As he entertained that thought, Brunetti was momentarily deflected from his desire for a coffee and paused to consider whether he had perhaps stumbled upon some cosmic explanation of current world history. He smiled, making a note to repeat the idea to Paola that evening, or better yet, to tell it the following night, when they were invited to dinner at her parents'. He hoped that the Conte, who appreciated paradox, would be amused. He knew his mother-in-law would be.

He abandoned his reverie and continued down the stairs of the Questura, eager for the coffee that would help him through the rest of the afternoon. As he approached the front door, the officer at the switchboard tapped on the window of his tiny cubicle and waved Brunetti towards him. When Brunetti was inside, the guard said into the telephone receiver, 'I think you should talk to the Commissario, Dottoressa. He's in charge.' He passed him the phone.

'Brunetti.'

'You're a commissario?'

'Yes.'

'This is Dottoressa Fabbiani. I'm the chief librarian at the Biblioteca Merula. We've had a theft. A number of them, I think.' Her voice was unsteady, the voice he had heard from victims of muggings or assault.

2

'From the collection?' Brunetti asked. He knew the library, had used it once or twice as a student but had not given it a thought for decades.

'Yes.'

'What's been taken?' he asked, preparing in his mind the other questions that would have to follow her answer.

'We don't know the full extent yet. So far, all I'm sure of is that pages have been cut from some volumes.' He heard her deep intake of breath

'How many?' Brunetti asked, pulling a pad and pencil towards him.

'I don't know. I just discovered it.' Her voice tightened as she spoke.

He heard a man's voice from her end of the phone. She must have turned away to answer him, for her voice grew indistinct for a moment. Then, silence from her end of the line.

He thought of the procedures he had gone through at the libraries in the city whenever he consulted a book and asked, 'You have records of the people who use the books, don't you?'

Was she surprised that a policeman should ask such a question? That he knew about libraries? It certainly took her some time to answer. 'Of course.' Well, that put him in his place, didn't it? 'We're checking on that.'

'Have you found who did it?' Brunetti asked.

There followed an even longer pause. 'A researcher, we think,' she said, then added, as if Brunetti had accused her of negligence, 'He had the proper identification.' He heard the response of any bureaucrat beginning to formulate a defence at the first whisper of an accusation of negligence.

'Dottoressa,' Brunetti began, using what he hoped was his most persuasive and professional voice, 'we'll need your help in identifying him. The sooner we find him, the less time he'll have to sell what he's taken.' He saw no reason to spare her this reality.

'But the books are destroyed,' she said, sounding anguished, as at the death of a loved person.

To a librarian, damage was as bad as theft, he imagined. Changing his voice to that of Authority, he said, 'I'll be there as soon as I can, Dottoressa. Please do not touch anything.' Before she could protest, he added, 'And I'd like to see the identification he gave you.' When there was no response, he replaced the phone.

Brunetti remembered that the library was on the Zattere, but the exact location eluded him now. He returned his attention to the guard and told him, 'If anyone wants me, I've gone to the Biblioteca Merula. Call Vianello and tell him to go over with two men to take fingerprints.'

Outside, he found Foa, arms folded, legs crossed at the ankles, leaning against the railing that ran along the canal. His head was tilted back, and his eyes were closed against the early spring sun, but when Brunetti approached, the pilot asked, 'Where can I take you, Commissario?' before opening his eyes.

'The Biblioteca Merula,' he said.

As if finishing Brunetti's sentence, Foa continued, 'Dorsoduro 3429.'

'How'd you know that?'

'My brother-in-law and his family live in the next building, so that has to be the address,' the pilot answered.

'I feared for a moment that the Lieutenant had made some new rule that obliged you to learn all the addresses in the city by heart.'

'Anyone who's grown up on boats knows where everything in the city is, sir. Better than a GPS,' Foa said, tapping his forehead with his finger. He pushed himself away from the railing and made towards the boat but stopped

4

mid-stride and turned to Brunetti. 'You ever hear what became of them, sir?'

'Of what?' a confused Brunetti asked.

'The GPS's.'

'Which GPS's?'

'The ones that were ordered for the boats,' Foa answered. Brunetti stood still, waiting for the explanation.

'I was talking to Martini a few days ago,' Foa continued, naming the officer in charge of procurement, the man to consult to have a radio fixed or get a new flashlight. 'He showed me the invoice and asked me if I knew whether they were any good or not. The model that had been ordered.'

'And did you?' Brunetti asked, wondering where this conversation had come from.

'Oh, we all know about them, sir. They're crap. None of the taxi drivers wants them, and the only person I know who ever bought one for himself got so mad at it one day that he pulled it off the windscreen of his boat and tossed it over the side.' Foa walked towards the boat, then stopped again and said, 'That's what I told Martini.'

'What did he do?'

'What can he do? They're ordered by some central office in Rome, and someone there gets something for having ordered them, and someone else gets something for letting the order go through.' He shrugged and stepped on to the boat.

Brunetti followed him, puzzled that Foa had chosen to tell him this, for he must have known that there was nothing Brunetti could do, either. That's how things worked.

Foa switched on the motor and said, 'Martini said the invoice was for a dozen of them.' He stressed the amount.

'There are only six boats, aren't there?' Brunetti asked, a question Foa didn't bother to answer.

'How long ago was this, Foa?'

'Couple of months. Some time in the winter, I'd say.'

'You know if they ever got here?' Brunetti asked.

Foa tilted up his chin and made a clicking sound with his tongue: he could have been a street Arab, so much did his gesture remind Brunetti of the way they dismissed the ridiculous.

Brunetti found himself at a familiar crossroads, where he could go forward only to move backward, move sideways to move forward, or just close his eyes and take a comfortable seat and not move at all. If he spoke to Martini and learned that the GPS systems had been ordered and paid for but were nowhere in evidence, he would create trouble for himself. He could begin to look around privately and perhaps prevent further looting of the public purse. Or he could simply ignore it and get on with more important things or with things that might be remedied.

'You think this is the beginning of spring?' he asked the pilot.

Foa glanced aside and smiled: their agreement could not have been more congenial. 'I think it might be, sir. I hope so. I'm sick to death of the cold and fog.'

As they completed their turn into the *bacino* and looked forward again, they both gasped. There was nothing theatrical about it, no attempt to make a scene or a statement. They did no more than express their human response to the otherworldly and impossible. Ahead of them was the stern of one of the newest, largest cruise ships. Its enormous rear end stared bluntly back at them, as if daring them to comment.

Seven, eight, nine, ten storeys. Was this possible? From their perspective, it blocked out the city, blocked out the light, blocked out all thought of sense or reason or the appropriateness of things. They trailed along behind it, watching the wake it created avalanche slowly towards the *rivas* on both sides, tiny wave after tiny wave after tiny wave, and what in God's name was the thrust of that vast expanse of displaced water doing to those stones and to the centuries-old binding that kept them in place? Suddenly the air was unbreathable as a capricious gust blew the ship's exhaust down on them for a few seconds. And then the air was just as suddenly filled with the sweetness of springtime and buds and new leaves, fresh grass and nature's giggly joy at coming back for another show.

They could see, scores of metres above them, people lining the deck, turned like sunflowers to the beauty of the Piazza and the domes and the bell tower. A vaporetto appeared on the other side, coming towards them, and the people on the deck, no doubt Venetians, raised their fists and shook them at the passengers, but the tourists were looking the other way and failed to see the friendly natives. Brunetti thought of Captain Cook, dragged from the surf, killed, cooked, eaten by other friendly natives. 'Good,' he said under his breath.

Not far along the *riva* of the Zattere, Foa pulled the boat to the right, flipped it into reverse and then neutral to let it glide to a stop. He grabbed a mooring rope and jumped up on to the pavement, bent and tied a quick knot. He reached down and grabbed Brunetti's hand to steady him as he made the jump to the pavement.

'This is probably going to take some time,' Brunetti told the pilot. 'You might as well go back.'

But Foa wasn't paying attention: his eyes were on the stern of the ship as it made its slow progress towards the dock at San Basilio. 'I've read,' Brunetti began, speaking Veneziano, 'that no decision can be made about them until all the agencies agree.'

'I know,' Foa answered, his eyes still on the boat. 'Magistrato alle Acque, Regione, junta of the city, Port

Authority, some ministry in Rome ...' He paused, still transfixed as the boat moved farther away, hardly diminishing in size. Then Foa's voice returned, and he named some of the men on these panels.

Brunetti knew many, though not all, of them. When Foa reached the names of three former city officials of the highest rank, he pounded on the pronunciation of each surname like a carpenter hammering the final nails into the lid of a coffin.

'I've never understood why they divided things up like that,' Brunetti said. Foa, after all, came from a family that had lived on and from the *laguna*: fishermen, fishmongers, sailors, pilots and mechanics for ACTV. They had everything except gills, the Foas did. If anyone were to understand the bureaucracy of the waters in and off which the city lived, it would be people like them.

Foa gave him the smile a teacher gives his dullest pupil: affectionate, poignant, superior. 'Do you think eight separate committees are ever going to reach a decision?'

Brunetti looked at the pilot as illumination came. 'And only a joint decision will stop the ships,' he said, a conclusion which caused Foa's smile to broaden.

'So they can consider and reconsider for ever,' the pilot said, in open admiration of the ingenuity of having divided the decision among so many separate governmental organizations. 'Getting their salaries, making inspection tours to other countries to see how things are done there, holding meetings to discuss projects and plans.' Then, mindful of a recent article in *Il Gazzettino*, 'Or hiring their wives and children as consultants.'

'And picking up small gifts that might fall from the table of the companies that own the ships?' Brunetti offered, though he knew as he spoke that this was not the sort of example he was meant to give to the uniformed branch.

8

Foa's smile warmed, but he said only, pointing along the narrow canal, 'Down there, just before the bridge. It's the green door.'

Brunetti waved his thanks for the ride and for the directions. A moment later he heard the motor spring to life, and when he turned he saw the police boat swinging out into the canal in a wide arc that would take it in the direction from which they had come.

Brunetti noticed that the pavement was wet, with large puddles against the walls of the buildings he passed. Curious, he walked back to the edge of the *riva* and looked down at the water, but it was more than half a metre below him. It was low tide, there was no *acqua alta*, and no rain had fallen for days, so the only way the water could have got there was by being washed up by a passing ship. And they were meant to believe, he and the other citizens the administration considered to be imbeciles, that these boats did no damage to the fabric of the city.

Weren't most of the men making these decisions Venetians? Hadn't they been born in the city? Weren't their children in the schools and university? They probably spoke Veneziano during their meetings.

He thought memory would return as he walked towards the library, but it all failed to become familiar to him. Nor could he recall whether the *palazzo* had been Merula's home when he lived in Venice: that was a job for the Archivio Storico, not the police, whose records did not go back a thousand years.

When Brunetti passed through the open green door, he told himself it looked familiar, though what it really looked like was any of the Renaissance courtyards in the city, complete with outside steps leading to the first floor and a metal-capped well. He was drawn to it by the beautifully-preserved carving, still safe inside these walls. Fat pairs of angels supported a family crest he did not recognize. The wings of some of the angels were in need of attention, but the rest of the carving was intact. Sixteenth century, he'd guess, with a garland of carved flowers encircling the well just under the metal lid: he surprised himself by having a strong memory of that, if of little else he saw there.

He started towards the remembered staircase, its broad marble handrail interspersed with the carved heads of lions, each the size of a pineapple. He climbed the stairs, patting the heads of two of the lions. At the top of the first flight, he saw a door and beside it a new brass plaque: 'Biblioteca Merula'.

He stepped inside into coolness. By this time in the afternoon, the day had grown clement and he had begun to regret wearing his woollen jacket, but now he felt the sweat drying across his back.

In the small reception area, a young man with a fashionable two-day beard sat behind a desk, a book open in front of him. He looked at Brunetti and smiled and, when he approached the desk, asked, 'May I help you?'

Brunetti took his warrant card from his wallet and showed it. 'Ah, of course,' the young man said. 'You want Dottoressa Fabbiani, Signore. She's upstairs.'

'Isn't this the library?' Brunetti asked, pointing to the door behind the young man.

'This is the modern collection. The rare books are upstairs. You have to go up another flight.' Seeing Brunetti's confusion, he said, 'Everything was changed around about ten years ago.' Then, with a smile, 'Long before my time.'

'And long after mine,' Brunetti said and returned to the staircase.

In the absence of lions, Brunetti ran his hand along the bevelled marble railing smoothed by centuries of use. At the top, he found a door with a bell to the right. He rang it and, after some time, the door was opened by a man a few years younger than he, wearing a dark blue jacket with copper buttons and a military cut. He was of medium height, thickset, with clear blue eyes and a thin nose that angled minimally to one side. 'Are you the Commissario?' he asked.

'Yes,' Brunetti answered and extended his hand. 'Guido Brunetti.'

The man took it and gave it a quick shake. 'Piero Sartor,' he said. He stepped back to allow Brunetti into what looked like the ticket office of a small, provincial train station. A waist-high wooden counter stood to the left, on it a computer and two wooden trays for papers. A wheeled rack with what seemed to be very old books piled on it was parked against the wall behind the counter.

There might be a computer, which there had not been in the libraries he had used as a student, but the smell was the same. Old paper, old books, had always filled Brunetti with nostalgia for centuries in which he had not lived. They were printed on paper made from old cloth, shredded, pounded, watered down and pounded again and hand-made into large sheets to be printed, then folded and folded again, and bound and stitched by hand: all that effort to record and remember who we are and what we thought, Brunetti mused. He remembered loving the feel and heft of them in his hands, but chiefly he remembered that dry, soft, scent, the past's attempt to make itself real to him.

The man closed the door, pulling Brunetti from his reverie, and turned to him. 'I'm the guard. I found the book.' He tried, but failed, to keep the pride out of his voice.

'The damaged one?' Brunetti asked.

'Yes, sir. That is, I brought the book down from the reading room, and when Dottoressa Fabbiani opened it, she saw that pages had been cut out.' His pride was replaced by indignation and something close to anger.

11

'I see,' Brunetti said. 'Is that what you do, bring books down to the desk?' he asked, curious about what the duties of a guard might entail in this institution. He assumed it was his position as guard that made Sartor so unusually forthcoming in speaking to the police.

The look the man gave him was sudden and sharp and might as easily have been alarm as confusion. 'No, sir, but it was a book I'd read – well, parts of it – so I recognized it right away, and I didn't think it should be left on the table,' he blurted out. 'Cortés. That Spanish guy who went to South America.'

Sartor seemed uncertain how to explain this and went on more slowly. 'He was so enthusiastic about the books he was reading that he made me interested in them, and I thought I'd take a look.' Brunetti's curiosity must have been visible, for he continued, 'He's American, but he speaks Italian very well – you'd never know – and we got into the habit of chatting if I was on the desk while he was waiting for the books to come down.' He paused, and when he saw Brunetti's expression, went on. 'We have a break in the afternoon, but I don't smoke and I can't drink coffee,' he said, then added, 'Stomach. Can't handle it any more. I drink green tea, but none of the bars around here has it, well, not a kind that I'd drink.' Before Brunetti could ask why he was being told all of this, Sartor said, 'So I have a half-hour and don't much want to go out, so I started to read. Some of the people who come to do research mention books, and sometimes I try to read them.' He smiled nervously, as if conscious of having overstepped some sort of class barrier. 'That way I have something interesting to tell my wife when I get home.'

Brunetti had always taken a special delight in the surprising things he learned from people: they did and said the most unexpected things, both good and bad. A

12

colleague had once told him how, when his wife was in the seventeenth hour of labour with their first child, he had grown tired of listening to her complain, and Brunetti had fought down the impulse to slap him. He thought of his neighbour's wife, whose cat was set free from the kitchen window every night to roam the rooftops of the neighbourhood, and who came home every morning with a clothes peg, not a mouse, in his mouth, a gift not unlike the interesting story Sartor took home to his wife.

Brunetti, interested in what he had to say, asked 'Hernán Cortés?'

'Yes,' Sartor answered. 'He conquered that city in Mexico they called the Venice of the West.' He stopped and added, afraid perhaps that Brunetti might think him a fool, 'That's what the Europeans called it, not the Mexicans.'

Brunetti nodded to show he understood.

'It was interesting, although he was always thanking God when he killed a lot of people: I didn't like that very much but he was writing to the King, so may be he had to say things like that. But what he said about the country and the people was fascinating. My wife liked it, too.'

He looked at Brunetti, whose approving smile to a fellow reader was enough to encourage him to continue. 'I liked how things were so different from how they are now. I read some of it, and I wanted to finish it. Anyway, I recognized the title – *Relación* – when I saw it in front of the place where he usually sits and brought it downstairs because I thought a book like that shouldn't be lying around up there.'

Brunetti assumed this unnamed 'he' was the man believed to have cut the pages from the book, so he asked, 'Why did you bring it down if he was working with it?'

'Riccardo, from the first floor, told me he'd seen him going down the stairs when I was at lunch. He never did that before. He always comes in soon after we open and stays

13

until the afternoon.' He considered that for a moment and then added, sounding genuinely concerned, 'I don't know what he does about lunch: I hope he hasn't been eating in there.' Then, as if embarrassed to have confessed such a thing, he added, 'So I went up to see if he was coming back.'

'How would you know that?' Brunetti asked with genuine curiosity.

Sartor gave a small smile. 'If you work here for a long time, Signore, you learn the signs. No pencils, no markers, no notebook. It's hard to explain, but I just know if they're finished for the day. Or not.'

'And he was?'

The guard nodded emphatically. 'The books were stacked in front of where he had been sitting. His desk light was turned off. So I knew he wouldn't come back. That's why I took the book back down to the desk.'

'Was this unusual?'

'For him it was. He always packed up everything and took the books back to the desk himself.'

'What time did he leave?'

'I don't know the exact time, sir. Before I came back at two-thirty.'

'And then?'

'As I said, when Riccardo told me he'd left, I went up to make sure and see about the books.'

'Is that something you'd normally do?' Brunetti asked, curiously. The guard had seemed alarmed the first time he asked this.

This time he answered naturally. 'Not really, sir. But I used to be a runner – a person who brings books to the readers and puts them back on the shelves – so I sort of did it automatically.' He smiled a very natural smile and said, 'I can't stand to see the books lying around on the tables if no one is there, using them.'

14

'I see,' Brunetti said. 'Go on, please.'

'I brought the books down to the circulation desk. Dottoressa Fabbiani was just coming in from a meeting, and when she saw the Cortés she asked to see it, and when she opened it, she saw what had happened.' Then, speaking more slowly, almost as if having a conversation with himself, he said, 'I don't understand how he could have done it. There's usually more than one person in the room.'

Brunetti ignored that and asked, 'Why did she open that particular book?'

'She said it was a book she'd read when she was at university, and she loved the drawing it had of that city. So she picked it up and opened it.' He thought a moment and then added, 'She was so pleased to see it, she said, after all these years.' Noticing Brunetti's expression, he said, 'People who work here feel that way about books, you know.'

'You said there were usually more people in the room?' Brunetti inquired mildly.Sartor nodded. 'There's usually a researcher or two, and there's a man who's been reading the Fathers of the Church for the last three years, sir. We call him Tertullian: that's the first book he asked for, and the name stuck. He's here every day, so I guess we've sort of begun to depend on him as a kind of guard.'

Brunetti forbore to ask about Tertullian's choice of reading matter. Instead, he smiled and said, 'I can understand.'

'What, sir?'

'That you'd trust someone who spent years reading the Fathers of the Church.'

The man smiled nervously, responding to Brunetti's tone. 'Perhaps we've been negligent,' he said. When Brunetti did not respond, he added, 'About security, that is. Few people come to the library, and after a while, I suppose we begin to feel as though we know them. So we stop being suspicious.'

'Dangerous,' Brunetti permitted himself to say.

'To say the very least,' a woman's voice said behind him, and he turned to meet Dottoressa Fabbiani.